I0683176

The Last Brass Ring

by Liz Hill

HOVEY
PUBLISHING
NORTH CAROLINA

ISBN: 979-8-9887674-0-4

Table of Contents

**For Anna, Elsie, and Marie
Who Took Their Secrets With Them**

"People are trapped in history, and history is trapped in them."
– James Baldwin

*"If we stand tall it's because we're standing
on the shoulders of many ancestors."*
– Yoruba proverb

1 – Funeral

On a hot, humid day in June of 1989, my great aunt Helen dropped dead of a heart attack in the meat aisle at the A&P. One minute she was reaching for a rump roast in a store she knew like her own Rosary, the next she was competing in a bake-off in heaven.

Aunt Helen is in heaven, of that I have no doubt. My concern is the hell she left behind for me in the person of her older sister, my great aunt Stella.

"Be reasonable, Lilli," my father pleaded. "Aunt Stella needs us, now she's alone."

I kept my face aimed into the wind as the Staten Island Ferry streaked away from the Manhattan skyline. My sandal beat a rhythm on the scuffed suitcase at my feet. Dad had coerced me into packing, but as far as I was concerned, my summer exile was not a done deal.

"I can't even imagine Aunt Stella without Aunt Helen," Dad said. "Even when I was a kid, they were as close as two sisters can be."

"And as different," I observed. No explanation was needed. My dad, along with anyone Helen had ever met, knew how much she loved everybody. She certainly loved me without question every time I showed up at the aunts' house, shipped off to the Island whenever my mom wasn't doing so great. Which was often. Nearly all the happy memories I had were connected to my Aunt Helen. Oreos and milk at midnight. Sunday afternoons at the kiddie rides. Scavenging shells at the beach. Scandalizing Stella by painting my fingernails blue. The sound of my Aunt Helen's laughter was the soundtrack of my childhood, and my throat seized at the realization that I'd never hear it again.

"You can't just dump me at Stella's, Dad. You know what she's like."

My father was hellbent. "It's been arranged, Lilli. She's expecting you. We're all she has now, right? We're her family."

Family. Like that explained everything. Like the very word was some kind of secret password to stability, to a certainty you could rely on. The only certain things about this family were the unspoken rules about what we never discussed. And that list changed or expanded without warning according to the whims and moods of its members.

"Family gives help where help is needed," Dad added.

I wasn't sure where this crap was coming from. I sure as hell did not remember a stampede of relatives being there for him when my mom was at her worst. Just the opposite, in fact. He correctly read my silence and changed tactics, his tone softening.

"Joe's got you a job down at the rides. How about that? You always did like the rides, Lilli."

The rides. True, I did always love going to the rides with Aunt Helen when I was little. Spinning on the teacups or riding the old carousel. But I wasn't little anymore. I was sixteen years old and headed for my senior year of high school. How could he think I'd find the rides fun at my age? "I don't want the stupid job," I snarled.

If we'd been at home he might have raised a hand to me, but as we were in public he just visibly stiffened. "You listen to me, Lilli. You're going to work the stupid job even if you hate every minute. Most people hate every minute of their job, but we have to work, don't we? You're nearly seventeen. It's high time you contributed something to this family."

I kicked my suitcase. He had no clue. To be completely honest, neither did I. None of us had any idea, that day, the extent of the contribution I was about to make.

Three hours later, I'd survived Aunt Helen's funeral mass in stuffy St. Mary's and was pouting my way to the cemetery in the limo's jump seat. The dull landscape of Staten Island rolled by the tinted windows, street after street of boring ranch houses. I could see where the owners tried to add touches to make their houses unique—American flags, pink or yellow aluminum siding, statues of the Virgin or St. Francis, bushes trimmed into the shape of birds. It was silly, really; the houses all looked basically the same. They had lawns the size of a postage stamp and narrow driveways parked with well-loved Fords or Chevys.

The occasional glimpse of kids splashing through sprinklers or wading pools reminded me again of my happy times on the Island. It was never good news when I was whisked off on the ferry from our apartment in the city. But Aunt Helen made it feel almost normal. She was the one who made it bearable. And now she was gone.

Aunt Stella sat across from me in the limo, her face pinched in her perpetual scowl. She wore a black dress, polyester knit with short cap sleeves, a string of pearls falling over her ample bosom. The dress looked a size too small, and though it was a modest length when she stood, her rolled-up stockings showed where her fleshy thighs met her kneecaps. Her feet were stuffed into black pumps. Her eyes were dry behind the giant gray plastic frames of her glasses, and I wondered if she'd cried for Helen, or if she just considered the loss of her only sister additional proof that there was nothing good to be expected in life, ever. That had pretty much been Stella's attitude for as long as I'd known her.

My dad fumbled with his cigarette pack and Stella reached a chubby paw toward him and smacked his hand. He pocketed the pack and turned his attention to the endless rows of green lawns, pretending he wasn't dying for a smoke, pretending not to care.

Dad was an expert at pretending. Whenever Mom had to go away, Dad always told me not to worry. Everything would be fine. He told me that for years, right up till the day she died. I don't think he really meant to lie. He wanted to believe that it really would be fine, to go about his business like nothing was wrong. I don't actually know for sure because we never talk about my mom. Nearly five years, and he never says he misses her, never mentions her name. Just goes on like nothing even happened.

My whole family is great at pretending. It's like they've sworn a blood oath to bury the past, the good along with the bad. Not that there was much good anyway. Stella wasn't wrong about that part.

With Dad ignoring her, Aunt Stella turned on me. "Lilli Rose, what have you done to your hair?"

I ran my fingers through the ragged super-short cut I'd given myself just yesterday. This morning I moussed it into deliberately uneven spikes and I was pleased that she seemed to hate it as much as I hoped.

"I was so tired of that big hair thing. It's passe. Out of style."

She frowned and studied me. "It looks ridiculous." This from a woman with a black lace mantilla bobby-pinned to her lacquered curls. "Like it was cut with an eggbeater. It's not even straight."

"It makes a statement. About the surprising unpredictability of life." Let her argue with that on the way to her only sister's grave.

We followed the flower-laden hearse through the cemetery gates as the rest of the motorcade trailed behind. I wasn't exactly eager to sacrifice the sanctity of the air-conditioned limo to follow the priest to the graveside, but I did my duty and found a place next to my brother Mike and Bernadette, his wife.

"Nice turnout," Dette whispered. "Aunt Helen would be pleased."

I surveyed the mourners, mostly blue-haired church ladies, friends from Aunt Helen's canasta club, and some cousins I hardly ever saw. Joe

Alonzo, the old guy who owned the rides where I was supposed to work that summer, stood next to Stella, his rosary beads twisted around his fingers. The back of his suit jacket was soaked with sweat and he looked like he'd rather be anywhere else. I knew the feeling.

"There's Darlene." I nudged Dette as my aunts' next-door neighbor arrived, dressed in a navy-blue dress and a navy hat trimmed with white silk flowers. Hers was the only Black face in the crowd, which I saw as both commentary on Staten Island's racial divide and tribute to my Aunt Helen's loving spirit.

"I hope Aunt Stel is polite," Dette whispered.

"And a donkey just flew out of that tree," I said. Dette looked up, then nudged me back as she got my little joke. When Darlene and her son Tyson moved into the neighborhood last fall, Aunt Helen baked a batch of her famous mint-frosted brownies to welcome them. I was the one who delivered them, over Stella's strong objections. "What good can come of that?" she asked.

"What harm?" Helen answered. "A nice plate of brownies to say welcome to the neighborhood. To say we wish them the best of luck and say we are glad they're here." To Helen that seemed as obvious and normal as getting up in the morning to brush your teeth. But it set Stella's teeth on edge.

"You will deal with the consequences of this. You hear me, Helen? You. Not me."

Aunt Helen just laughed. "There won't be consequences."

"There are always consequences," Stella announced. "Always."

Later on, Helen tried to explain away Stella's attitude. "She's not prejudiced. You know how she is. Prickly. With everyone."

As if I hadn't noticed. The brownies had given me an excuse to meet Darlene and Tyson, who was about my age. Since then, I'd seen him a couple of times in the neighborhood, at the deli or sitting on his front stoop. I wouldn't call us friends, but we got along okay.

As the priest began the service, Stella swiped at a tear and dabbed her sweaty face with a lace hankie. An odd sense of sympathy crept over me. I tried to shrug it off. I couldn't let myself get mushy. Mushy wouldn't get me through a summer with Stella Whitaker, the great aunt from hell. I had to be strong. Stay strong. Let her know I was in charge of myself and no one was going to tell me what to do.

My brother offered to drive me to Stella's in their minivan, but even with the kids at a sitter's, the van would be a heady blend of diapers and formula.

"I'll stick with Dad. God knows what he and Aunt Stel will come up with if I leave them alone."

"Suit yourself, Squirt," Mike said. "By the way—what the hell'd you do to your hair?"

"Cut it with an eggbeater."

"Looks it."

Dette shot Mike a how-could-you look. "I think it's cute." She steered him toward their van. "And that's a cute top, too. Brings out your peaches and cream complexion."

My brother's wife always found something nice to say but she had no idea how little time I had to pack for this nightmare, or how little I cared about my peachy Irish skin. Still, I thanked her before following Dad and Stella to the limo.

The car's frame sagged as the driver helped Stella into the car. Lulled by the air conditioning, she dabbed at tears, sniffling. My father, pulling out all his emotional stops, reached out to pat her hand. She met him at his own level and ignored him. After a few snuffly minutes Stella turned her attention to fretting about the food back at the house.

"It'll be fine, Aunt Stella," Dad assured her. "People don't come to eat, they come to offer condolences."

This was a silly thing to say to Stella, whose relationship with food outweighed her relationship with anyone.

"Nonsense," she sniffed. "A funeral repast is all about food. People take comfort in it. I just hope those dimwit friends of Helen's did a decent job of setting it up. Didn't just throw it out on the table like some Polack affair."

I bit my finger to keep my mouth shut.

"It'll be fine, Aunt Stel," Dad repeated.

"Lilli Rose!" Stella shrieked. "Take that finger out of your mouth."

I tapped my lip a few times before I lowered the finger, oh-so-slowly, from my face, folding both hands deliberately in my lap. I aimed my best Aunt Helen smile in her direction. She scowled back.

By the time we arrived at Stella's the mourners were circling for the attack around the overflowing dining room table. Three old birds from Helen's canasta club swarmed Stella but even as they twittered in sympathy my aunt peered over their heads, hawklike, inspecting, giving no hint of approval before waving them off. She headed for the kitchen, where Dad was already helping himself to a drink.

"A bit early for that, isn't it, Stan?" she shrilled.

"Tough day," my father explained. He retreated to the dining room, tinkling the ice cubes in his tumbler of scotch. Every day was a tough day for Dad.

"Hey, Squirt." Mike punched my arm in greeting. "Still time to grab that suitcase and run."

"Run where?" I asked.

Dette raised her chin and nodded toward the staircase up to the bedrooms. "You could carry your sister's suitcase up," she told Mike. "It's the least you can do."

"Thanks, Dette, I've got it." I grabbed my case and headed up, ready for a break from them all.

At the top of the steps, I closed my eyes and inhaled the familiar mixture of moth balls, flowery soap, and musty drapes. When I was little and things were a mess at home, this jumble of smells was my safety. I arrived totally sure the world was ending, and Aunt Helen showed me why I was wrong. She had a way of making the insanity seem totally logical, a talent no doubt learned through years of surviving this family.

How was I supposed to live without her?

Aunt Helen encouraged me to cry when my Mom died.

"You'll never actually get over a loss like this one," she explained. "You just go on living and time takes care of the rest. But you have to cry. If you don't, the sadness and tears will fester inside you. They'll turn ugly. Crying helps."

Stella, in contrast, accused Helen of "coddling the child" and allowing me to "wallow." Her sage advice for me was, basically, buck up.

I threw the suitcase on one of the twin beds in "my" room. It was Helen and Stella's girlhood haven and still had the old white chenille bedspreads, worn soft from dozens of washings. I wandered down the hall to Helen's room. It looked the same as always, the bed made up with a yellow flowered cover and tons of ruffled pillows. A paperback romance lay on her night stand, a tasseled bookmark stuck where she left it the night before she died. I touched the bookmark, sad that she'd never get to the happy ending, half expecting her to appear at the door to ask me to run out for bagels. Except I knew, of course, I wasn't getting a happy ending either.

A lacy dresser scarf covered the bureau, her silver comb and brush set aligned in perfect forty-five-degree angles to her jewelry box. I picked up an atomizer and squirted my wrist, pressing it to my nose for a rush of Helen.

I set the bottle down and ran my hand across the top of the double frame that held my brother's wedding picture and the latest Sears shot of my tiny niece and nephew. Next to it was my graduation picture from junior high. What a mess: my mother's gold cross rested in the hollow of my throat and I wore a half smile that didn't hide the braces or the pain I was carrying.

I turned the picture face-down. Not a year I cared to remember. I studied the wood-framed snapshot on the opposite end of the dresser. Me, Mike, and my parents, posed on Stella and Helen's front sidewalk. I'm in kindergarten, Mike is twelve or so, and from the clothes I could tell it was Easter: Mom in a navy pantsuit, a ruffled pink dress on me, jackets and ties on Dad and Mike. I don't remember that specific day but it looks like it might have been a good one. My father and mother are both smiling. One of her hands rests on my shoulder and the other rests on Mike's, and Dad has an arm around her waist. We look connected. We look like an ordinary family. Maybe, that day, we actually felt like one.

I set the frame down and picked up a smaller frame that held a faded black-and-white snapshot of two little girls, hands entwined, dark ringlets peeking from the edges of their small felt hats. Helen and Stella. I had examined this photo many times as a kid. Even now I can't quite believe that the girl with the angelic smile is really my great Aunt Stel.

"It can't be her," I insisted to Aunt Helen. "This little girl is smiling."

"Your Aunt Stella smiles," she explained. "You just aren't around to see it."

Because she never smiled at me. Or at any of us, because she hates us. I never actually said that to Helen. If I had, she only would have defended her sister, no matter how mean or selfish she seemed. And hate was not a word Helen used. It was not in her vocabulary. Love. Patience. Forgiveness. These were the guideposts of her life. A life that was now gone. Forever.

I set the photo back in its place. I could cry now, if I wanted. I was entitled to cry. I had lost the person who loved me most in the world. I fingered my gold cross, staring out the window, daring the tears to come. Nothing happened.

A door banged shut outside. Tyson Davis settled on his back stoop, leaning back on his elbows, his long legs snaking down the steps. I called to him through the window.

He jerked his head in my direction, squinting. "Your aunt'll give you hell, she hears you hollering like that."

"She's bound to give me hell for something. There's tons of food downstairs. Want anything?"

He shrugged. "Can you bring it out? Ma went to work. And I'm not dressed for a funeral."

"Give me a few."

I was glad to have some kind of useful task and maybe someone to talk to who wouldn't be judging every word that came out of my mouth. I went downstairs and waded into the crowded living room and almost made it to the table before a red-finger-nailed claw snagged my shoulder.

"Is that little Lilli?" she cooed, lips curling into a crooked half-smile as she looked me up and down. "Why, of course it is. You remember me, your father's cousin Barb?"

I remembered all right. Dad always said she was born with a pole up her ass that went straight to her nose and pushed it up in the air. "Sure," I said. "Hello"

"My, you've really grown up. Lost that baby fat. And what have you done with all your pretty curls?"

"Hacked them off, obviously."

She barely contained a smirk as she continued to size me up. It didn't feel like she was admiring my brush of freckles or my peachy skin. And when it came to skin she had nothing to smirk about. All those hours on her boat at the Jersey shore were totally wrecking her face and her own hair looked like August grass that hadn't seen a sprinkler lately. She wore a pink and blue flowered dress with big shoulder pads and lapels trimmed in white piping. I considered telling her she could use a little baby fat herself, anything to keep that loose skin from sagging all over the place, but I knew better.

"Your dad tells me you'll be staying with Aunt Stella for the summer. Good for you, Lilli. She'll be so alone now. You'll have a chance to get to know each other better."

Who was she kidding with this crap? "It's not like I have a choice."

She tilted her head in question. I noted my father on the sofa, sitting up and taking notice.

"It's more my dad's idea," I said. "It's kind of a huge sacrifice for me, giving up my normal life in the city to stay in this hellhole with that—"

"Lilli Rose." My father's scotch glass banged the coffee table. "That'll do."

"Nice to see you," I mumbled to Barb, moving on to the food. I built two monster sandwiches and added a generous pile of chips to each plate. I then grabbed a couple of Cokes and headed for the back door.

When he saw me coming, Ty hopped the fence that divided his yard from Stella's and we sat on the back steps. He wore a sleeveless tee and baggy basketball shorts and his untied white Jordans resembled clown shoes on his long feet. I picked at some chips and watched Ty dig into his

8

sandwich. He wasn't a bad looking guy: his nose was angular, almost regal, and his black hair was cropped short, trimmed just to the tops of ears that sat close to his head. Ty's skin was the color of milk-laced coffee, and I knew this was because his Dad was white. Stella made sure we noticed that fact the day they moved in, though it didn't seem to me that Ty's Dad was around much.

Ty caught me looking at him and stopped chewing. "What're you staring at?" he asked, his mouth filled with sandwich.

"Nothing much." I didn't want him getting all full of himself.

He swallowed and took another bite. "So how long you staying this time?"

"The whole summer. My father thinks it's a great idea. I'll be working at the rides."

"Me too. My second summer with Joe. It's a dump, but there are worse places. You'll see." He popped the last bit of sandwich into his mouth. "Me and Ma? We were betting Stella wouldn't let you take the job."

"Why not? The way she goes on about how lazy we all are I'm surprised she didn't find me a job in a coal mine or something."

Tyson laughed. "You know how she is. With riff-raff like me working down there, you know, it might not be cool."

"Not a proper place for a young lady, you mean? I've been hearing that crap my whole life. A pre-recorded Stella lecture." I pinched up my face and spoke through my nose in a shrill voice. "Beds are for sleeping, chairs are for sitting. Young ladies should act like ladies. Helen, you'll spoil that child rotten!"

Ty laughed again but not before he glanced toward Stella's back door.

"She'll let me work, all right, but she might be sorry that I'm not gonna be here to run out to get her Lotto tickets or a hot bagel whenever she needs one."

"Like every five minutes?" We cracked up again. "I bet Joe talked her into letting you have the job," Ty said. "She's got the hots for Joe."

I snorted. "As if she knows what's hot."

"It's true. Wait till you see her when Joe's around, she 'bout falls apart."

"Maybe she just likes cheap toupees." Joe's wavy black hair was obviously a rug and he had a nervous habit of petting it like a dog. I expected Ty to laugh. He didn't.

"Don't dis' Joe. He's all right. He went out of his way to hire me on last year. Oh, I know your Aunt Helen had something to do with that, her and my mom, always planning my life for me. Ma told Helen I was saving for a Game Boy and she came back the next day with a phone number.

Joe. Ma made me do the calling and I had to go meet him and all, but he hired me. He didn't have to do that. There's plenty of Italian kids down the beach, but Joe took a chance on me." He downed the last of his soda. "I gotta respect that. Even though—"

He glanced away, his face twisted into a grimace. He blinked his eyes a few times and I couldn't help but notice how his long lashes brushed the tops of his round cheeks like two big brooms. Most girls would kill for lashes like those.

"Even though what?" I asked.

"Nothing. It's just, I do a lot of, like, trashy work. Sweeping and emptying cans. Ma says it's good for me to get a little dirty. First job can't be your best job, she says. Put in the time, then you climb."

"Climb what?"

"Heck if I know. Anyway, Joe's okay. And I ain't kidding, Lilli. Joe knows how to handle your aunt. You could learn a thing or two from watching him."

I bristled. "You don't think I can handle Stella?"

"Not like Joe."

"Better than Joe. You just watch."

"Yeah, I'll be watching all right." He hoovered up the rest of his chips and winked. "From a nice, safe distance."

I yanked the empty plate out of his hand. "Be a lot safer in your own yard, I guess."

Ty just chuckled as he brushed crumbs from his lap. "My mother's right about one thing. You and Stella? You really are two of a kind."

Stuart: Dreamers

My name is Stuart McGee and I've been dead a long time.

You've heard a story like mine before. A war, young men, big dreams, death. A short life in one act, over almost before the curtain went up. But, dead as I am, I play an important role in this story.

Back in the nineteen-forties, when I was young and very much alive, I fell in love with Stella Whitaker. God, she was a gorgeous woman. Like a willow she was, tall and solid, yet soft and graceful, with flawless pale skin set off by wavy black hair and brown eyes that never missed a trick. But what caught me at first was her smile. It was a beacon of joy that lit her face from her full rosy lips to the arch of her dark brows. Truly, that smile was a dazzler.

When I first saw Stella I was just a kid myself, barely twenty, running my legs off at my job, rolling stock certificates in a big wheeled wagon from one Wall Street house to another. On the eight o'clock ferry from Staten Island to the city, I watched Stella and her sister Helen chatter with friends, their musical laughter rolling out on the sea air as they arranged their hair and rouged their cheeks and made sure their stocking seams were straight.

Believe you me, I was no Casanova. I watched Stella for two whole weeks before I was brave enough to say a single word. But one sunny morning, I summoned my courage.

"Isn't it a lovely day?" Harmless and banal, but sure it became a lovely day when she rewarded me with a quick flash of those lovely dark eyes and that incredible smile. For the next few days, I tipped my hat, edged a bit closer. Finally one day I settled a few seats away on the same bench as the girls. Helen glanced my way. I smiled. She turned away with a giggle, but then tapped Stella's knee and tilted her chin my way.

It may have been the longest twenty minutes of my life, but when the engines cut and the boat drifted toward the dock in Manhattan, Stella's friends practically pushed her toward me, scattering and waving, leaving us to each other at last.

"Are you walking up Broadway?" she asked, her lilting voice magic in my ears.

"Sure," I said. It was a lie. I would have walked to Times Square if she suggested it. We talked congenially all the way to her office. It was instantly clear to me that Stella wasn't just beautiful; she was smart too. A high school diploma, more than I had, and a better job than mine, at an insurance company. And we were Irish, the pair of us! I wasn't overly handsome but I was young and brash and I wasn't about to let that stop me. I intended to woo this wonderful girl.

That evening we met again on the homeward ferry, and a few days later I invited her to lunch, then a movie, then dinner. Within a few weeks we were keeping steady company, and love wasn't far behind.

When I was alive and Stella was a black-haired beauty, the dark threat of war couldn't dim our hopes. Even as friends and the brothers of friends began shipping overseas, dying overseas, we made idiotic, optimistic plans. When my draft notice came and off I went to basic, still the dreams sprouted like weeds, thick-rooted and determined. And if any seeds of sensible fear or caution dared poke up their heads, our dreams just choked them out. We wouldn't hear of it. Our happiness would surely win.

I last saw Stella just before I shipped out to the European front. We were as happy as two lovers could be, that night. We'd no notion of what lay ahead, and I wish with all my heart that everything had turned out right.

I'm a dreamer. I know. I always was.

But believe it or not, so was Stella Whitaker.

2 - Purge

"Lilli Rose! I won't have you lazing in bed all day."

I rolled over, squinting. It was daylight, but still early. I had no urge to get up. Aunt Stella stood in the doorway, and I mean the whole doorway, every inch of it filled with pink flowered house dress.

"It's Saturday," I said, folding the pillow around my head.

"And tomorrow's Sunday, and yesterday was Friday. Would you like a weather report as well?" She shuffled into the room, pink slippers chafing the carpet, and snapped up the shades on both windows. "Sunny. Hot. And we have a lot to do. Look alive, Lilli. I'm not boarding you here for your pleasure."

In case I thought it was my pleasure to be here. The clock on the night stand read 8 a.m. "Give me half an hour to take a shower and grab something to eat."

She gave a prim nod. "There are rolls and bagels from yesterday." At least I knew she wouldn't starve me to death. She began vigorously smoothing the chenille spread on the other twin bed, erasing any evidence of my butt.

"Beds are for sleeping. Chairs are for sitting," I said.

She was not amused. "I see you grasp the concept. Now let's see if you can put it into practice." She shuffled out again.

I buried my face in my pillow. Day two. Any vacation that starts with a funeral is bound to be fun, right? Yesterday, Stella told me she saw Ty hop the fence. She warned me away from him. When I asked her why, she said Helen told her the boy's mother kept him on "a short leash" and wouldn't be too pleased if she saw him hanging around with me. I was pretty sure Stella was the one who would be displeased if Ty and I became friends, but I didn't push. I avoided her the rest of the afternoon and around dinner time I pleaded exhaustion and escaped upstairs with my Walkman. A few hours later she climbed the steps, and soon after her snores penetrated my closed door like toxic waste.

At least tomorrow I could go to work. Pretty sad state of affairs when I was looking forward to that. Joe had delivered a set of completely hideous uniforms and suggested I start today. But Aunt Stella told him it was "too soon." Too soon what— to let me out of her sight?

Somehow I had to get through this summer without going crazy or killing Stella. My first instinct was to block her at every turn and challenge every decision; to basically be so difficult she couldn't stand to have me around. That might buy me a ticket home within a week or two, but Dad would return the favor by making my life hell for having "let the family down." Besides, I did need that job. It would be a long summer in the city with no pocket change to speak of. And if I wanted any school clothes beyond Basic Dork, I had to have some cash.

No, this situation called for a little finesse. I had to at least make it look like I was doing everything Stella asked. Could I somehow manage to do as I pleased while appearing to be cooperative? That might just throw her off balance enough to back off and leave me alone. I could say yes when I didn't really care one way or the other. Let her think she was the boss but not actually let her boss me around. No matter what Ty thought, I knew I'd win in the end.

Down in the kitchen, I slathered a bagel with tons of butter and jelly and ate slowly as I scanned the pages of the Daily News. If you believed half of what you read in the paper, this city was going to hell in a handbasket. Muggings, murders, riots, robberies, and the candidates in the upcoming mayoral election screaming at voters with their solution to make it all go away.

"I'll be in Helen's room," Stella said. "Come up when you're done. And don't dilly-dally."

I gave her a thumbs up and flipped the paper shut. It was all nonsense and I had enough to deal with right here. I knew she was anxious to steamroller through Aunt Helen's things but I wasn't so eager. I could still feel the sting of what happened after my mother died.

The day after her funeral, I was sent to the Island to spend a few days with Aunt Helen while my dad handled "things." I didn't mind. Helen was the most stable, loving person in my life and I had no desire to sit around my apartment thinking about my mother and mentally rehashing who was to blame for any of her problems. Too often the wheel of guilt spun and spun until it stopped at me, and I had no idea what to do with all those feelings.

Aunt Helen helped me get through that week, but when I got home the next weekend, I walked in to find mom's younger sister Pearl standing on a step-stool cleaning our kitchen cupboards. When she saw me she hopped down and slipped off her rubber gloves.

"Welcome home," she said. "I'm just here for a few days helping your dad with—things."

Things.

I accepted her hug and poured myself a glass of Coke. She sat down and we stared at each other for a couple of minutes. I had no idea what to say, and I guess she didn't either.

She finally said, "I put something aside for you." She went into my parents' bedroom. Her eyes glistened with tears when she came back. Her hand closed over mine and she dropped something into my palm. I opened it to find the plain gold cross that had always graced my mother's neck.

"She struggled," Aunt Pearl said. "But never forget that she loved you." She lifted the cross from my hand and fastened it around my own neck, where it's been ever since.

I was touched, thrilled even, to have something of my mother's hanging so close to my heart, chosen just for me. The thrill lasted till sometime later that day when I realized that gold cross was it. Everything else my mother had owned, every stitch of clothing, pair of shoes, book, painting, every damned thing, was already packed off to Goodwill or shoved down the building's trash chute.

"But nobody even asked me," I protested. "About anything."

"It's what your father wanted," Aunt Pearl explained when I questioned the decision. "Anything else was too painful."

As usual, my pain was not considered.

The next day Pearl went back to Pittsburgh where she lives with my grandmother, and I haven't seen either of them since. Every year, they send a birthday card with a twenty dollar bill tucked inside. It feels a little like hush money. Don't ask too many questions, because we won't answer them anyway.

I snarfed the last of my bagel and ran my mother's cross along its slender gold chain. No sense stalling. If I didn't get up to the bedroom soon Aunt Helen might end up like my mother, nothing but a memory beamed into the clouds and forgotten.

Slowly, I climbed the steps to my fate. Stella was in Aunt Helen's rocker, staring out the window.

"Reporting for duty, ma'am," I said, saluting.

She jumped. "Don't sneak up on me." Her hands flew to her face as she turned away.

She grabbed a tissue, frantically rubbing her eyes. I realized she'd been crying, sitting in that old rocker crying, and she didn't like being caught.

I started to say something nice, something comforting, but my instincts told me to pretend I didn't see a thing. And anyway, once her eyes were dry she was back to her stony old self, ordering me around as usual.

"Let's start with the closet," she said, throwing open the door. She settled back into the rocker and indicated that I should lay Helen's brightly colored wardrobe on the bed for her inspection. Within an hour the closet bar held nothing but empty hangers and the clothes had been sorted into two piles: giveaways to relatives and giveaways to the needy.

I eyed the second pile warily. It was hard to believe there was anyone that needy. "Shouldn't we make a trash pile, too?"

"Trash? These things are much too nice for trash. Why it's a shame I can't keep some of them for myself, but they'd be a little snug."

A little snug? Like cramming an iceberg into the freezer. "I only meant, some of this stuff looks a little worn."

She sniffed. "The trouble with you is, you never had to do without. Plenty of people have nothing, and when you have nothing, these things look pretty darned good. Can you reach that top shelf?"

"Not even on tiptoe." I carried a straight back chair from the hall to use as a step stool and hefted a cardboard box filled with books.

"Hey, neat," I said, poking into the box as soon as I hit the floor. "These look like old yearbooks."

"That's none of your concern." Stella tried to wrench the box from my hands but it was heavy and I was stronger, so I held tight.

"Can't I at least look?" I said, exasperated. "Why is this family always so anxious to bury the past? It's like we're trying to erase history or something."

She winced like I'd stuck her with a pin. "We are not erasing anything. If I know Helen, that box is nothing but silly cartoons and ancient news clippings. You know what a sentimental fool she could be."

"I know. I liked that about her."

She ignored me. "Put the box over there."

I remembered my vow to appear cooperative and put it in the corner as commanded.

"Now, hand down those shoeboxes."

I hopped to and passed them down one by one. Judging by their weight the boxes actually contained shoes. But the last one was suspiciously heavy. Instead of handing it to Stella, I jumped down and slipped it onto the bottom of the pile, noting its color.

"That's it," I said, brushing the dust from my hands.

Stella surveyed the stacks of clothing and instructed me to fill plastic trash bags with the giveaways, marked with an appropriate label. She opened the top shoebox and frowned. "All the shoes can go. Helen's feet were like a little doll's. Someone with tiny feet will get a windfall but it's no one I know."

"Okay," I said, relieved she didn't insist on checking every box. "I'll take care of them, Aunt Stella. Why don't you take a break? Go have an iced tea or something?"

She sighed and gently replaced the cover on the shoebox. "I do have some calls to make. Just pack it up and put the bags back in the closet for now. We still have the bureau to deal with, so there will be more."

"No problem." I began to fold the clothes and place them into the big black trash bags, thankful that she considered this job simple enough to entrust to me.

She shuffled out and began her slow, heavy descent. The second she was out of earshot I jerked the heavy shoebox from the bottom of the pile. Just as I suspected, it wasn't shoes. It appeared to be a treasure trove of snapshots and some letters tied together with blue satin ribbon. Two small books were wedged against the back of the shoebox. I pulled out the first and opened it.

Helen Whitaker - PRIVATE!

I flipped through the pages of tiny Catholic-school handwriting, my pulse quickening as I scanned a few entries.

January 10, 1941. The wind has finally stopped howling and left us with piles and piles of fluffy snow. I coerced Stel into building a snowman. He has a carrot for a nose and one of Da's old scarves to keep out the chill. It felt wonderful to come into the warm house after.

April 13, 1941. A beautiful Easter Sunday. I colored eggs last night, even though Da and Stel both teased me for being too old. Never!

A pot banged downstairs and I slammed the book shut. It could take me hours to properly digest these treasures from Aunt Helen, and I sure couldn't do it when Stella might come charging in like some wild-eyed nun hoping to catch me with my pants down. I returned the diary to the shoebox, slapped on the lid and slipped down the hall to my room.

The box found a home in the back of the closet behind the wool suits and winter coats. I would need to stay alert in case Stella got the urge to annihilate this closet too. But for now, I floated back to Aunt Helen's room feeling like I'd single-handedly saved an endangered species from extinction.

I concentrated long enough to load two more bags, but that heavy cardboard box full of books called to me from the far corner. One ear tuned for sounds from downstairs, I tiptoed over. The first book I touched was a yearbook: Curtis High School, 1937. I scanned the pages in search of a Whitaker and found Aunt Helen on page sixty-seven. She looked plainer than some of the other girls, with stick-straight hair and no lipstick. But she had the same soft eyes and wise smile that I always loved. Next to her picture was a quote:

"Life is mostly froth and bubble,
Two things stand like stone:
Kindness in another's trouble,
Courage in your own."

The name underneath it was Adam Lindsay Gordon, whoever he was, but the quote was pure Aunt Helen. I wasn't surprised she chose a poem. She loved poetry. She had a few well-worn anthologies and sometimes she would read aloud from them. When she read those words, they were nothing like they looked on the page. I could see them floating in the air like clouds that suddenly came together and formed a picture you could feel inside. She told me she used to write poems when she was younger but she didn't anymore. When I asked her why, she just lifted a shoulder.

"Other things need my attention," she said. "And there are plenty of good poems out there to enjoy."

The steps creaked. I closed the book and slipped it back in the box next to some photo albums that were screaming my name. Man, this box was pay dirt, but it wasn't mine just yet. Quickly, I crammed the rest of the clothes into bags and shoved them into the closet, barely finishing the last one as Stella appeared.

"Lord, child, aren't you finished yet?"

"I had to go to the bathroom," I lied.

She narrowed her eyes and peered over my shoulder at the box in the corner. "Have you been poking around in Helen's trash?"

"It's not trash," I protested. "It's memorabilia."

She pushed past me to the box. "I'd appreciate it if you'd carry this to my room." She drew herself up, daring me to disobey. "Your Aunt Helen was a wonderful woman. But she was also a total sap and it never did her one ounce of good." I didn't move. She used the toe of her slipper to shove the box an inch closer to me. "Do I have to carry it myself?"

I couldn't shake the feeling that something was being stolen from me, something I didn't even know I owned. Right then and there I promised myself that one way or another I was going to get a good look at that box. Aunt Stella had to go out some time. Or maybe one day when she was in the right mood—not that her moods varied that much between bad and worse— she'd let me have a peek. For now, remembering my vow to appear helpful, I dutifully lugged the box to her room.

When I came back she was positioned in front of Helen's bureau to continue the purge.

"What's next?" I rubbed my hands together. With a shoebox full of treasures stashed safely in my closet, I could afford to look like an eager-beaver. Stella thought she had me pinned securely under her big, fat thumb. She had no idea that I was already wiggling loose.

3 – Amusements

On Sunday, my first day of work at the rides, I stood in front of the mirror in Stella's spare room trying to decide if pride would allow me to actually wear the regulation dorky uniform. Baggy red shorts that looked like a gym suit gone bad and a white T-shirt emblazoned in red with Island Amusements. I don't exactly love my thighs—who does? —but if Madonna slithered onstage wearing this outfit her most loyal fans would boo her right back off. It was that unflattering.

Whatever. At least this job got me out of the house. That was some small comfort. I grabbed my fanny pack and bounded downstairs. Stella was bent over the newspaper at the kitchen table, working her way through an Entenmann's crumb cake as she read. Spongy pink rollers hung at odd places on her head, performing spot repair on her perm. She glanced up, chewing, and watched me pour a glass of juice.

"What mass are you going to?"

"Uh— well—" I sipped my juice, stalling. "I hadn't actually planned to—"

Stella arched an eyebrow.

"I went to mass on Friday, right? The funeral? A high mass. That counts double." I gulped the rest of the juice. "I'm almost late for work already. Maybe next week."

"There'll be no maybe about it."

I fled down the brick stoop toward the bus stop. Stella and Helen had lived in this same house since they were little girls. It was a two-story aluminum sided house with a high brick stoop with a wrought-iron rail. Its stamp of uniqueness was the kelly green shutters with shamrocks carved into the outside corners. The sun had faded the green to an uneven mess that looked like a leprechaun's suit had accidentally landed in the bleach load. The block still looked tidy enough, though Stella and Helen often discussed the number of homes that were rentals now. The old owners died, and too often their kids saw dollar signs of opportunity where their parents saw only a home. I suppose Tyson and his mother were beneficiaries of that kind of deal, moving into a rental next to the old Whitaker house.

Tyson was already waiting for the bus, also in uniform with a Giants cap covering his head. He mumbled a "hey" and checked his watch every couple of seconds until the bus finally came, then plopped into a seat across the aisle from me. We stared out opposite windows as we wound our way through the old beach neighborhoods.

"Did you know South Beach used to be a resort?" I asked Ty.

He didn't even glance my way. "Yeah? Where's the golf course?"

"Not a golf resort. A beach resort. Aunt Helen told me all about it. People used to come here from the city in the summer and rent bungalows."

No response. Clearly, morning was not Ty's best time. I squinted out the window trying to imagine some of the romance Aunt Helen had painted: lovers strolling hand in hand on the boardwalk, sharing a horse on the old carousel, escaping the steamy sidewalks of summertime Manhattan. What I saw this morning did not inspire romance. What were once summer bungalows had been converted to year-round residences with picket fences around their tiny yards. It seemed like every other corner had a store that sold milk, cigarettes, bagels and cold cuts, the New Yorker's staple goods. As we got closer to the rides, we passed a dilapidated boardwalk where a few old men were out for a morning stroll. The sandy beach was littered with cans and cups and the water was so polluted only crazy people swam. As far as I could tell, the shabby park where Ty and I worked was the last vestige of amusement in the area, and that was really pushing it.

Ty rang the buzzer as the front gate of the rides rolled into view. "Here's your resort," he said, pronouncing it REE-zort.

"Doesn't look like it's changed much since I was little." I followed him across the street. I hadn't been there in years but the place had always been dingy and past its prime. The front gate was flanked by a cardboard cut-out of two sequined clowns, once bright magenta and chartreuse, now as muted as baby clothes.

"It's not much to look at. But it beats being home with the old lady, huh?" Ty pushed open the gate for me. "The office is in the back. I gotta clock in. Joe probably needs you to do some paperwork."

Pollution haze reflected weakly off the sequined signs and the eerie stillness buzzed in my ears. We passed the kiddie roller coaster and an assortment of boat and helicopter rides, the kind that circled so slowly that all but the smallest riders were bored to tears. At the snack bar, a Black girl behind the counter poured pink liquid into a soda machine. She called hello to Ty, and I noticed she opened her big brown eyes wide, then looked down and away really quick. Ty was oblivious. He said hello but kept on walking.

"Who's that?" I asked when we were safely out of earshot.

"Nobody." He reconsidered. "Khamille. With a 'K' and a 'H'. She works here."

"No kidding. I thought she snuck in to steal pink drink mix. She nice?" He shrugged. "Find out for yourself."

"She likes you." The words popped out before I could stop them.

Ty stopped and squared his scrawny shoulders. "Who are you, Dear Abby?"

"No, I— I can just tell that she—"

His eyes were black bullets. "You wanna talk to Khamille, you wanna get tight with her, go ahead. She's friendly, you'll see. Big mouth like yours. Just leave me out." He strode off.

I wasn't sure what made him so mad or how to make it right. It dawned on me that maybe he thought I was making assumptions because he and Khamille were both Black. That wasn't it at all. I saw with my own eyes, that girl was flirting with him. But I didn't know her and I didn't know Ty well enough to understand what was going on.

To be honest, I didn't have much experience with guys, especially Black guys, even though there are plenty of Black and Hispanic kids in my school. Me and my biology lab partner, Ayesha, got along fine. Sure, she made me slice open the frog belly for the dissection, but that had nothing to do with race. It was about who was less likely to puke when the green guts spurted out. We all get along okay in class, no real problems. But in study hall, in the cafeteria, places where we can choose where to sit, we don't mix it up much. They sit at their tables and we sit at ours. There are no actual lines, but we all seem to know where the invisible lines are and when to cross. That's just how it goes. I never really gave it much thought before.

Ty had disappeared in the direction of Joe's office, returning a couple of minutes later. I watched as he unlocked the door of the ticket booth and stepped inside. He came out wearing a red apron and swept the sidewalk in front of the booth. He seemed to be looking everywhere but my direction. Okay, at this moment Ty was just like every guy I ever knew, black, white, or purple: dancing the awkward ridiculous dance of getting goofy around a girl and trying to pretend it wasn't happening.

I crossed the yard to the ticket booth. "I'm sorry, Ty. I don't even know Khamille, so just ignore me, okay?" He finished sweeping up and put the broom away without looking at me, proving that he wasn't actually paying me one ounce of attention. Then he nodded and said, "Joe's waiting for you. I'll take you to the office."

I took that to mean I was forgiven, for now at least. We made a left and walked past a big plywood structure, obviously hiding something under construction.

"What's that?" I asked.

"The old carousel. They're restoring it. Been working on it all winter. Joe's planning a big grand opening for the Fourth of July."

Memories of the huge old carousel, with its multicolored menagerie whirling round and round, flooded me. The very first time my Aunt Helen buckled me onto my favorite red horse, I felt big, important, like I was really somebody in this world. I could still hear the loud, tinny music that made my skin prickle, and still feel the power of the jeweled horse beneath me, the magical escape from reality.

"That was my favorite ride when I was little. I can't wait to see it again," I told Ty. "I love it. That music. What did my Aunt Helen call it? A calliope."

Ty laughed. "Yeah, well, let me know how you feel about the ka-lie-o-pee when you been sitting in that ticket booth for eight hours listening to it."

"I won't care," I said.

He laughed and turned toward the office.

"I won't," I whispered again to myself. And I meant it.

Joe's office was in a small yellow shack wedged between the bumper cars and the big new video arcade. The door squeaked as we opened it. Joe hunched over an adding machine, wreathed in smoke from the cigarette burning in his ashtray, his black polyester jacket draped over the back of the chair. What sounded like opera music blasted from a small boombox behind him. He glanced up, shaking a stubby finger as a signal for me to wait.

When he finished entering a string of numbers, he tore off the machine tape then stamped out his cigarette with one hand and used the other to smooth the thick black pelt on his head. He reached over his shoulder and turned off the screechy soprano. When he lifted his arm I had a good view of the yellow sweat-stained armpit of his short-sleeved white shirt.

"What is it with kids these days?" he asked. "That video arcade makes more money than the rest of the place put together. What kind of kid sits in front of a TV screen shooting at space monsters when he could be riding a roller coaster?"

"A normal kid," Ty mumbled.

"Hell-o Lilli," Joe sang, ignoring Ty. "Uniforms fit okay?"

I nodded. "Just fine." This wasn't the time to tell him what I really thought of his uniform.

"Ty, we were busy last night. Angelo could use some help on clean-up crew, the place is a mess. Why'n't you see what he needs then check back with me when Angelo's done with you?"

I recalled what Ty had said yesterday about dirty work. But he just told Joe, "You got it. See ya later, Lil." And he was gone.

"Nice boy," Joe said. "I liked him the minute I met him. You don't see a lot of his kind with that kind of respect."

"His kind?" I asked.

Joe smoothed his hair, dimly aware that he might have said something offensive. "Kids his age, I mean."

"Oh." I nodded. I was sure that was just what he meant. "Kids my age, you mean."

He yanked a chair to his desk. "Sit down, sit down," he said, patting the yellow vinyl seat. "Let's talk about Island Amusements and your future."

I didn't care for the implication that my future was in any way tied to this dilapidated park. But I needed the job and Joe was actually a sweet old guy, so I decided right then and there not to give him a hard time. Of course, that didn't mean I'd let him push me around.

"I'm really looking forward to working here," I said, digging deep into my sweetness reserves. "I have a lot of good memories from this place."

"You don't have to tell me!" Joe clapped his hands like a little boy. "We always rolled out the red carpet for you, Lilli. And for Helen, of course." He crossed himself and mumbled, "God rest her soul."

I didn't want to think about Aunt Helen right now so I kept the conversation rolling. "Ty was telling me you're restoring the old carousel."

"Ai, Maria," he said, throwing his hands up and pinching his cheeks. "It's bee-yoo-ti-ful. But it's been such a bi—"

He slammed the brakes on the swear word. As if I'd never heard it before? Joe was a funny guy.

"The workers are slow as sh—" he shook his head, stopping himself again. "Slow. They were gonna be done for Memorial Day when we opened for the season, but now it looks like we'll be lucky to make July Fourth. Can you believe it? The season's half gone already and the darned thing's still not ready."

"Will it be ready by the Fourth?"

"It better be, or somebody's gonna hang. The carousel people keep making excuses. Keep telling me how important it is to do the job right."

"Carousel people?"

"Yeah, the Carousel Society. Bunch of guys who are crazy about old carousels. I think they're crazy, period, but who am I to complain? They're the ones who came up with most of the cash to pay for the project. They took the ponies off to be fixed up at some warehouse in Brooklyn. The whole carousel's pretty much back together, just needs a little touch up, but now they tell me there's some missing parts they can't seem to get their hands on." He sighed heavily. "Coulda bought a whole new carousel, the money we're dumping into this one."

"You couldn't buy a carousel like that, Joe."

Joe's face lit up like his eyes were neon. "Ain't that the truth? Plenty of people excited about it, too. In fact, I mapped out a whole PR campaign around that merry-go-round, that's why I'm so pissed it's not ready yet. That thing's got history. It's vintage, know what I mean? It was one of the few to roll out in the lean years just after the First World War. It's not in a class with some of those old pre-war classics, but it's a beauty. Not another one like it anywhere, I can tell you that. The stories those little ponies could tell if they could talk, huh?"

"Yeah," I said. "Sad tales of being tortured by generations of little brats."

Joe threw back his head and laughed. "You. You remind me of your Aunt Stel, anybody ever tell you that?"

"Only all the time," I said. "And I'm not that thrilled to hear it." I leaned forward. "Joe. Do me a favor. When the carousel opens? That's where I want to work."

His eyes narrowed and I could see him mentally rearranging staff. Then he nodded and stuck out a stubby hand. "You got a deal, kiddo."

His handshake was as clammy as I expected.

"You oughta check it out today on your lunch hour. Some of the carousel guys will be in there. Just tell them I said it was okay for you to nose around. In the meantime, let's start you out at the snack bar. It's always busy on a Sunday, and Khamille could use the help. She can show you the ropes so you'll be able to work it alone when she's in school. She's a good kid, Khamille. Hard worker."

"For someone of her kind?" I asked.

Joe opened his mouth to answer, then seemed to decide I was only teasing. "You!" he said, waving a chubby fist at me. "You just remember, I'm the boss around here."

"Yes, sir," I said, grinning. "Just like my aunt Stella is the boss at home."

4 - Carousel

The park had sprung to life by the time I finished filling out Joe's forms. The gates opened at ten, still twenty minutes away, but loud music blared from overhead speakers and the motors on rides idled, spewing smelly fumes.

A middle-aged woman in the red-and-white Amusements uniform stood in front of the snack bar, nursing a styrofoam cup and wolfing a donut. Khamille leaned on the counter, a portrait in boredom. Her chin rested on her hands, her lips pursed into a pout. She glanced at me as I approached. She didn't bother to turn as I came through the back door.

The smell of hot dogs and cotton candy hit me full force. How could anyone work in here all day without puking?

The visor on Khamille's red-and-white striped cap faced backwards, toward me. It covered most of her hair but one braid poked out and grazed the top of her left shoulder. The braid had a few gold beads twisted into it.

I sidled up next to her, noting that I stood at least four or five inches taller, which made her just a hair over five feet. "I'm Lilli Whitaker. Today's my first day working here."

"Is that right?" She sized me up. "You didn't just wear that outfit 'cause you liked it?"

The donut-eating woman snickered. "Khamille, don't start with her, now. She's new." She winked at me. "Believe me honey, we all hate these uniforms. But you'll be glad you got it when it's ninety-eight and the sun's beating down, I can tell you that. I'm Bev, by the way." She licked the donut grease from her fingers and extended her hand, then thought better of it and just waved.

"Lilli. Nice to meet you." Bev had a half-grown-out bleached-blonde perm. Her face was ruddy pink with a light coat of sparkly sweat, and I could see her pores from four feet away. But she seemed friendly. I wasn't sure how to read Khamille.

"You're Joe's cousin, right?" Bev asked.

"Not exactly. My aunts know him. My great aunts, actually. They've known Joe since he was a kid."

"That's a long time to be friends," Khamille said. It sounded like she thought that was something to admire.

"Yeah, it is. He was pretty close to my Aunt Helen. She just died."

"Sorry for your loss," Khamille said.

Our eyes connected for an instant and I could feel my throat start to tighten, thinking about Helen being gone. Uh-uh, that wasn't going to happen, not here. "Anyhow," I said, averting my gaze, "Joe's a funny guy sometimes, but he's okay."

"World is full of funny guys," Khamille said. "That one treats Khamille fair, and that scores big points."

It was a little weird to hear her refer to herself as Khamille but I let it slide. We'd just met and I was glad she liked Joe. "Ty said pretty much the same thing."

"Did he now?" Khamille made herself busy arranging the napkin and straw holders, making sure I saw how completely disinterested she was in Ty. It just made me more certain that she liked Tyson; she just wasn't about to let me see it.

Bev gulped the rest of her coffee and headed off. Suddenly Khamille was all business.

"C'mon then. Let's show you the ropes before we get busy." She handed me a striped cap, the two gold bangles on her right wrist clinking together. "Health department says we got to cover our heads. It's not pretty but it's legal."

I donned the cap and listened as Khamille explained the cash register and the general flow of things behind the counter.

"There's a few tricks." She ticked them off on her fingers. Her nails were filed short with no polish. "Make sure they don't fool you into giving them change for the wrong amount. Like saying they gave you a ten when you know it was a five? And don't put too many hot dogs on the grill at once or you'll have to throw out a bunch at the end of day. Joe will not be happy. Check the drink bubblers every hour or two so they stay full and icy cold. And try to be patient with the kids who can't decide what they want.

"It's not brain surgery," she concluded. "You'll learn as you go. Oh, and you can eat pretty much whatever you want. Not that you'll want to."

We both laughed and shared a smile. Hers was wide with a small space between her front teeth. On most people that might have been seen as a flaw, but on Khamille it looked just perfect.

The weather turned hot and sunny, a nice Sunday afternoon for fresh air and hot dogs. Apparently the nauseating wiener-and-pink-drink odors that flipped my stomach when I walked in were a kid-lure, causing instantaneous whines of hunger in almost every one that passed by. Thank God, my brain suppressed the smells after the first hour so they had no effect on me as we worked together to handle the lunch rush. I wouldn't exactly call it a crowd, but we served a steady stream of customers.

When it quieted down, Khamille announced her lunch hour. "You're in charge," she said, settling into one of the folding chairs in the back of the wagon. "Khamille is here only if she's needed." She pulled a flattened sandwich from a brown paper bag and nibbled as she opened a small paperback.

"What are you reading?"

"Out to lunch," she sang, then flashed the cover of the book at me. "But since you asked. It's Maya Angelou's autobiography."

"Maya who?"

She gave a small, undeniable eye roll. "She's a Black writer. Poet. You wouldn't know her."

She was right, I'd never heard of her.

"I'm taking an AP course this summer. College credit even though I'm still a senior at Curtis High."

"Cool. I'm going to be a senior too." No response. "Good book?" I wasn't much of a reader but it felt polite to ask.

"This woman?" She tapped the page with her index finger. "Survived some serious stuff. Serious. She's an inspiration."

She went nose-down into the book and I turned away, leaning on the counter to size-up the patrons. The kids reminded me of myself when I used to visit here with Aunt Helen, filled with anticipation, all antsy and excited. I understood now that it wasn't the rides themselves, it was the thrill of being taken to the rides. The place was absolutely no big deal but kids still seemed to love it.

After a while Khamille closed her book. "Your turn."

"Okay. I'm gonna go check out the carousel. Joe says that's where I'll be working when it opens."

"Is that so?"

Her tone made me wonder if my news was somehow an insult to her and the snack bar. "I'm not totally sure," I said, hoping to smooth things over. "It sounds like they've done a lot of work on it. Fixing it up."

"It looks pretty good." She glanced toward Joe's office shack. "But I don't know. Joe's so excited about that carousel. Like a fresh coat of paint and some publicity could really change anything around here."

"It might."

"You never know," she said, but her expression told me she did know. Change was hopeless and Joe was bound to be disappointed. "You be back in a half hour, you hear?"

"No sweat. There's no way it'll take me that long to look at an old carousel."

It took me a while to find an entrance on the face of the plywood barricade but I finally spotted a dangling padlock that indicated a doorway. I stepped in and let out a long low whistle at my first glimpse of the newly painted horses. I expected a buffed-up version of the shabby old machine of my childhood, but the shabbiness had been zapped, replaced with a glorious glitz and glitter beyond my imagination. Brilliant blues, golds, and reds slapped me in the face, demanding my full attention. Glassy-eyed ponies dared me to board their bright saddles and I stepped forward, hand outstretched, ready to ride wherever they'd take me.

"Whoa, there," a husky voice called from behind me. "Carousel's not open yet."

I turned, prepared to defend my rights, and another shock wave hit. The voice belonged to a tall, thin guy with wire-rimmed glasses perched on a perfectly formed nose. His face was surrounded by masses of sandy-blonde hair, thick and wavy, barely contained in a loose ponytail at the base of his neck. A blue shop apron covered his jeans and he juggled a jar of paint, a wad of rags, and a handful of brushes in his long-fingered hands.

Talk about demanding your attention. I had a sudden flash of fingers, my fingers, combing, twisting, dancing in that tangle of hair. I drew a breath and prepared myself to speak. To say something that would make this guy remember me.

"Joe invited me to check out the carousel," I told him. "I'm going to be working here after the Fourth."

He looked me up and down, noting the unfortunate uniform then nodding. "Joe's the boss." He stepped carefully onto the carousel and squatted to inspect the decorative side panel of one of the chariots, ignoring me. His fingers were smudged with paint, so he used the back of his hand to brush back a lock of stray hair and slide the glasses up his perfect nose. As he raised the brush with his multicolored fingers, I stepped closer.

"Careful," he warned. "A lot of this paint is wet. It's oil. It won't wash out, and it's all so shiny you can't tell the wet from the dry."

"Thanks," I said. "I'd be really bummed if I got paint on this nice new uniform."

He acknowledged that with a short laugh and a shake of his bushy head, but still didn't turn to look at me.

I didn't like that. I wanted to see his eyes again, fix their color and size and shape in my brain. "Did you paint all these horses yourself?"

"Some," he said, still intent on his work. "Not all."

"Show me your favorite."

He faced me then. His eyes were blue, clear deep blue as vivid as the trim on the painted pony over his left shoulder, and they told me he didn't like being interrupted. "You know anything about restoring carousels?"

"No," I admitted. "But I figure if I'm going to work here this summer, I better start learning." It was lame, but it was something. "People might ask questions." It occurred to me that it would be less obvious if I just lay down at his feet and begged, but I really didn't care. I wanted this guy to like me.

He set his brush carefully on the pile of rags. "I'm Jesse."

"Lilli," I replied to his unspoken question.

He nodded. "I suppose I could take a few minutes to explain what we've been doing."

"That would be great," I managed. Other adjectives sprang to mind, but I muzzled myself and tried to focus.

He explained that it had taken eight months of work in a little shop in Brooklyn to undo the years of damage to the carousel. "We attacked it horse by horse. This one here's my favorite." He crossed to the one with a saddle trimmed in the same blue as his eyes. "I did most of the work myself."

"How long did it take?"

"Sixty or seventy hours."

"Are you kidding? For this one horse?"

He laughed. "It was a wreck. The ears and legs were practically falling off the old guy and he had about twenty coats of cheap park paint." His palm slid lovingly down the gilded trim of the saddle. I forced myself to concentrate on what he was saying. "When I finally got him stripped, the detail on the original paint underneath was incredible."

"Is this your job, fixing up old carousels?"

"Don't I wish. I'm in art school. I'm a painter. I work on this kind of project when it comes along, which isn't very often. It's—" he hesitated, looking for the right word. "Kind of a—a calling."

"A calling?"

He rested his hand on the pony's neck and nodded.

I thought that was the most amazing thing anyone had ever said about their work. I stepped up onto the platform next to him and tried to think of something else to say. "It's so quiet in here. Almost too quiet. It feels weird. I love hearing that — what do they call it? Calliope? That music thing that blasts your brains out? I love that."

"Me too." His nod turned eager. "Only it's not a calliope, it's actually a band organ."

"Well, excuse me."

"Common mistake," he said. "You want to hang out with a carousel expert, expect to be corrected."

I liked the sound of that. Hang out. "What else can you teach me?"

"This band organ is European, like a lot of them, and it plays rolls, like a player piano. Joe's planning to use it for the grand opening, but after that he'll use a modern sound system to blast you off your horse."

"He will? That doesn't sound like Joe."

"Band organs sound great and everyone loves them, but maintenance is a royal pain in the butt. Expensive. A plain old sound system's a lot cheaper to run."

"Now that sounds like Joe," I said. He laughed then, a sound that bubbled out like cold water from a fountain. I suddenly understood I was dying of thirst.

"I like Joe," he said. "He really looked hard to find the money to restore this carousel. And poured in plenty of his own. He seems to think if he can recapture the old magic, things will be just like they used to be around here."

"You don't agree?"

"I want it to be true." He shook his head. "You should've heard him arguing with the insurance man about the ring machine."

"The what?"

He pointed to a metal pole sticking up from the ground near the plywood shell. "This carousel used to have a ring machine, before the war. You know, grab the brass ring, get a free ride?"

I had no idea what he was talking about. He crossed to the edge of the platform and leaned way out, crooking a red-streaked finger to snag an imaginary ring.

"That used to be a thing?"

"It did. I understand they stopped it during the war. At one point Uncle Sam took anything that could be put to better use, and the brass rings were considered recreational metal."

"They took something as small as that?"

"Hey, bullets were essential, carousels were not. What can I say? Anyway, Joe was hot to get the ring machine up and running again. The carousel people could repair it, but the insurance premiums were sky high. Joe was pissed but he had no option. No ring machine."

"That must have been hard for Joe. But still. The horses do look gorgeous." I ran my hand across the nose of a dappled gray horse, enjoying the smooth, fresh feel of the glossy paint. "Do you ever feel sorry for these ponies?"

"Sorry? No way. They look better than they have in years, all spiffy and shiny-brand-new."

"Yeah, but that only makes it harder. They're all decked out and ready to roll, and they just have to stand there and wait till somebody hits that big button. And even when that big bell rings all they do is go around and around and around again. They never really get anywhere." I knew I was thinking about my own life. My own stupid, boring, nowhere life.

Jesse took a step closer, his lanky frame towering over me. I stared hard at the horse's sad black eyes, not daring to look up at Jesse's baby blues. I felt suspended, afraid to even breathe. Finally I heard him sigh, and maybe I imagined it, but the feathery touch of his breath brushed my own fingertips.

"I don't see it that way at all. These horses? They love going around and around and around, making people laugh and smile. They can't get enough of it, Lilli."

At the sound of my name, I turned to him and right away I fell into those deep blue pools.

"They love it because it makes people happy. They're like little joy-spreaders, doing exactly what they're meant to do." He reached his hand toward the dappled gray, stopping just short of touching it, of touching me.

It was wonderful.

It was terrible. I had to get out of there.

I yanked back my hand and cleared my throat like I was trying to dislodge a giant hairball. "I better get back to the snack bar. Khamille's probably clocking my lunch hour with a stopwatch." I hopped off the carousel. "It looks terrific, really. You guys did a great job." I walked on shaky legs to the plywood door and felt around for the handle, waving once I finally found it.

"Maybe I'll stop by for a Coke," he called. "Later."

Friendly, I thought. And obviously a whole lot calmer about the whole thing than I was.

I shut the door behind me and collapsed against it, my heart thrumming in my chest. I was panting like a squirrel who just escaped a Doberman.

I closed my eyes against the sudden glare of the sun and inched my way along the flimsy plywood wall, trying to restore a normal flow of oxygen and brainwaves.

"What's up?" a voice called. "Those ponies stampeding in there or what?"

Ty set down the carton he was carrying. His smug little grin made me wrestle my self-control.

"I was just checking out the new carousel."

"Yeah. And what did you think of him?"

I swallowed hard. It couldn't be that obvious. Ty must have been spying on me. I felt exposed, vulnerable, and in the next instant, furious. "You mind your own business, Tyson Davis. You get all bent out of shape with me when I ask you the tiniest question about Khamille. You don't get to pry into my life. You hear me?"

Ty just smiled his annoying little smile and batted those long lashes of his. "Loud and clear." He picked up the carton. "See you later at the bus stop. Maybe. Have a nice day," he said, tipping his Giants cap.

"Stuff it!" I shouted as he sauntered off, whistling. I stalked across the park, following the scent of hot dogs and cotton candy, which my forgetful brain had now re-labeled "disgusting new scent." I stomped into the snack bar trailer, slamming the door behind me.

Khamille didn't flinch. She finished giving a customer change then turned in my direction, looking me up and down. "Something wrong?"

"Tyson Davis," I replied.

"Not much wrong there as far as Khamille can see."

I folded my arms across my chest. It was a little annoying, the way she used the third person to make pronouncements that made her sound like Queen of the Universe. I wasn't surprised that she would take Tyson's side, given her own obvious feelings for him. But could I trust her with anything about Jesse? I wasn't sure.

"What'd you think of the new carousel?" she prodded.

"Beautiful. Knocked me over."

A chubby middle-aged man stepped up to the snack bar and eyed the menu on the wall behind me. I quickly washed my hands and slapped on an apron, then nudged Khamille out of the way so I could wait on him. Anything to get me moving, get my head back in gear. Khamille busied herself in the kitchen and didn't ask any more questions.

The man was short, barely a head taller than the counter. His receding hairline of dull reddish hair was slicked back with the kind of hair goop nobody used anymore. A few unruly tendrils curled into small knots at the back of his neck. He studied the menu and shook his head.

"This menu hasn't changed in years."

I shrugged. "People seem to like it. Kids, especially."

He nodded. "I'll have to bring my grandson." He ordered a hot dog and an orange soda, and I got busy filling his order.

"I hear they're re-doing the old carousel," the man observed. "Any idea when it'll be done?"

"Grand opening on July 4." I traded his hot dog and soda for his crumpled bills.

He smiled and nodded again. "I'll have to come back. Keep the change." He took his food to a bench across the way.

I tossed the extra money into our tip jar then continued to brood. I couldn't decide which had set my pulse racing. Was it Tyson's superior attitude, or was it because he was right about Jesse? Just when I had managed to convince myself I didn't actually care what either of them thought of me, I spotted Jesse coming toward the snack bar. I felt my pulse kick into high gear as he drew closer.

He plunked down two singles. "Large Coke. Extra ice."

My hands shook as I pulled the spigot. Khamille had my number in less time than it took to wipe the foam head from the cup.

"Need any help?" She flashed a toothy smile.

"I'm fine." I set the cup on the counter in front of Jesse.

"Thanks." Jesse took a long pull on the straw. His Adam's apple bobbed as he swallowed. "I'm done for the day. Won't be back till the opening."

I nodded. I could feel Khamille's eyes on us.

"The grand opening," he added, making sure I really understood. I got it. His words were practically branded on my eardrums. "Will you be here?"

"Probably," I said. For sure, I wanted to scream. "I'll be at the carousel from the day it opens."

"Well," he said, toasting me with his cup as he walked away. "See you both then."

Khamille's shoulder grazed mine. "Lordy," she said, chuckling softly as Jesse headed back toward the carousel. "It all makes perfect sense now."

There was no point in trying to deny it to Khamille. I flopped into a chair and fanned myself with a paper napkin. "I think I'm going to faint."

"You'll be fine." She sat next to me. "I've seen worse."

"You have?"

"Sure. On TV, you know? Those animal mating dances on the educational channel?"

She laughed, not a mean laugh, but it set my teeth on edge. I hate it when my feelings threaten to overwhelm me. I hate it even more when someone thinks they know how I'm feeling. And I really hate it when they're right. "You get just as bad around Ty," I said. Okay, I hadn't actually seen that but I had a pretty good suspicion based on what I had seen.

"I definitely do not." She waited a beat. "So. What's this guy got going for him? Besides the obvious."

"He's a painter. He's in art school. College, I guess? Did you see the work he's done on those horses? It's gorgeous. And he's—"

"Sort of gorgeous himself."

I kicked my sneaker against the wall. "I hate this!" I drew a ragged, frustrated breath and blew it out. "It's always like this, and I hate it." I had barely met Jesse and already I could feel myself losing control.

"Always?" Khamille asked. "For example— like what?"

I rolled my memory over the not-too-long list of love-life mistakes. "Like last Christmas. There was this guy at school? His name was Roger. I didn't even like him that much. But he started flirting with me and all of a sudden it was like whoosh. Zero to sixty. High gear, too fast, racing along like a Gypsy cab at 3 a.m."

"And?"

"And it lasted exactly ten days. He just started flirting with another girl and that was that."

"Sad."

"Yeah."

"And you're still here, right? Still alive. Still Lilli."

I took a long breath and exhaled with a big sigh. "I guess."

"For sure. Listen. You want some advice?"

I shrugged. I was probably going to get it whether or not I wanted it.

She raised her chin and focused on the spot where Jesse's back had just disappeared. "First off, he's a little old for you."

She was right, but I didn't want to admit that.

"But let's put that aside for now. Because in Khamille's book? There's nothing wrong with seeing what you want and going for it. Sure, keep your eyes open. Play it smart. But don't just give up before you start."

"I don't know," I began. "It's just—"

"Never mind it's just. You listen to Khamille. If you want to win a race?" She nodded with certainty and nudged me with her shoulder. "First thing, you have to show up at the starting gate and be ready to run."

Without another word she made herself busy in the back, leaving me to regain what was left of my composure.

5 – Plans

The next two days at the rides passed quickly. Jesse hadn't come back, but the snack bar kept me busy. Not exactly swamped with customers, just enough to keep me from dying of boredom. On Tuesday evening when I turned off Bay Street into Stella's quiet tree-lined block, I could feel time skidding to a halt. I tried to slow my pace to the rhythm of the neighborhood, but I felt like a thoroughbred at a pony ride. Today the most exciting activity was the corner house, where a couple of squealing kids tossed a big pink ball around on the lawn while an old man watched from a green-webbed lawn chair. Close second was a few houses up, where a woman in a purple sundress sprayed her petunias and geraniums with a green hose. For sure, if I had to spend every night hanging around here with no one but Stella for company, I'd be stir-crazy in a week.

I paused in front of Ty's house. He had today off, so I hadn't seen him. On a whim, I turned in and climbed his front steps, hoping we could at least make a plan to do something interesting. Through the screen door, I could see his mother on the sofa reading. She looked up when I knocked.

"Hey, Darlene," I waved. I wondered if that was too casual. "Miss Davis. Is Ty around?"

She closed her book and set it aside to come to the door. "Sorry, he's out right now."

"You know if he's working tomorrow?"

She tilted her head thoughtfully. A lot of Black ladies were letting their hair go natural these days, but Darlene's hair was straight and usually slicked back off her face with a hairband. Maybe the nursing home where she worked made her wear it that way. Or maybe she was just more traditional.

"He is," she answered. "Ten to three, I think. Did you need something?"

I wasn't sure how to proceed. Ty and I were still a little touch and go and I didn't want him or his mother to think I was desperate. Then I realized maybe I was a little desperate, facing evening after evening with Stella. I just wasn't sure what to do about it.

"Nothing special. I just wanted to say hello."

"Well, come on in for a minute. It's hot out there."

I stepped in and she invited me to sit near a fan that was blowing warmish air around the room. They had just moved in that day last fall when I delivered Aunt Helen's brownies. The place had been full of unpacked cartons and bags, but it was clear they were settled now. The living room was homey, with a sofa and two chairs that were a lot newer than anything in Stella's house.

"The place looks great," I said.

"Thanks. We like it."

The wall by the dining room was covered with big framed photos of family events that included a lot of bridesmaids in colorful dresses. I homed in on the wall beside the front door where a cluster of frames hung with the unmistakable look of school pictures.

"Are those Tyson?" I asked.

She nodded. I stood to get a closer look of everything from that little six-year-old missing his front teeth to a more recent one where he was apparently attempting to grow a mustache. It looked more like the glass had a smudge near his upper lip.

"I'm glad he decided to shave," I said.

"You and me both."

I sat down again. On the table behind the sofa was a large framed photo of a younger Darlene, nose to nose with a toddler. They looked completely delighted with one another.

"Is that you and Tyson?" I didn't really need to ask; the eyelashes were a dead giveaway.

She turned to look at the photo. Her expression softened. "I love that picture. Wasn't he a beautiful boy? He still is. Tyson got the best of me and his daddy. My brains, thank goodness, but his dad's looks." She turned back to me. "How is your aunt? She must be so lonely. It's good you're here with her."

"I guess. It's not exactly fun."

She laughed. "She's not the easiest person. Not as easy as Helen for sure. Rest her soul." She shook her head a few times. "How's the job? Going okay?"

"I guess. First job and all. You know."

"I do. A little hard work never killed anybody your age. Do the time, then you climb."

I recognized the motivational lecture Tyson referred to the day of Helen's funeral. "It's kind of fun, actually. Working with Tyson." It suddenly dawned on me that she might think I had, like, a crush on

Tyson, which was pretty far from the truth. But then I thought about Khamille, who actually did like Ty. "And there's another nice girl we work with. Khamille?"

I was surprised to see Darlene's face cloud with suspicion. "Khamille?"

"Yeah, she's really nice, she's smart and—"

"I know Khamille," she said.

And I don't like her, was what she didn't say. So she and Ty both had a problem with Khamille. I just wished I understood more about why that was. "Miss Davis. Is there some problem between you and Khamille?"

Darlene's whole attitude toward me had flash-frozen. "Not really."

"Because I don't want to keep stepping on toes if —"

"It's not your concern," she said, her tone final.

"Oh." I didn't know what else to say. "Okay."

She stood, a clear signal for me to leave.

"I'd better get on home. Stella will be worried. If Tyson wants to hang out some time—maybe a movie? Tell him to just let me know."

"I'll tell him you stopped by." She walked me to the door and did everything but push me through it. "Regards to your aunt."

She retreated without another word. I wondered if Khamille knew how Ty and his mother felt about her. I wasn't sure how to find out, but I needed to try, since I had to work with Ty and Khamille all summer. I trudged toward Stella's taking some comfort in knowing that at least there would be something decent for supper. At least this summer I was learning to calibrate my expectations.

I found Stella parked in the old gray arm chair in the sunporch, the window AC roaring and a floor fan ruffling the hem of her housedress. She glanced over the top of her Staten Island Advance, sausage fingers clutching the newsprint. The sour look on her face made me wonder whether there was more bad news in the obituaries or if she'd just spotted a dog squatting on her lawn.

It turned out to be worse than either of those things.

"Go wash up," she said. "We'll eat in a few minutes."

I started to climb the staircase to my room.

"And by the way," she added. "I told Joe you need tomorrow afternoon off."

I whirled around. "Why?"

She didn't look up from the paper. "I've been invited to have lunch with Helen's canasta club, and I have no intention of going alone."

She couldn't mean what I thought she meant. "What's that got to do with me?" I struggled to remain calm as I backed down the steps.

"What do you think? You're coming with me."

I dropped onto the couch. "No way."

She turned a page of the paper and scanned it casually. "And I expect you to dress decently. Hair combed, spit polish. I won't stand for less."

"You won't need to. Because I won't be going." My Aunt Helen's canasta club used to be the highlight of her month. Once when I was visiting, the club met at Helen's, and I still remember how the ladies cooed and fussed when she introduced me, like I was some kind of pet monkey. It was unbearable when I was nine, never mind now.

I had to think fast. "I don't play canasta, Aunt Stel. And besides, don't they need—like—an even number or something? To play?"

Stella waved her arm. "They haven't actually played canasta for years. It's too mentally challenging for them."

I suppressed a smile.

"These get-togethers are just an excuse to gossip while they rave about each other's fancy recipes and their brilliant grandchildren." Stella frowned.

"Yeah, well, whatever. Just count me out."

Stella dropped her hands to her lap, crumpling the paper in the process. "Lilli Rose," she said sharply. "Let's see if we can't agree on something for a change, shall we? My sister Helen thought the canasta club was wonderful, and they worshipped the ground she walked on. But collectively they are without a doubt a bunch of addle-headed dodos. You and I both understand that."

Her cheeks blazed with anger. I had to admit it was a relief to see her mad at somebody besides me.

"They think they're doing me a favor by including me in their little club, now that Helen is gone."

"So? Just say thanks, but no thanks."

She folded the paper with a sharp snap. "You think I didn't try? The more I refuse, the more convinced they are that I'm so grief-stricken I can't think straight. So, I'm going tomorrow, just once, to shut them up and to show them I am just fine. And you are part of what they need to see. That I have company and I am not bereft." She raised a finger and tapped her chest. "So if I go," she aimed the finger at me like a fleshy gun, "you go. Got it?"

I got it all right. I didn't like it but I got it. I took a breath and tried to sort out the jumble of feelings swirling inside me like a fizzy Coke. It was actually kind of refreshing for Stella to be this straight with me. It showed a certain respect for my opinion, if you looked at it in the right light.

"What time is this sorry little affair?" I asked.

"Don't be flip, young lady," she snarled. So much for mutual respect. "Twelve-thirty. Now go wash up." She tossed the paper aside, heaved herself out of the chair and shuffled toward the kitchen.

Great. I had been promoted from errand girl to companion. We were, at least, agreed that this debacle would only happen once. Meanwhile, tomorrow was sliced up like a picnic watermelon, a huge chunk cut right out of the middle and barely a nibble of time on either end. I went upstairs and splashed water on my hands and face and ran my wet fingers through my hair until it stood on end. My only hope was if Ty had a good idea for some fun tomorrow night. Assuming I survived the day.

At the kitchen table, I stabbed a slice of meatloaf with my fork, spooned out some mashed potatoes, and poured a puddle of brown gravy to dip them in. I poked at my plate, trying not to stare as Stella filled hers and covered everything with about an inch of gravy. She wasn't a bad cook but it was amazing how absorbed she got when she ate. She seemed to forget there were other humans in the vicinity.

I decided to make some conversation, especially now that we were united in mutual anticipation of tomorrow's trauma. "So was Joe okay when you told him I couldn't work tomorrow?" Joe was always a safe topic.

She shrugged, dabbing her lips with a paper napkin. "He was fine. He'd never say so but the place is empty half the time. He can certainly get along without you for one afternoon."

I couldn't argue with that. "The rides should be pretty busy on July Fourth, though." I felt a flutter in my stomach at the mention of that magical date. "That's the grand opening of the old carousel."

"Hmmph." Stella shifted her attention from meatloaf to potatoes. At least I think it was potatoes. The food all looked the same buried under that gravy.

"I saw the carousel on Sunday," I continued. "It's gorgeous. They really did a nice job."

"Joe told me all I need to hear about it." She licked her fork and waved it at me for emphasis. "I'd never say this to Joe, but I think it's a complete waste of money."

"Why? It's a beautiful old carousel. A lot of people are looking forward to the opening. Joe thinks it will bring people to the rides who haven't been there in years."

She snorted again. "Joe Alonzo lives in a dream world. He's always been that way. He's as bad as Helen was. When he was a kid, he used to save his SkeeBall tickets for ridiculous prizes. Do you know he actually asked me if I wanted to be interviewed for some silly article he was planning for the Advance? Reminiscences of the old days. Completely ridiculous." She took a piece of Wonder bread to mop the gravy on the rim of her near-empty plate.

Joe asked Stella to be interviewed? That was weird. As far as I knew she hated the rides and always had. She couldn't possibly have anything positive to say. "Maybe he was trying to be nice," I suggested. "You know, like the canasta club?"

She harrumphed again. I actually felt a little sorry for Stella. She was used to being left alone, and now that Helen was gone suddenly everybody was trying to be her friend. Which was crazy. Stella needed friends like a millionaire needed subway tokens. What was the point?

"That would be fun though, wouldn't it?" I goaded. "Being interviewed for the paper?"

"No, it would not be fun."

"Come on. People would love to hear about the good old days. I know I would."

"The old days were not all good. This business of romancing the past just drives me nuts."

"Aunt Helen would have done it, I'll bet."

Her fork clattered to the plate. "You're right. Of course she would. As I've said, my sister Helen, may she rest in peace, was a sentimental sucker. But in case you haven't noticed, Helen is unavailable at the moment."

I certainly had noticed. I chewed a mouthful of potatoes and suddenly had one of my little brainstorms.

"Hey, Aunt Stel, if you're not interested in that article in the paper maybe you could ask Joe if I could be in it."

"And what could you possibly have to say?"

"I don't know. Fresh angle. New employee. Maybe get my picture taken or something?" The idea excited me. "Maybe I could get my picture taken on Jesse's horse."

Her eyes narrowed. "Who's Jesse?"

"Oh, just a guy I met at work." I was so into my idea I plunged right into the jungle, heedless of the land mines ahead. "He helped restore some of the carousel horses. He's an artist. He's really nice."

"Is he, now?"

"Yeah, and you should see how amazing his work is, it's like—amazing."

"Amazing." She pressed her lips together. I had a sudden sinking feeling about the expression on her face. "Perhaps it was a mistake to allow you to work at Joe's."

"Mistake?"

"Already being influenced by God-knows-what kind of eccentric Beatnik artist."

"No, no, he's nothing like that, he's—"

"He's what? What do you know about him?"

I knew there was no point in defending him. Only Jesse could have made me forget that mentioning b-o-y-s, especially boys that Stella had never met, was a recipe for disaster. Because if she hadn't met them, she couldn't tell if she approved of them, and she believed she had the right to approve or condemn everyone.

"I should have known better than to try to have a normal conversation with you." I was angry, too, and I didn't care if she knew it. "It's not what you're thinking, Aunt Stel." Actually it's even worse. I think I'm in love with this guy I barely know and I'm not even going to see him for another whole week, but I'm not about to tell you that. "I talked to Jesse for like, ten minutes, tops. He taught me about the carousel. Explained what they did, how they restored the horses to look like new. I'll be working there soon so I needed to know all that."

She gazed at me in stony silence, unimpressed.

"It wasn't any big deal."

She pushed her chair back from the table. "See that it remains so."

I stared at my plate, insides churning. Stella's standards were whacked out. Completely out of touch with my reality, that was for sure. Still, I had made a mistake. Everyone in my family knew enough to color the truth to make it more palatable to Stella. How could I have forgotten? I hadn't done anything wrong, but she made it seem like I was consorting with the devil, as she might have put it. Imagine Joe even asking her to be interviewed. What was he thinking? This woman had never had a bit of fun in her entire life.

At the rate I was going, this canasta club tomorrow could be the highlight of my summer social life. By the time July Fourth rolled around she'd probably have me chained up at night. But she was not going to win. I shoved my plate away, more determined than ever to make sure that statement came true.

Stuart: The Brass Ring

In June of 1942, Stella and I spent every Sunday afternoon at the South Beach boardwalk. I wasn't in uniform yet, but I'd been processed and scheduled for basic, which won me the admiration of others and filled me with an ill-founded sense of pride. While basic training loomed ahead, actually going off to war was still a distant nightmare that Stella and I had yet to face.

"Riff-raff and hooligans," Stella's father said whenever we mentioned the boardwalk. He sat in his tattered armchair in the sunporch, square in the path of the faintest breeze that might find its way through the wide open windows. A burly man with a fading fringe of red hair, he favored ragged undershirts and cut-off trousers, and clutched a can of Piels tightly in his fist. One ear cocked toward the radio, he swigged and smoked his way through his days, pounding the arm of his chair and swearing at the announcer if the news or sports was particularly vexing.

Life hadn't been kind to Paddy Whitaker. As a young lad he sailed from Ireland, leaving behind generations of sadness and starvation. Forever, so he hoped. He soon landed himself a job, and then a wife who gave him four little ones. But the crash of '29 threw him back to hard times. More lean years, barely scraping by, and just when things were fattening up again, Paddy lost his wife to a sudden fever. Grief led him to develop a stronger interest in drink than he ever had in his children. Stan, his eldest, fled as soon as he could, while Helen and Stella, still in their teens, held the house together for their youngest brother, Harry.

The war brought more work to everyone. But by that time, the job was more than Paddy could manage, no matter the pay. The girls had finished school, found jobs, and somehow managed to keep hearth and home going.

By the time I came onto the scene, some six years after their mother's death, an uneasy peace had formed at the Whitaker house. Helen tried to keep things cheery, coddling Paddy and Harry, who was now sixteen and heartily resisted her attempts at mothering. Stella lived in a social whirl, always out with this friend or that, and with an illogical, yet unshakable, faith that life would be kinder to her than it had been to her father.

"Oh, Da." She bent to kiss him lightly on his stubbly face. "The boardwalk is perfectly harmless fun. Don't fret so." Stella had grown expert at sidestepping her father's gloomy observations. She was respectful, as any proper daughter would be, but overall she paid him very little mind and did mostly as she pleased.

"You ought to come with us some Sunday," I suggested, just to see Stella blanche. I knew old Paddy'd never say yes and thank God I was right. The old man waved his arm in disgust, his deep scowl broadcasting that I wasn't quite approved of, never mind my ideas about where to take his daughter. He gulped his beer and swore at the Dodgers' pitcher as we waltzed hand in hand out his front door.

We stood together at the corner bus stop, arms entwined around one another. We weren't particularly worried if the bus was late. What was the rush? We were together, we were in love, and ahead of us we had nothing but forever.

We had no idea what was actually ahead. But nothing could stop us that summer.

"Stella!" someone called from the window of a Chrysler. "Hop in, we're headed to the boardwalk."

"Louise! Zig!" Stella tugged me toward the car, already overstuffed with young bodies. "That'd be swell."

"You sure there's room?" I asked.

"Sure, pile in, we'll just cuddle up," Zig said, pulling Louise a little closer. She giggled and we squeezed in, Stella in front, me in the back beside two fellows and a girl. "We'll be there in a jif." Zig hit the gas. Peals of laughter filled the car as we jammed into each other at every corner, and when we tumbled out at the boardwalk ten minutes later, I felt I'd been permanently creased at the ribs.

Stella thanked Zig for the ride and the group broke up.

"Have fun you lovebirds," Louise said, shooing me and Stella away.

The offshore breeze was a heavenly relief and we stopped here and there to try our luck at the games of chance. For weeks we'd tried to win a doll in a pink ruffled dress that we could have bought three times over for the number of nickels we plunked down as they spun the wheel. We were no luckier today.

A couple passed by, clinging to one another, and though we both knew that look of time-running-out, we did our best to ignore it. The radio news, the newsreels of war, the grim telegrams our friends' families were party to, they didn't seem real yet. The only thing real was our blossoming romance.

"How about a little SkeeBall?" I asked as we neared the alleys. Stella groaned, knowing I would want to play till my arms ached. I was pretty good, and we were getting close to collecting enough prize tickets to cash in on something big. "Come on, I thought you wanted that nice blanket? Or those fancy mixing bowls? Can't win them without tickets."

She hugged me, and I knew both our heads were filled with dreams of the bed, the kitchen, the house that would one day become our home. With Stella cheering me on, I plopped the first nickel into the machine and began rolling balls up the alley.

"There's Joe," she said after the first game. "I've got to go say hello."

She strode quickly toward the pimply-faced kid, waiting until he was between throws before tapping him on the shoulder. "How's our little man?" She playfully ruffled his jet-black curls.

Joe Alonzo lived up the street from the rides. He was still in high school, no more than 15, and we saw him so often at the SkeeBall alleys that we'd more or less adopted him. Joe was awkward and chubby from too much of his Italian Mama's homemade pasta and sausages, but he was a SkeeBall champ. He flashed the pile of tickets he'd won that night, blushing at her attention.

"I'm saving for a set of records," he said. "The great operas."

Stella laughed. "Operas! Joe, you're so serious, sometimes I wonder what will become of you."

Joe blushed again. "I'll be a soldier like everyone else, I guess." He rolled another one square up the middle for 200 points.

"No, no," Stella said. "The war will be over long before you're ready, Joe."

"Gosh, I sure hope so." It was the patriotic thing to say, but he didn't mean it. Kids Joe's age couldn't wait for their chance to kill some Nazis or Japs. Hell, guys my age were chomping at the bit to get overseas. God knows why.

Turns out, Stella was right; the war was over before Joe and his friends had their chance to die, and they all felt cheated. When God designed young men he overdid the lust for danger, that is the long and short of it.

"See ya, Joe," Stella said. "It's time for a ride on my carousel." She took my arm and tugged me toward the noisy old machine. It was, without a doubt, her favorite part of the boardwalk.

Stella raced aboard, scrambling to get to her favorite red-saddled horse before anyone else. Sometimes we both squeezed onto it, me on the rear of the saddle and she sideways in front of me, my arms a protective armor around her waist. But that Sunday night, I clambered on to the horse beside her, a blue and gold stander on the outside perimeter of the carousel.

"I'm going for the brass ring," I announced.

"Are you, now?" she teased. "Careful you don't break your neck trying."

I laughed. The carousel's engine clicked into gear, the music blared and the park whirred past in a blur.

Snagging a ring required split-second coordination, reaching out just so to pull it from a metal tube placed far enough away to make reaching it near impossible. With every pass I'd lean way, way out, and each time Stella squealed as if the fall would kill me if I tumbled.

That Sunday turned out to be the last before I left for basic. On the third go-round I nabbed a ring, but it was only made of iron. I'd done that plenty of times before, the worthless iron ring, but I'd never snagged the brass. But that night changed my luck. On the fourth try, I leaned out and pulled hard, and in my hand was something shiny. Something real.

"It's the brass!" I waved it above my head. Stella cheered and clapped, and other riders applauded.

I could have turned in that ring and gotten us a free ride on the carousel. But I didn't want to. The brass ring felt like an omen, a blessing on my journey, on our entire romance. The old carousel wound down, the music slurring as it slowed. We hopped off. I showed the ring to Stella. She slipped two fingers through it and it was still far too large. She laughed then took it off her hand, kissed it, held it to the sky for a blessing and pressed it into my palm.

"Doesn't it feel magical?" she asked, echoing my very thoughts.

"It does indeed." I slipped it into my pocket. We were starry-eyed, impractical lovers, and despite our faith in the future, nothing went as planned from there on out.

But that ring?

We were spot on in that regard. It was, indeed, endowed with special powers.

6 – Canasta

Considering how she supposedly felt about them, Stella took long enough getting ready for her debut with the canasta club. She baked and frosted a cake before her nine o'clock hair appointment, and came home around ten with a hairdo that looked even stiffer and poofier than usual. Then she took the world's longest shower, probably trying to figure out how to get wet without damaging the 'do, no small feat. When she finally padded past my open bedroom door, her face the same rosy pink as her chenille robe, I was tempted to deliver her own "wasting more water than a leaky faucet" lecture.

"Lilli Rose." Her voice sliced through my headphones. "We are leaving at 12:15."

"I know. It's not even eleven."

"May I remind you that I expect you to be properly dressed for the occasion?"

"I'll be ready." I cranked up the volume on my Walkman as she stomped off, closing her bedroom door with a slam.

I took off the headphones when I was sure she was out of earshot. I heard her window fan revving like a race car, attempting the hopeless job of trying to keep her cool and dry as she dressed. A mental image of my aunt Stella wiggling into panty hose floated into my head. I shook it loose and decided maybe it was time to get ready.

A lot of geniuses claim their best ideas come to them in the shower, and I guess I'm no different. By the time I shut the water off, I practically ran back to my room to dress, because I dreamed up a way to make this afternoon more mine than hers. I moussed my hair into nice, stiff spikes, making sure they didn't all point in the same direction, and put on my jewelry, giggling as the little devil inside me danced and waved his pitchfork in encouragement.

Stella was still primping next door as I slipped downstairs. When she finally descended, her stockings shushing like a steam engine, I was ready and waiting. She wore a dark blue dress, and she dropped into her armchair, prepared for the battle between her broad feet and her Navy-blue pumps, when she caught sight of me on the sofa in the living room.

She shrieked. I do not exaggerate, she actually screamed like she'd spotted a decaying corpse on the couch.

"What's wrong?" I asked, all innocence.

"I thought I told you to dress decently."

"I am dressed decently. My knees are covered, and I am wearing a skirt."

I wasn't lying. My knees were covered with hot pink leggings, and my skirt was a yellow mini topped with an oversized purple and white striped top that hung almost to the skirt's hem. I wore plain white sneakers with yellow slouch socks folded over the hem of my leggings. My right ear lobe sported an earring of pink feathers that cascaded almost to my shoulders, and my left ear held several silver ear cuffs. My hair was fairly exploding from my scalp, and I'd added pink stripes to my black fingernails, a sort of fantasy zebra effect. My white lipstick made my lips disappear right into my pale face. When I had inspected the total picture in the mirror upstairs, I thought I looked perfect for the occasion.

Apparently Stella did not agree. She lumbered toward me. "I will not allow you to go with me looking like that." Ordinarily, I'd take that as an insult. This time I knew I couldn't lose so I kept my cool.

"Suits me," I said. "I'll just stay home if that's what you want."

That wasn't what she wanted, and I knew it, but I also knew she hated the sight of my mis-matched Bohemian self. What a dilemma. She stood over me, huffing like a locomotive.

"You better put your shoes on," I said calmly. "We'll be late."

She dropped into her chair again. "You are an incorrigible spoiled little heathen."

"Why, thank you."

"You get up those stairs right now and comb that hair. And put in some normal earrings. You look like you escaped from an asylum."

Another touchy subject, but again I held my tongue. "You know, Aunt Stella," I said, "I think there's an angle to this you haven't considered."

"Oh really?"

"You told me the other night you didn't really want to go today. Right?"

She answered me by shoving one foot into her shoe, which fit about like Cinderella's glass slipper fit the stepsisters.

"Is that still true?" I demanded.

"You know it is," she replied, wincing in pain.

"Well, what do you think the ladies will think of my outfit? Do you think they'll like it?" I stood up and twirled around. I wiggled my butt just for effect. "Do you think they'll, like, want to know who does my hair?" I presented my freshly polished fingers. "Or my nails? Do you think they'll want to invite me back next month?"

I saw her lips purse as she grasped my point. Her brow furrowed, and finally the familiar scowl appeared. "It's embarrassing. They'll think I have no control over you at all."

Correct, I thought, but I had the good sense to keep my mouth shut. "What's a little embarrassment if this is the end of the line for canasta? The club meeting to end all club meetings?"

She stuffed her other foot into the shoe and let out a huge sigh. "You are in league with the devil. But I am simply too tired to argue. If you are not embarrassed to show up looking like a color-blind ragamuffin, why should I be? Go get that cake plate on the kitchen counter. And get a move on, or we'll be late."

Okay, so she couldn't bring herself to agree that my plan might just work. But she must have been thinking about it, because instead of lecturing me all the way over on proper behavior, she drove the fifteen minutes in silence, tapping her fingers on the steering wheel every time we got caught at a light. Poor thing, she was really struggling to figure out the rules for this one. I mean, how do you behave in a room full of women who only invited you to their stupid luncheon because they pitied you? With or without me, she had a problem.

Personally, the only thing I was worried about, besides being forced to eat something gross, was being bored to death. I didn't really care what any of these ladies thought of me. Whatever happened, I could handle it.

We turned into a neighborhood that felt a lot ritzier than my aunt's. Stella and Helen had always lived in Rosebank, an older neighborhood a few miles from the ferry on the east side of the Island. It was a neighborhood originally settled by Irish and Italian immigrants, and you knew that because there were two Catholic parishes, one for each group. The houses in the area were so close to each other you could see right into the living room of the house next door if you cared to look. Stella made kind of a hobby out of looking, though she called it "keeping an eye on things." I called it plain old nosy.

This ritzy neighborhood had large brick houses with long green lawns that reached toward the wide street. Plenty of privacy here. I guess most of the canasta club had already arrived because the driveway was parked full, making it necessary for us to find street parking.

"Drat," Stella said, checking her watch after she successfully parallel parked on the third try. "Now we are late."

We walked up the curving path that wound to a red front door and rang the bell. A perky lady in a pink pant suit answered.

"Why, Stella," she said, "you're—." Then she looked at me and her mouth fell open. She closed it and tried to smile, but her face transformed instead into something out of a wax museum.

"Afternoon, Anne," Stella said, acting like everything was perfectly normal. "This is Lilli, my nephew Stan's youngest." Anne gave a half nod and fondled her pearls, that frozen smile still plastered to her face. When she didn't move after an uncomfortable wait, Stella shoved her gently aside and led me into the front hall.

The noise level in the living room would have roused Aunt Helen in her grave, but we ignored it and went straight toward the kitchen, away from the chattering crowd. A few seconds later, Anne sprinted after us, letting the screen door slam as she raved about how yummy Stella's cake looked. I strolled over to the kitchen counter, filled a glass with ice, and poured myself a Coke.

"Please help yourself," Anne chirped, as if I hadn't already. "And please, pour a little something for your Aunt Stella." She draped an arm over Stella's shoulder. "We're so thrilled you're joining us," she said, with a little squeeze. "Helen would be so pleased."

Stella stiffened slightly, her eyes desperately roaming the assortment of bottles on the counter. "I'm sure she would. Helen loved her canasta club. Frankly, I think she was glad for an excuse to be away from me for a few hours once a month."

Anne laughed, a little too fast and a little too loud.

"Poor Aunt Helen," I said. "I sure wish she could be here instead of me."

Stella came toward me and slipped an arm around me to give me what looked like a gentle, loving squeeze, but which really included fingernails digging into my bare skin.

"We all do, dear," she said, then uncapped the bottle of pink wine she'd been eyeing and filled a crystal glass to just below the rim.

"Well, as much as we miss Helen, we're glad to have you both," Anne said. She strapped on a ruffled apron like something out of a Rockwell painting and yanked open the oven door, releasing an inferno into the already hellish kitchen. "Now go on out and be sociable," she said, shooing us like naughty kittens. "I know everyone wants to see you."

I suppose we could have hidden in the hall until someone noticed us but we continued bravely toward the noise.

"Don't embarrass me," Stella hissed.

"I won't if you won't." We passed through the doorway to a long, narrow living room that felt very different from Stella's place. It had plush furniture, newly-upholstered in a pink and mauve floral print. The end tables overflowed with framed pictures of smiling kids and babies, Anne's children and grandchildren, and the paintings on the wall were framed in gold, like they belonged in some museum. The mauve sculptured carpet was dotted with folding chairs and small snack tables, arranged especially for the hors d'oeuvres. Eight or nine old ladies perched around the tables munching crackers like cackling birds pecking seed from a backyard feeder. It was hard to believe that so few women could make such an incredible racket.

"Stella!" A woman on the sofa was waving furiously. "Come here and let's get a good look at that grand-niece of yours." She patted the sofa and scooted over, clearing enough space for Stella to squeeze in between her and a bent white-haired woman in a green flowered dress.

I followed Stella into the room. The lady in the flowered dress gave me a dazed smile, and the other women just peered curiously over the rims of their Irish crystal glasses as they sipped their wine. The noise level dropped a notch and I felt their eyes glued to me as I sat in a folding chair beside the sofa. They were too polite to stare for long but when the conversation resumed I thought it seemed a little louder than before. I folded my arms across my purple-striped stomach, reminding myself that I didn't care what they thought.

"I'm Louise Hunt," the woman on the couch said after my aunt settled in next to her. She wore a baby blue pantsuit that matched her huge blue-rimmed glasses. She looked familiar, and I realized I had seen her at Helen's funeral last week. Was that only last week? It felt like forever.

"You're Lilli, right?"

Stella set her wine on the coffee table and busied herself smearing creamy dip on a cracker. I was surprised she wasn't trying to answer for me. Mrs. Hunt looked at me expectantly and I decided she had a friendly face. I nodded and said it was nice to see her again.

"Those leggings look really fun. And those colors. Wow! I have a granddaughter about your age. Heather. She likes bright colors too. Her hair is a lot— longer." She took a sip from her glass. "But never mind. I just think it's lovely that you're able to spend this summer with your aunt."

Before I could say anything, the old woman in the green flowered dress perked up. "Oh I know," she said suddenly, to no one in particular. "Don't you just hate that?"

I stared at her, amazed not only that she was so perceptive, but willing to speak up about it. Then she added, "Every summer, no matter what you do, those ants get in everywhere."

Stella rolled her eyes and bit into another cracker, dip pooling in one corner of her lip. Mrs. Hunt giggled. "Mother doesn't hear much anymore, I'm afraid," she said. "But she loves to chat. Just speak up and go along with her, all right? Now Stella," she turned toward my aunt and grabbed both her hands. "Tell me how you are. Really."

I braced myself for the lash of Stella's acid tongue, but she surprised me again by answering in a voice so soft and low that only Mrs. Hunt could hear. They began to talk seriously, and it dawned on me that maybe Mrs. Hunt really was Stella's friend. The idea had never occurred to me.

I tried but I couldn't hear their conversation any better than Mrs. Hunt's mother could, so I leaned back and twirled the ice cubes around my glass. My feather earring dipped dramatically each time I leaned forward to scoop chips from the big glass bowl on the table. That made the other ladies look my way, and I wondered how many of them had granddaughters like Mrs. Hunt who still had big hair and stupid denim skirts. Or if any of them would know the difference between hopeless and hip.

Mrs. Hunt's mother didn't seem to care. She patted my knee and winked, as if we both understood that we had the last word on ants. Her shaky hands lifted her glass of pink lemonade and she took a tiny sip, carefully wiping a drip on her skirt with a crumpled paper napkin she pulled from under her belt. "That's a nice hat," she said, pointing to my hair. "I had one like that in the twenties, in my trousseau."

I noticed a couple of the ladies suppressing giggles. They watched with interest to see how I would handle this one. "Thanks," I said. What was I supposed to say? Louise had told me to go along with whatever her mother said. I didn't want to burst the sweet old thing's bubble and besides, she wouldn't hear me anyway.

"Those were wonderful times," she said. Her faded blue eyes looked beyond me, as if her life was projecting on a movie screen just over my shoulder. "Wonderful times. We had all the money we could spend, and we were so crazy in love we didn't even care when we lost it all."

"That's baloney," another woman chimed in. "She's getting too old to remember it straight. It mattered, plenty, let me tell you. I was only a kid in the Depression but we grew up fast. One day life was fine and the next, bam, we had to worry about everything."

"It was scary," said a red-haired woman. "You kids today don't know how scary. When it finally came, the war was a piece of cake compared to the Depression."

Another one took exception to that, and they started to compare hard luck stories. I could have shared a few childhood tales of my own if anyone asked me. Coming home from school to find my mother passed out cold with a bottle of pills beside her. Or spray painting the kitchen windows black while blasting Bob Dylan from a boombox. But no one asked. They bickered back and forth and just when I was beginning to wonder how I could survive on chips and dip, Anne came in and sang a little song.

"Come to the table all who are able," she warbled, and they all chirped with amusement and fluttered toward the dining room. While everyone scrambled for seats, Stella disappeared down the hall to the powder room. By the time she came back I was settled between Anne and a lady in a turquoise nylon warm-up suit that rustled every time she moved. The only empty seat was at the far end. Stella flopped into it. She was too polite to make a scene, but from the look on her face it was clear she hated having me out of earshot for the whole meal.

"I'm Roberta," the lady in the turquoise suit said, extending a diamond-decked hand in my direction. "You must be Stella's grandniece."

"Yes," Anne chimed in, "Tell us, Lilli, what are you doing to keep busy this summer?"

The interrogation began. I explained about my job at the rides, and after a few more questions I found myself telling them about the carousel restoration and the grand opening. My head was filled with visions of Jesse but, of course, I was careful not to mention him.

"Oh, what fun," Roberta said. "I think I'll take my grandbabies when the carousel re-opens. We all used to spend every weekend at the boardwalk, years ago, but I haven't been down there in ages."

"It was quite a place then," Anne added. "People flocked to that beach. Quite a place. So fun! Nothing like today."

"Aunt Helen told me all about it," I said, hoping to forestall another black-and-white documentary.

"Your Aunt Stella could tell you plenty, too," Anne said. "She and Louise ran with a crowd that practically lived there, way back when. Dancing and carrying on, oh it was some wild fun for sure."

"Really?" I asked. Wild fun? Now this was news. I stole a look at Stella, seated between Louise and the red-haired woman, who was yap-yapping and waving her hands for emphasis. As usual, Stella was focused on her meal, ignoring the redhead, and I watched as she arranged the food on her plate.

It was hard enough trying to get my arms around the idea that Louise was actually her friend. Now these women were trying to convince me that Stella used to be fun. A lot of fun, in fact. It was pretty easy to imagine Louise flirting and cavorting, but Stella? Stone statues didn't dance. That was all there was to it.

"It's hard to believe, isn't it?" Anne sighed. "When you see that beach today?"

"Hard to believe." I nodded, still staring at Stella.

Roberta tapped the edge of her lip with a long red fingernail and squinted toward my aunt. "You know," she said. "I just got a crazy idea. Why don't I call Joe and suggest that he invite Stella to that grand opening?"

"Oh," I said quickly. "She'd never go"

"Don't be so sure about that," Roberta said. "Your Aunt Stella was quite the social butterfly, in her day." Her eyes had a faraway look, like she saw a fairy princess at the other end of that table instead of a miserable old woman.

"You don't believe it," Anne said, as if she were reading my mind. "But it's the truth. I think it's a great idea to take her to the opening. Roberta, why don't you call Joe tonight? He can talk her into anything."

I shook my head. "Joe already asked her to be interviewed by the Advance about the old days. She flat out refused."

"Did she?" Anne said. "Hmmm. Well, some of the memories might be —" she trailed off.

I waited. Might be what?

Roberta nodded. "Difficult. Still, wouldn't it be fun to see if we can wake up any of the old romance in her?"

"Romance?" The word just slipped out of me. To be honest, I'd been imagining what having Stella at the grand opening of the carousel might do to my own chances for romance, and it wasn't shaping into a pretty picture: me and Jesse, reunited under the eagle eye of Aunt Stella. "I'm not sure she cares much for romance. You should hear how she freaks out whenever I mention boys."

Roberta laughed. "Oh, she's all bark and no bite."

"Easy for you to say."

"It's about time Stella had some fun," she continued, her voice dropping. "At least Helen got out once in a while. But Stella? All she ever did was work, after she lost him...."

Anne shook her head. "She was never the same. Her poor heart was broken."

The two of them exchanged a look that set my curiosity juices flowing.

"Wait. You mean Aunt Stella's heart?" I asked.

They suddenly got very interested in eating again.

I leaned toward Roberta. "What are you talking about? Who got lost?" I asked, firmly but without raising my voice. I was very aware of not drawing attention from Stella's end of the table.

Roberta seemed to have gone deaf. "I think I'd like just a dab more Jell-O salad. Anne, that just hits the spot in this heat."

"Excuse me," I said, tapping Roberta's blue nylon sleeve. "Did someone die? And break her heart?"

"Here you go, Rob," Anne said, passing the bowl of jiggling green stuff to Roberta.

Roberta took the bowl from Anne and served herself a small mountain of Jell-O. "You know," she said to Anne, oblivious to the fact that I had spoken, "Getting back to Helen and Stel. The thing I wonder is, what if their mother had lived? Do you ever think about how different their lives would have been?"

Anne nodded solemnly, helping Roberta to steer the conversation away from the danger zone. "Such a wonderful woman. The good ones always die young."

Like the one who broke her heart? I asked myself, knowing even if I had spoken they would have pretended not to hear.

Anne clucked her tongue. "It was that miserable father of hers that put their mother in an early grave," she said, pointing her fork for emphasis.

Roberta nodded her assent. "If he wasn't already dead, why— I'd like to have him skinned, the old coot."

"Excuse me, but who are you talking about now?" It was exasperating, the way they danced around me like I wasn't even there.

"Your great-grandfather," Anne said softly. "Paddy Whitaker, may God rest his tormented soul."

"You never knew him, of course," Roberta said. "He died long before you were born."

I nodded. Somehow, we had crossed out of forbidden territory and were back again on ground they considered safer. But it was still of great interest to me. "Even my grandfather was dead before I came along. His name was Stan. My father was named for him. Aunt Helen told me that."

I realized that everything I knew about my family history, which wasn't much, came from Aunt Helen. It honked me off to realize that these women knew more about my relatives than I did. "We don't talk much about the family," I explained. "Sometimes it feels like there's nothing in my past but tombstones and cardboard boxes."

Anne and Roberta exchanged glances then, and Roberta stole another look at my aunt. "Well, there are things it's better not to know. Paddy Whitaker was lethal. Believe me. Lethal."

All three of us were staring at Stella now. Anne and Roberta's faces dripped with pity, while I struggled to process the image they had painted of a young and carefree Stella. Aunt Helen never hinted at Stella's broken heart, though I knew she was always tolerant of her sister's deep and constant bitterness. Helen must have known a great deal more than she ever let on. I regretted not asking her a thousand questions when I had her ear, but it was too late now. And it was obvious there were certain boundaries I was not allowed to cross. It made me furious. As I pushed my plate away, I had a sudden vision of those boxes I unearthed from Helen's closet. So far, there had been no time to explore them. That would change, and soon.

Stella must have felt our eyes on her, because she looked up from her near-empty plate and glowered. "Lilli Rose, I hope you're behaving yourself down there."

Anne's cheeks turned as pink as her pantsuit.

Roberta went for the Jell-O dish again. "Don't worry, Stel, she's being a perfect little lady. Lilli, more Jell-O?"

"No thanks," I said. "I've had all I can take." I pushed my chair back from the table, my insides churning.

The conversation continued behind me as I crossed the living room. I stared out at Anne's wide lawn, my hot breath making a damp circle on her picture window. I should be used to it by now. The silence and secrets. The things we did not discuss, often discovered only when you stumbled on the wrong question. The way we pretended my family tree was as green and healthy and perfectly trimmed as the trees that lined Anne's street.

It killed me to hear people I just met referring to names and events that had never even been whispered in my presence. My lethal great-grandfather. This mysterious long-lost breaker of Stella's heart. The romantic Stella Whitaker herself. I could even add my own mother to the list of mysteries we couldn't discuss. It was like I lived alone in the shadow of a dark, angry cloud while everyone around me pretended it was a glorious, sunny day and I was the only one who felt any need to carry an umbrella.

I clenched my fists at my side. Maybe they were bluffing about how much they really knew. Maybe they were scared of Stella. Maybe they thought I didn't deserve to know, or that I wasn't strong enough to handle it.

So what. So I didn't know a lot about Paddy Whitaker, and I'd never heard a word about Stella's broken heart. I didn't need these old ladies to spill their secrets. I didn't need their help. If I wanted to find out, I was smart enough to do it on my own. And by God, I would.

7 – Escape

At three o'clock I was still trapped in Anne's living room, leafing through a magazine with one eye on the clock. It was a New Yorker—the only other option was *Modern Maturity*— and I studied the cartoons wondering which New York these people lived in. I was about to go out for a walk around the block when the commotion in the dining room told me the canasta club's post-lunch gossip fest was finally breaking up.

They hugged and made see-you-soon promises as they gathered their belongings. I found the cake plate in the kitchen, pleased to see there was still a decent sized wedge left, and took my place next to Stella to say our goodbyes.

"It was so sweet of you to invite us," Stella told Anne at the door. "And I know Lilli feels just the same as I do."

"Exactly," I said. I knew the goal was to appear grateful without actually saying we couldn't wait for next time, so I followed her lead and smiled.

"We'll see you again soon," Anne cooed, wrapping Stella in one of those mysterious old-lady hugs where the arms go out but no one actually touches. She didn't even try to hug me, but I wasn't sure if it was my earrings or hair or if she was afraid I might grill her with questions in front of my aunt.

As our car pulled away, a hurricane-force sigh gushed out of both of us.

"Well, that was fun," I said. "When do we get to do it again?"

"Don't be flip."

"Come on, Aunt Stella, don't be like that. I did my part, didn't I?"

We pulled up to a light and she stared straight ahead, tapping the steering wheel.

"You're not going to pretend you enjoyed it, are you?" I asked. "That you're looking forward to going again next month?"

She stared at the light, waiting for it to change. "Don't worry. They'll forget me by then. When somebody dies everyone's tripping over each other in sympathy. But it doesn't last. Pretty soon they'll leave us alone.

All alone." She was staring right at the light when it changed but she didn't make a move toward the gas pedal.

"It's green," I prompted. We lurched forward. What she said made sense. When my Mom died the relatives called Dad constantly at first, but he was so busy dealing with all the "things" he had to do that he had no time to talk. A few weeks later, when the only thing left to do was stare at the TV and drink scotch, the phone went silent. Five years later, it's still silent.

But I didn't want to talk about that with Stella. I couldn't remember ever talking with her about my mother, before or after. Helen was the one who understood. I always felt like an afterthought to Stella. A nuisance she had to deal with. I didn't expect any sympathy from her, now or ever.

I did see a little crack in her armor, though. A hint of emotion. So I decided to probe, very gently, about what I learned at the luncheon.

"That Mrs. Hunt is nice, huh?" I said. "I didn't mind sitting next to her."

She nodded. "Louise and Helen were always the obvious standouts in that group. They somehow managed to use the brains God gave them."

"Have you known Mrs. Hunt a long time?" I fished, wondering what kind of saint you had to be to stay friends with Stella for years and years.

"Long enough," she said. "She went to high school with Helen."

I flashed on the yearbook we unearthed last Saturday morning. "Hey," I said. "I bet her picture's in Aunt Helen's yearbook. Let's look it up when we get home."

"To serve what purpose?"

To keep me from going nuts, I thought, though I knew that wasn't high on her list of concerns.

"Just for fun," I said. Another high runner on her to-do list. She didn't answer, just sighed again, and I decided to drop it for now. I knew that box of goodies was in her room. When the coast was clear I could check it out on my own. As we pulled into the driveway the real question just popped out of my mouth.

"Hey Aunt Stel. Was your father a nice guy?"

Stella's foot jammed the brake and I lurched forward so fast my seat belt locked up. Her face contorted like something out of an old sci-fi movie, where there's a special effect of the monster's face superimposed on the human one, just for a second, before it slinks away again. In an instant her face snapped back to her normal scowl. It all happened so quickly I wasn't sure if I'd seen her usual flower-wilting anger or if my question had caused genuine pain.

"My father's been gone for many years," she replied. "Why do you ask?"

"One of the ladies was talking about him," I said. "And about when you were young. At the rides."

"Which lady?"

"I'm not sure," I said, trying to be vague. "There were so many."

"Which lady?" she repeated, making it clear I needed to come up with an answer.

"I think her name's Roberta," I said, caving without a fight. I didn't really think Stella would stalk Roberta and blow her head off, but if it was Roberta's head or mine, my choice was obvious.

She cleared her throat delicately. "As I believe I made clear, most of the canasta club are empty-headed fools. The things they say have very little connection with reality. You shouldn't pay attention to half of it."

"You're right." I nodded. I knew I could safely ignore way more than half of what I had heard. But I also knew by Stella's reaction that what they told me was part of the other half, the important half, the half I was desperate to know. They were telling the truth. And I wasn't about to let that go.

She heaved herself out of the car and walked slowly up the front walk, scooping the mail from the mailbox as she passed it. She flipped through the pile and stopped suddenly, frowning. She held up a small envelope, using her thumb and forefinger like tweezers, then passed the letter to me like it had cooties.

I set the cake plate on the front stoop and took the letter, surprised that anyone would write to me here. Then I saw it had no stamp, just the word "Lily" printed in pencil on the front. Somebody had hand-delivered it to the mailbox. I tore it open and read the scrunched-up script splattered across the blue lined paper.

"Mom said you stopped by looking for me. If you want to hang out later let me know. If you want to hang with Khamille here's her number. If you want to hang with both of us, forget it."

Ty had signed it and scrawled a phone number beneath his name.

"Well?" Stella asked.

"It's from Tyson. Next door." I stuffed the note in my pocket.

"Hmmph," she snorted. "Now we're having secret communications with riff-raff. I warned Helen about this kind of thing, but she never listened to a word I said."

"It's not secret communications," I snapped, "And he's not—" I started to argue but she was already climbing the stoop like a mechanical toy whose batteries were dying. Something had sapped her strength, and I had a feeling it was not just lunch with the canasta club.

As soon as we got inside, Stella complained of a headache and went off to her room. I turned on the TV to watch a soap and consider my escape alternatives for the evening. Ty's attitude really bugged me. Without over-thinking it I picked up the phone and dialed Khamille's number.

It rang a long time before a sleepy male voice answered. I asked to speak to Khamille.

He dropped the receiver with a clatter and called for her. I could hear sounds in the background, a TV, coughing, footsteps shuffling. But no one came to the phone. I tried calling hello and whistling into the receiver. Nothing. After another minute or two I hung up. It was almost four, and I realized Khamille might still be at work. I'd have to try her again later.

Everyone on the soap opera was still stuck in the same lousy love affairs, so I turned the TV off and headed upstairs to try a little exploring.

I listened for those window-rattling snores from Stella's bedroom, and was relieved to hear them competing with the roar of her window fan. It's great she was fast asleep, but the box of old yearbooks was in her room, so that was on hold for now. But Aunt Helen's shoebox was hidden in the back of my closet, just waiting for me. As I pulled it out I felt the same thrill that filled me on Saturday when I first found the box. It didn't matter whether this treasure chest was filled with diamonds or writhing snakes, I intended to explore it.

I pulled out a packet of black-and-white snapshots, their edges curled with age. The rubber band that held them disintegrated in my hand and the pictures scattered onto the rug. I pawed through them, searching for faces I recognized. There was one of a smiling girl in a graduation gown standing next to a stern looking man. I figured that was probably Helen or Stella with their father. I built a little family tree in my head, coming to the conclusion that he was my great-grandfather.

What had Roberta called him? Lethal. I squinted at the picture, trying to see the poison in his eyes, but I couldn't tell much from the tiny black-and-white. His expression reminded me of Stella's, like the world was an unfit place and he hated the fact that he was trapped in it.

The rest of the pictures were mostly groups of young people, clowning around, smiling with their arms draped around each other, a few goo-goo-eyed couples leaning into each other. A lot of the guys were in uniform, and the girls wore super-retro calf-length skirts and blouses with wide shoulders. All the girls must have been wearing lipstick because even in these small photos their smiling mouths were the most prominent feature.

There were no names or dates anywhere so I just gathered the pictures and stashed them back in the shoebox, swapping them for the diary I had found the other day. Carefully replacing the box's lid, I shoved it deep into the closet again, then grabbed a magazine and nestled the diary behind its cover. It was unlikely that anyone who moved as slowly as Aunt Stella could sneak up on me, but I had to be careful.

I passed the private warning on the inside cover without another thought. Reading this diary wasn't hurting anybody. Helen wouldn't have minded my snooping, I was sure of it. Why else would she have written anything down, unless she wanted someone to find it? Besides, she was dead, and if I was expected to carry on the family name, I had the right—actually, more of an obligation—to investigate.

Helen started this diary in January of 1942, and for about a month there was an entry for every day. I read the first few pages word for word and after a while I started to wonder why she bothered with that warning. Her writing was a flowery scroll that bled across the lines, making it nearly impossible to decipher. On top of that, most of what I was reading was totally boring stuff about what she wore to which movie. I wasn't sure what I expected, but this wasn't it.

To keep myself from dozing I flipped ahead, looking for interesting parts. In the middle of June she had a short entry: *Da's out of sorts. Maybe it's the heat. If only he would stop the drinking. But it's worse when he doesn't. It's hard to know what's best. I don't want to worry Stel, she seems so happy.*

Wasn't that just like my aunt Helen, trying to decide what would make everyone else happy, keeping her worries to herself? It gave me goosebumps. I read on, and found a few more entries about family, but the details were sketchy, as if she was afraid to write too much. I flipped almost to the back of the book and finally hit the jackpot on July 30.

I'm very worried about Stel. She's trying so hard to be brave, but it's finally hitting her— Stu will be shipping out soon. Basic training is only half the reality. There's no pretending any longer that he won't be in danger, or that the risks are low. How I hate this war!]

Stu. Could that be the name the ladies wouldn't say, the person Stella had lost?

I scanned through to the end of the diary, but the last entry was in the middle of August and I saw no further mention of anyone named Stu. Well, it was a start, and it made sense. This Stu, whoever he was, had shipped out some time in 1942. Roberta said he died young. Killed in the war? That was the logical explanation. I thought about never seeing Jesse again. I barely knew the guy, but even so, I'd be gutted. Heartbroken in a way that might change me forever.

I closed my eyes and thought about that snapshot of Stella and Helen on her dresser. Two smiling little girls, holding hands. I tried to picture Stella holding hands with a guy, laughing, having fun, stealing kisses, even. It wasn't an easy thing to imagine. I had known Stella my whole life and could hardly recall a song or a smile, never mind a whole day that she was happy. It made me sad to think about it.

I hopped off the bed and went to the closet, ready to dig out the other diary and read the rest of the story. But the other book was from the previous year, 1941. Dang. It might be fun to read someday, but if I wanted to understand what happened with this Stu person, Helen's diaries were not going to help. I'd either have to make up the ending myself or coax it out of someone who knew.

Thumping sounds floated through the wall of Stella's bedroom. I stuffed the diary back in the shoebox, slammed on the lid, and shoved it back. I plopped on the bed and whipped open the decoy magazine. I don't know why I was rushing; the hotter it is, the slower she moves, and it was another few minutes before I finally heard her shuffling up to my bedroom door.

She had changed into a house dress, another in an endless stream of pink flowered affairs, and her arms were folded tightly across her chest, hiding something. She seemed to be hesitating about crossing my threshold, which was curious since she usually barged right in. I sat up on my bed and tilted my head, trying to project just the right tone of youthful innocence and curiosity. She looked doubtful but after a few seconds she stepped into my room.

"I found Louise Hunt," she said. "In the yearbook."

I leaped to her side. "Cool. Let's see."

She had her finger in the right page, so I'd be sure to understand that this wasn't blanket permission to randomly examine the entire book. She pointed to a picture halfway down.

"Louise Schact," I read.

"Hunt is her married name."

No kidding, I thought. Louise had a hairdo identical to most of the other girls, flat on top, parted on one side with ripples of curls exploding from her ears to her chin. Even as a young girl, Louise projected a soothing, sort of motherly look.

"Was that hair fake?" I asked.

"What do you mean? Was it a wig? Of course not."

"No, I mean, they all have the same hair. It didn't just grow that way, did it?"

"Of course not, we had a permanent wave. That was the style."

"Oh, a perm," I said, nodding. My own hair had been permed before I cut it last week, tired of looking the same as all the big-haired girls at my school. From the looks of these pictures the chemicals must be wildly improved since the 1940s, because none of the girls I knew looked like their hair had fried from sticking their finger in a socket. But all I said was, "I had a perm last year. They're in style again."

"You know what they say, what goes around comes around," Stella said.

The quote Louise had chosen was Rudyard Kipling. I read it aloud with the drama I felt it deserved. "'Land of our birth, we pledge to thee, Our love and toil in the years to be; When we are grown and take our place, As men and women with our race.' That's pretty heavy."

"It's quite a famous hymn. Which you might know if you went to church." Aunt Stella slapped the book shut, and with it my opening to ask more questions.

"It's just, Louise didn't seem so serious."

"We were all serious. Not like you kids today. We didn't have an easy life, and we didn't expect it to be all fun and games down the road."

"But you must have had some fun. In school? With your friends?"

She shrugged. "I don't remember. It was a long time ago." She turned toward the door. "No use talking about it now."

Her shoulders drooped.

"Hey, Aunt Stella?"

She paused but didn't turn.

"Thanks. I know you don't like to talk about it, but it means a lot to me, to learn a little about those times."

Her lips turned into a half-smile. "I'll go down and fix us something to eat."

It was after five, and I decided to try Khamille again. This time a woman answered, and I heard some muffled conversation before Khamille came to the phone.

"Khamille? It's Lilli."

She paused for an instant. I figured she was probably wondering how I got her number.

"Hey, Lilli. Missed you at work today."

"I was with my aunt," I explained. "Sometimes it's not such a big advantage to have her so tight with Joe. She just calls him and goes, like, Lilli can't come in, and that's that."

"Must be nice. So what's up?"

I asked her what she was doing tonight, trying to explain how much I wanted to escape without sounding too pathetic.

"Sounds good," she said. "It was quiet at work so I caught up on my reading for school. So yeah, might be fun to get out."

We agreed to meet at the ferry terminal, where most of the bus routes end, and decide what to do once we got there.

When I hung up I swapped my garish skirt and leggings for a pair of jeans. In the kitchen, two burgers sizzled in a pan under Stella's impatient eye. I set the table, trying to stay out of her way and in her good graces so she wouldn't fuss about me going out. As we ate, I told her I was planning to see a movie with a friend.

"Which friend?" she asked suspiciously.

"Her name's Khamille. I met her at work."

"Sounds Italian." She didn't look entirely happy about that fact.

"I don't think she's Italian." I left it at that. What Stella didn't know couldn't hurt her. Or me.

"I'll be glad to meet her when she picks you up."

"We're meeting at the ferry."

Her mouth turned down. "At the ferry? That terminal is filled with low-lifes. Why can't you meet here?"

"She suggested the terminal. We both know what bus to take to get there."

Stella chewed ferociously, trying to work out a way to put the kibosh on our plans. "Where does this girl live?"

"I'm not sure, really. Some place where the bus goes to the ferry."

"Hmmph. That could be just about anyplace."

"Yeah, well, I didn't think I needed to ask. She works for Joe, Aunt Stella. Who cares where she lives? We're just going to a movie." I carried my plate to the sink.

"Which movie?"

"We're not sure. Something fun? Don't worry, they don't let teenagers into X-rated films."

"Well, I should hope not!"

Before she could get started on that one, I went into the living room and tore the movie page from the paper. I stuffed it into my purse, figuring Khamille would know how to take the bus to any theater we chose.

"See you later," I called.

"Don't be late," she called back.

"Depends on the movie. Gotta run. Thanks for the burger!" I slammed the door behind me, not waiting for her reply.

It was less than twenty minutes by bus from Stella's to the ferry terminal, and I arrived a little early. As I walked up the bus ramp into the huge old building, commuters streamed past me in the other direction, on the way home from their workday in the city. They plodded toward the ramps, their faces haggard. Even the young men and women looked exhausted. And bored. I couldn't imagine doing the same thing every single day, riding the bus to the ferry, the ferry to Manhattan, sometimes taking a subway uptown after that. Spending your day at the same desk, then turning around at 5 o'clock and doing it all again in reverse. Stella and Helen had done just that for years. And obviously thousands of people still did.

For the second time today, I felt filled with an almost unbearable sadness. It was becoming obvious to me that Helen and Stella never had a chance to be happy. They were young when their mother died and left them with a lethal father. Then the war came. It seemed like life just overwhelmed them. Was I headed for the same fate? Could I do this for myself, knowing that the deck was stacked against me? Everything I saw and every new fact I learned about my family and its past seemed engineered to make me feel like crap.

I shook the feeling off as best I could. Tonight, at least, I would try to have some fun with Khamille.

I headed for the newsstand where Khamille and I had agreed to meet. The ferry terminal was a cavernous old building, edged with bus and train ramps on one side and ferry slips at the other. Like so many old places in New York, there were things about it that hinted at former grandeur; speckled marble floors and carved wood molding at the top of paneled walls, and benches made of smooth dark wood. The building housed a pizzeria and two or three snack bars, newsstands, a flower shop, and a couple of souvenir stands that sold plastic Statues of Liberty and I Love NY shirts. Even if it had been a once-grand place, today's ferry terminal wasn't a place anyone wanted to linger. You grabbed a cup of coffee or a slice of pizza, shoved a quarter into the turnstile and ran for the doors to the ferry.

I was glad to see Khamille waiting for me, studying magazine covers at the newsstand. She wore jeans and a plain white tee with the sleeves rolled up. I snuck up behind her and poked my finger into her back like a little gun, giggling when she whirled on me, scowling.

66

"Khamille is not laughing," she said.

"Aw, c'mon. I was kidding."

"You think it's funny?" She waved a hand at the headline on the Daily News, which screamed something about another subway shooting. "Not funny."

"Okay, okay, sorry." I whipped out the movie listings I'd swiped from Stella's paper.

"That Spike Lee movie's supposed to be good," I suggested.

"Due respect? You're not ready for that one. Tom Cruise, maybe?"

I wrinkled my nose. "Not my speed."

"And no Dead Poets for me, thank you very much."

It was clear our taste in movies had no overlap, and as we stood debating whether any of them was worth another bus ride a loud *brrring* sounded in the inner terminal, signaling that the doors to board the soon-to-be-departing ferry were about to close.

"Hey," I said. "Let's take the boat to the city."

"Why?" Khamille asked.

"Just because," I said.

A young couple scurried past us and slid through the turnstile, hustling toward the doors, which were starting to close.

"Hold it!" the man yelled.

"Hurry up." A deckhand motioned them to hurry.

I yanked Khamille by the arm, slipped a quarter into the turnstile for her and another for me, and dragged her through.

"Move it, ladies," the deckhand called. "Doors are closing."

We slid through the door and ran down the gangplank to board. The deckhand on shore whistled, and another deckhand closed the gate on the back of the boat.

"You sure you know what you're doing?" Khamille asked.

"Ya kidding? This is your island." I gestured toward the front of the boat. "Mine's over there."

"Okay then." She smiled her wide grin. "Let's have some fun."

8 - Encounters

The ferryboat pilot gave a long pull on the horn as we chugged away from the dock. Khamille and I reacted with reflexive squeals then collapsed into each other laughing. We had boarded the Verrazano, one of the older, smaller boats. We stepped through the doors to the inside cabin, immediately hit full force with the familiar smells of a snack bar.

Khamille stuck out her tongue. "Spent all day with hot dogs. Now all night too?"

"It's only a twenty-five minute ride," I said. "Let's go upstairs. We can sit outside."

She followed me up the wide metal staircase to the ferry's top deck. This level had three sets of long wooden benches, one by each window and one in the center. At rush hour, those benches held hundreds of people, packed shoulder to shoulder, but this off-hour return trip to Manhattan carried no more than a few dozen. I loved the dark wood of those old benches. The new boats had plastic bucket seats that made it feel like a floating subway car. We passed through the heavy metal bulkhead doors to the outer deck on the left side of the boat. When I sat down on the bench my insides rattled with the vibration of the clunky old engines.

"This is the statue side," I said, pointing to Lady Liberty in the distance. "You'll have a great view."

"Saw it up close once. Third grade class trip."

"Me too," I said. Me and every school kid in New York City, but I thought pointing that out might sound a little snippy. "At least we can breathe out here."

The night was warm but there was always a breeze on the ferry, one that carried the unique diesel and salt smell of New York harbor. I took a deep breath and congratulated myself that I was out with a friend, away from Stella's clutches for the first time in six days.

I stood up and raised my arms. "Free at last, free at last, thank God almighty I'm free at last."

Khamille smirked. "Calm yourself, girl. It's just a boat ride, not the March on Washington."

I sat, willing myself to keep grinning. "I know. I know. I'm just... trying to be happy."

"Well don't try so hard. Just be happy."

She made it sound easy. "It's my aunt. She's killing me. She's miserable all the time. She's never happy, ever. I've known that pretty much all my life. But today, we went to a lunch with a bunch of my Aunt Helen's friends—you know, my aunt that just died?"

Khamille nodded.

"And those ladies, they told me a few things that made me wonder."

"Like what?"

"They talked about my great-aunt's younger days. They said my Aunt Stella used to be fun."

"What, like, a party girl? That's good, right?"

"It's weird. I mean, Helen, sure I'd believe that. But Stella? She's just an old grump, always has been."

"She wasn't always old, Lilli. Nobody's born old."

"Well a grump, for sure. She's never been anything but miserable to me or anybody in my family. But these ladies, they hinted at some stuff about a broken heart. And then they just clammed up and acted like they never said a thing. Pass the Jell-O. Nice day, isn't it?"

"So just ask your auntie about it."

"It's not that easy. My family doesn't talk about stuff. I mean never. It's like we're all trapped in a well of deep, dark secrets."

"Every family has secrets," Khamille said.

"They do? Yours too?"

"I guess."

"Like what?"

"You think Khamille is gonna tell you her family secrets? They're secret. For a reason."

"See now?" I stood up and grabbed the railing. "That's what I mean. Just when you think you hit on something important, something that will explain things, they circle around and burrow back into that dark hole and bury the truth again. Those ladies today, they told me it's best not to know some things."

"Uh-huh. My mother always says some things are best forgotten."

I threw myself back on the bench beside her. Without giving it any thought, I blurted, "My mother's one of the things my family expects me to forget. "

"Say what?"

I realized I hadn't told Khamille anything about this part of my life. Well, too late now. Might as well explain.

"I don't have a mother anymore. She died. Almost five years ago."

Khamille regarded me for a longish minute and I could see pity in her eyes. I turned away. This is one reason I never talk about my mother. I hated being pitied. Finally, Khamille spoke. "I didn't know that. I'm sorry. That must be tough."

I shrugged. "She had a lot of problems. She was sick a lot."

"Still. She was your mother."

"Yeah." I slid my mother's gold cross back and forth along the chain at my throat. Even though I was the one who started the conversation, I really did not want to talk about this. My mother was never anyone's idea of a good mom. Even when she was home and taking all her meds, she mostly watched TV or sat at the kitchen table. Drinking coffee. Playing solitaire. When she was in trouble she could be absent for weeks at a clip, sometimes in the hospital, sometimes just off somewhere. My dad and my brother Mike were the ones who made sure I was dressed and fed and shuttled off to school. And by second grade I pretty much did all that for myself.

"I bet you still miss her."

"You sound like a social worker." After mom died, I saw the school social worker once a week for a while. She was nice enough, but she asked a lot of questions that had no easy answers. How were things at home? Was there someone I could talk to about my feelings? Did I miss my mom? I wasn't sure what to say. I loved my mother. I knew that. But I also knew she was never completely mine. There was always a part of her I couldn't quite reach or rely on.

But there was a truth I could share with Khamille. "I miss my Aunt Helen. She was more like a mother to me, really. I miss her like crazy."

Khamille was quiet, just listening.

"I found her diary. And some letters. I'm hoping they help me put the pieces together, to understand my own history better. The things those ladies were saying today? I can feel it in my bones there's a story there. Something important. Something that matters to me. Does that make sense?"

"Of course. The ancestors are calling and you want to get to know them."

I laughed then, thinking she was kidding. But her brown eyes probed mine under her heavy brows. She was serious.

"In African culture, the ancestors are very important. We learned about it in Black History class. The ancestors stay connected to us. Like, forever. They die, but they're still with us. For better or worse."

"Like ghosts?"

"Not exactly, but okay. If that helps you to imagine them. Benign ghosts. What do you know about your ancestors?"

The word lethal sprang to mind, as far from benign as you could get. Any connection I had to my ancestors did not feel like something that fed me from afar. More like a tube that sucked me dry without my realizing I was hooked to it. But I kept that to myself. "I've never really thought much about them. They came from Ireland. They were poor. They liked to drink." I shrugged. "That's the gist of it."

"But they were strong, yeah?"

"Strong?"

"They had to be, to get here from Ireland, on their own. To cross the ocean and get away from their troubles to something better."

I hadn't considered that, but she had a point. They had to have some moxie to up and sail to America instead of starving to death at home. "Maybe," I allowed, not quite convinced.

"No maybe about it. Khamille's ancestors? Especially the women? They were amazing."

"How do you know?"

"For one thing, we're still here. My ancestors were forged out of steel. Cast iron. Indestructible. They had to be."

We were approaching Liberty Island, now close enough to clearly see the statue's torch pointed high into the sky.

"Give me your tired, your poor, your huddled masses yearning to be free," Khamille quoted from the famous poem I knew was on the base of the statue.

I had passed that green lady so often I took the sight for granted. But I'd never realized how the sight of her stirred a little pride in me. To be a New Yorker. American. Free.

Khamille shook her head. "Unless you look like me. Or my ancestors. They were tired and poor all right. Definitely yearning. And definitely not free."

That brought me up short. I realized I had no idea what it felt like to be descended from people who had actually been enslaved. I'd never really thought about what it meant to be Irish, or white for that matter. It was just who I am.

"My ancestors left some strong lessons," she continued. "Everybody from my mama on back made one thing crystal clear: Khamille, if you want it, you better work for it, cause ain't nobody going to hand it to you. Oh, and another thing? You're gonna have to work twice as hard as some folks to get it. At least twice as hard. But don't let that stop you."

I nodded slowly, trying to take in the meaning of her words.

"You want to understand your family? Your auntie? You gotta ask. Don't be afraid to poke around. Do some digging. Do the research then decide what to do with it. Am I right?"

She was right. I felt a little chill run through me because I had come to the same conclusion that very afternoon. Okay, my life wasn't like Khamille's, but what she said made sense. When Roberta clammed up after dropping all those hints today, I knew one thing: if I wanted to understand my family history, it was up to me to root it out. Nobody was going to hand me an explanation on a silver platter.

We were quiet then, lost in our own thoughts as the ferry made its way toward Manhattan. I watched a line of seagulls drifting up and down behind the boat, getting a free ride on our air currents. I wanted my own life to be that easy, to just drift along, lifting a wing now and then to steer myself a little to the right or left. Most of the time I felt more like a park pigeon, the kind with a peg-leg and one eye missing, hobbling around hoping someone would throw me a scrap. I was tired of that. I was itching to soar.

"Hey," I turned to Khamille. "I forgot to ask you, who's the guy who answered the phone when I called today?"

"My mother answered when you called."

"No, I tried earlier, and a man answered. I guess you weren't home yet."

Khamille's eyes narrowed and she looked away. "Must have been JT. My brother." She fiddled with her bracelets. "He didn't say anything nasty did he?"

"No. He sounded like I woke him up. He put the phone down and kind of forgot about me. I just hung up."

"Yeah, that's JT. He probably was asleep. He and my dad both work nights."

I wanted to ask her more but she suddenly stood up. "Great view from here. Look at those Twin Towers." She gestured toward the approaching skyline. For someone so jaded about the tourist sights when we boarded she seemed awfully interested now. I'm not totally stupid. I figured she didn't want to talk about her brother so I dropped the subject. I guess we were both entitled to our secrets, and we both seemed to have enough of them. We rode the last few minutes in silence, enjoying the view and the breeze and each other's company.

The engines cut, and we drifted toward the ferry slip. We went inside and joined the other passengers making their way down the steps to the main level, ignoring announcements warning everyone to stay off the staircases until we had docked. The entire boat shuddered as the engines reversed and we gripped the handrails on the steps as the boat gently bounced off the pilings and settled into the slip.

"So, what do you want to do?" I asked as the big steel ramps lowered from the slip to the bow of the boat.

"You're the tour guide," she said. "You tell me."

"You got bus tokens?" I asked.

"I have a transit pass. My dad works for the TA. In Brooklyn."

"Cool. Well then, let's go to my neighborhood."

"All this talk of family got you homesick?" she teased.

"Who said anything about family? I said my neighborhood. Come on."

Khamille and I hurried down the concrete ramp that circled the building then headed toward Water Street. Downtown was pretty quiet at this hour, all the Wall Street bankers safe at home in the suburbs and outer boroughs. A small group of guys gathered around a boom box near the edge of Battery Park. They were fifty feet away, but I could feel their eyes on us. As we passed them, they whistled and made smoochy sounds. I ignored them but Khamille turned to sneer in their direction, which only made them whoop a little louder.

We rounded the corner to stand at the east side bus stop.

"Disgusting." Khamille made a face. "On top of being ugly and immature, they're blasting such bad music." She rolled her tongue and made fast motion with her hands, imitating the sound of the electronic drum beat.

"It's dance music. Got a good beat."

She clucked her tongue. "Like all we gotta do is shake it till we make it."

I laughed.

"Honestly," she said. "They think they're attractive? They're like babies in a playpen. Bring Khamille a serious man. You feel me? Somebody serious. Somebody with a mind that's looking ahead, planning some kind of future. Somebody with a — I don't know how to say it—"

"A calling?"

"Yeah, like that. A calling." She leaned back and opened her eyes wide, quizzing me. "Where'd you come up with that?"

"Jesse. That's what he says he has. A calling. To be an artist."

She hit me with a wink. "See now? That is the type of serious substantial man worth pursuing. You better look out, my friend. Somebody might snatch your Jesse away."

My mouth opened in shock, and she just about fell over laughing. "You're a goof," she said. "I have no interest in Jesse, he's all yours. And by the way, he wasn't around today, so you didn't miss anything."

"He said he wouldn't be back till the grand opening."

"Just figured you'd want to know he was telling the truth."

A bus with a giant Dinkins for Mayor poster on its side pulled up and we boarded. The ride from South Ferry to the lower east side wove through Chinatown and Little Italy. Khamille stared out the window, fascinated at the bustle of the crowded streets. She acted like she knew her way around the city but from the look on her face, my guess was she didn't cross the bay too often.

We got off on Second Avenue just at the edge of my apartment complex. "Here we are." I felt anxious being here with a new friend. It all felt familiar to me, the small tidy stores, the background noise of taxi horns and sirens, restaurant smells mixed with car exhaust. But I wondered how it felt to her. Her sharp eyes seemed to be drinking it all in. Though she didn't say anything, I was glad to see her give a little nod of approval.

"Where do you live?" she asked.

I pointed east, to the maze of high-rise apartments that stretched for blocks and blocks. "Stuyvesant Town. My parents moved in with one of my mother's aunts before I was born. When the aunt died, my folks just stayed. You know how it works. You gotta have connections. Nobody vacates rent control."

"Got that right. Looks pretty nice."

"It's okay. Come on," I said, rushing her along. "Let's hit Java Jive. We call it Java Junk, because it's filled with all this old coffee stuff. Weird looking grinders and pots and posters. But it's got a good vibe."

We stepped into the shop and inhaled the scent of good, strong coffee.

"Cool, huh?" I asked.

"Kinda homey," Khamille said. "Smells a whole lot better than snack bar wieners."

We placed our order at the counter and scoped out a place to sit. I spotted two girls from my English class at a back table. I wasn't sure I wanted to—or was invited to—join them but Valerie waved and Jenny patted the chair beside her.

"Friends?" Khamille asked.

"From school." I felt torn. Part of me was hoping this would happen, that we'd run into somebody and hang out. But I really didn't know Val or Jenny that well, or how they'd feel about Khamille. Val and Jenny wore crop tops and denim cutoffs, and I could see their eye shadow from across the room. Their hair, the same big hair I had until I hacked it shorter to tick off Stella, was puffed and plumped into submission. Khamille in her beaded braid and plain white tee and me in my jeans and spiked hair, it suddenly didn't feel like such a great plan to throw us all together.

But here we were. Khamille followed me over to their table. Val and Jenny looked up from their coffee. We sat down across from them and I did quick introductions all around. There was an awkward silence. They sipped their coffees while I stared at the giant chocolate chip cookie that sat untouched between them.

"I love their cookies," I said. "Khamille, you want to share one?"

"Oh, you can nibble ours," Val said, pushing the cookie to the middle of the table. "We're just picking at it anyway."

I could have wolfed that thing down in one bite, and I bet Khamille could've too. Neither of us touched it.

"New haircut?" Jenny asked.

Before I could answer, Val added, "Cut it yourself?"

Was it that obvious? I nodded. "I wanted it to be shocking."

"You got your wish," Val said.

Jenny delivered a warning elbow to Val's ribs. "Haven't seen you around," Jenny said. "Where you been hiding?"

"Staten Island."

I might as well have said "Ryker's Island" from the look on Val's face. "Ewww. Whatcha doing over there?"

"My father's aunt died, and I'm staying with her sister for the summer. She's old. Needs some help."

"I'm sorry," Jenny said.

"Is there anything to actually do there?" Val asked. "On Staten Island?"

Khamille sat up straighter and I could almost see her hackles rising.

"I have a job. Khamille and I work together, at a little amusement park near the beach."

"It sounds....interesting," Jenny said, but it was clear she didn't think that at all.

The guy at the coffee counter called my name and I rose to get our drinks. I loaded up on sugar packets and napkins and when I came back, Khamille had somehow switched the topic to her upcoming summer school class on African American poets and writers.

"Summer school, huh?" Val asked. "So, did you like—flunk English?"

"Pardon?" Khamille asked. "Why would you ask that?"

Val shot a panicky look at Jenny. "That's the only reason anyone goes to summer school. Isn't it?"

"No it is not," Khamille said.

"She's going to be taking a college-level class," I said.

"AP. Advanced Placement? I'm a senior and I have plans to go to Hunter College next year."

"Oh. Sorry." Val pulled her cookie back and broke off a big chunk, completely disinterested.

"So what are you guys up to this summer?" I asked.

They shrugged. "Just normal summer stuff. My dad rented a beach house down the shore, last two weeks in July."

"Sounds fun," I said. It actually sounded like a dream, nothing normal about it. This encounter was starting to depress me. Just when I thought I couldn't feel much worse, I heard a familiar laugh behind me. It grated my ears like a subway on a sharp curve.

"Don't look now." Val's voice dropped to a whisper. "It's Roger."

"And his annoying new girlfriend," Jenny added.

I didn't need to turn, because Roger waltzed past us with a willowy blonde on his scrawny little arm. He passed by without a second glance, for which I was grateful.

"That's the big crush you told me about? From last Christmas?" Khamille whispered.

I nodded.

"Must have been temporary insanity."

I could have hugged Khamille for saying that.

Roger and the blonde crammed into one armchair. He nuzzled her neck with a disgusting slurping sound that rivaled the espresso machine. Val and Jenny pasted sad, sympathetic looks on their faces but it barely covered the amusement underneath. They knew the whole story, and I was in no mood to relive it.

Khamille took charge. "So Lilli, how's Jesse?" Before I could concoct an answer, she added, "Jesse's an artist who's been working on restoring the old carousel where we work. He's a serious artist. Not just a talented artisan. A real man. He's to die for. And he has it bad for our girl here."

"Does he now?" Jenny asked.

"For real," Khamille said. "I try flirting with the guy but he only has eyes for Lilli."

I could feel the blush crawling up my neck. Val started to giggle. "I see that look on your face," she said. "You got it bad."

"Oh, he is bad, Lilli's Jesse is." Khamille gave me a nod and one of her generous smiles.

I glanced at Roger and the blonde, now sucking face like crazed Hoovers. I realized it didn't upset me one bit to see them together. I was so over Roger. He actually seemed completely unappealing. But I wanted what he and that blonde had, I wanted someone. I wanted to feel that desire coursing through me. I wanted that kind of attention, connection, passion. I wanted what Khamille was implying I had with Jesse to be one hundred percent true.

I snapped back to reality when Khamille's chair made a loud scraping sound as she pushed it back from the table. "Well, we'd better get moving. Lilli wants to show me around the 'hood."

We said our goodbyes and stepped outside to the busy sidewalk. The night air cleared my head a bit, but not totally. I waited until we were out of viewing-range of the front window before I grabbed Khamille's hand and gushed my thanks. And an apology.

"They were so rude," I said. "About summer school? And Staten Island?"

"They were."

"But we set them straight."

"Maybe. Didn't seem to Khamille like they actually cared much about anything but themselves. Advice? If those are your friends? It's time to find some new ones."

"We're not that close," I admitted. It was my only defense. But the truth was, I was as close to Val and Jenny as to anyone at school. Friends were hard for me. I was never sure what to say, how much to show, how much to hide. And there was always something to hide. So far, it was easy with Khamille and I was grateful for that. She didn't put on airs and she was always crystal clear about what she thought.

"Thanks for being my friend," I said. "Seriously."

She shrugged me off. "Can we go to your place? I'd like to see it."

My building was only a short walk but I wasn't sure how I felt about dropping by. "I might give my father a heart attack. He'll assume my aunt threw me out."

"But she didn't. So that's okay, right?"

I hadn't planned to stop at home even though we were close. But honestly, all our talk about the ancestors had my mind whirling like a carousel on crack. I couldn't stop thinking about my mother, and that felt really strange.

"Okay," I agreed. "Just a quick stop. There actually is something I want to check out."

At the next block we made a right and wandered into the high-rise maze of Stuyvesant Town. We passed a few joggers and people walking dogs along the network of sidewalks inside the complex. In my building we rode the elevator to my floor. Khamille followed me down the hallway. The air smelled spicy, from my neighbors' Indian cooking. I unlocked the door and called Dad's name. He was on the sofa watching TV, his scotch glass and a bowl of chips on the coffee table. He bolted upright when he saw us.

"Lilli. What the hell? Who the hell is this? Is everything okay?"

"Yeah, yeah, fine. This is my friend Khamille. We work together. We were just in the city so I thought I'd pop in."

Khamille said a polite hello. Dad shook his head, trying to comprehend this interruption. "You could've called. Save me from a heart attack." He was trying not to stare at Khamille and I was pretty sure why that was. "It's crazy out there these days. You watch the news? Read the papers? No time for two girls to be wandering around alone."

"We're fine. Had a coffee and ran into some girls from school. I won't be long, just need to check something in my room."

"Yeah, yeah. Whatever." Dad took a gulp of scotch. "Jesus. Give a guy a heart attack."

We hurried down the hall. I switched on the light in my bedroom. It looked just as I'd left it, a little rumpled from packing in a hurry but basically not too embarrassing.

"Don't mind him. He's—"

Khamille waved her hand. "Trust me. I get it. My dad would be just as freaked out if I brought you home without warning." She picked up a framed photo from my bedside table. "This you and your mom?"

"It's me and Aunt Helen," I said. "In front of her and Aunt Stella's house."

She studied the picture. "You look happy. Cute."

"Whatever." I took the picture from her hand and placed it back on the table.

She turned to home in on a collage thumb-tacked to my wall.

"What's this?" she asked.

"Nothing," I said automatically. She pulled back and pursed her lips at me. "Okay, it's a collage."

"No kidding." She turned to study it again. Not that there was much to study. It was just pictures and words cut from old magazines and glued haphazardly to a piece of black construction paper.

"A school counselor made me do it," I explained. "After my mom died. It's nothing."

She backed away and nodded. "I like it. The black background. The way the girl in the middle is almost obliterated by all these different ideas." Her finger jabbed at the individual words and phrases, all different sizes and colors, pasted one on top of the other. *Lost. Family. Mother. Future. Where to? Alone. Courage.*

I hadn't really seen that collage in who-knew how long. It had hung on my wall for a few years now and I didn't even notice it anymore. It was embarrassing. It made me sad to look closely at it. It was like shining a light on all the bleak and hopeless feelings I was trying to get beyond.

"Let's just say I knew what the counselor wanted to see." I hated all those stupid questions. What was your mother like? What do you miss most about her? If you could change one thing what would it be? Like I could wish it all away by wanting things to be different. "They wanted feelings. I gave them feelings."

"You sure did," Khamille said. She stood straight and looked around the room again. "I like your room. It feels like you."

"What's that supposed to mean?"

She smiled. "Chill, girl. It's like— I don't know. It's a little messy but it's kind of a good mess. A mess with heart and soul."

"Thanks. I think." We giggled. "You keep your room in perfect order, am I right?"

"Close to perfect," she laughed. "I'll show you around one day. You can decide for yourself. Did you find what you came for?"

"Not yet. Follow me."

I crossed the hall and flipped on the light. "This is my brother Mike's old room. Dad calls it 'the study' now, but I don't think he studies much except the bills and the racing form."

Khamille watched as I opened the top drawer of the desk. "What are you looking for?"

"Old pictures. I think there are some in here." I rooted around, but all I found were pens and pencils, old bills and scrap paper. The next drawer held envelopes and stationery, and the bottom drawer was stuffed with old junk of Mike's— Matchbox cars, toy soldiers, and about a thousand magic markers.

I slammed the drawer and rustled through some stuff on the bookcase shelves, but didn't find anything there either. I surveyed the small room, hands on hips, not wanting to accept the obvious truth: if there were any old photos my Aunt Pearl or my dad probably threw them out or hid them so well I'd never find them.

I heard footsteps in the hall. Dad appeared in the doorway. "What the hell are you doing?"

"Nothing. Never mind."

"That's my private desk," he said. "You don't need to be poking around in it."

"I thought I could find some pictures of me. When I was little. I thought it'd be fun to show them to Khamille."

"Pictures?" He looked from me to Khamille and back again. "You show up without any warning looking for pictures? I don't know about any pictures. I'd have to look around, I'd have to see where—"

"Never mind," I snapped. "I'll just grab a couple of things I forgot from the bathroom and we'll be out of your way."

I brooded for the whole bus ride to South Ferry. Khamille watched the city lights roll past, and seemed to understand she shouldn't bug me. Less than a week ago I left Manhattan, unhappy to be leaving behind everything important in my life for a summer filled with nothing. Tonight made me wonder if I even had a life here. Or anywhere, for that matter.

The ferries only ran once an hour in the evening so we had to wait almost a half hour for a boat. There were no benches in the waiting area, a brilliant plan the city devised a few years ago because the place had become a hangout for street people. Tonight there were a few hundred commuters milling around, watching the big clock over the doors to the slip and practicing that New York etiquette of refusing to look anyone in the eye.

"You okay?" Khamille asked me.

I nodded. I felt empty and a little numb. But I wasn't sure Khamille could help. I wasn't sure anyone could help.

Khamille yawned. "Man, I'm tired. And I have to show up at school tomorrow for official registration."

"What is this class you're taking? College level? AP?"

"It's a special program. So when I get to Hunter after graduation next year, I'll already have credits. I need some serious scholarship money and my advisor told me these classes would help."

I nodded. It didn't surprise me that Khamille had a plan for success. I remembered what she said earlier about working for what you wanted.

Plus I knew this much: if you had a plan, you had a better chance of staying in charge. That was important.

The "Next Boat" sign lit up over one of the big doors, and the waiting crowd swarmed around it. In a couple of minutes the doors slid open and we poured through. As we headed toward the boarding ramp, Khamille suddenly stopped and let the people flow around her. She fixed her eyes on something or someone up ahead.

"What's wrong?" I asked.

"Nothing."

I knew she was lying. Her whole body had tensed up and her lips were pressed together. I looked into the crowd ahead but couldn't tell what had shaken her.

"Is there a ladies room on the boat?" she asked.

"Yeah. But it's kind of gross."

"Lead the way."

As I led her toward the door to the ladies room, she kept an eye on the crowd. We ducked inside and quickly moved away from the door into the room and out of sight.

The front half of the rest room had long make-up mirrors and stools, while the rear half had two rows of stalls. The stink hit me square in the face, but I wasn't sure if that was the room's usual scent or the air around the woman slumped on one of the stools. She snored lightly, her upper body sprawled across the counter in front of the mirrors and the plastic bags that held worldly goods clutched tightly between her knees.

Khamille seemed unfazed by the woman, but was definitely not her usual cool and collected self. She plopped onto a stool and folded herself into a little ball.

"Don't you have to go?" I asked. "I don't want to sit in here for the whole ride."

"Wait outside, then. I'm staying put."

The whistle blew, signaling our departure. We both jumped. You really had to be a hardcore ferry rider to take that blast in stride.

"Khamille, please tell me. What is the problem?"

"Trace," she mumbled.

"Huh?"

She turned to me. Her eyes, usually bright and inquisitive, were clearly troubled. Her body tensed and she focused on the door to the restroom as if she expected the devil himself to waltz right through it. "It's Trace," she said. "Not somebody I want to run into, okay?"

"Okay," I said. "I guess this is our night to avoid old friends, huh?"

She didn't smile. "He's not my friend. He was never my friend. He knows JT."

"Your brother?"

She stood up and began to pace. Her voice migrated from fear to cold hatred. "JT isn't like Trace. Not at all. But lately — my brother has changed. He has new friends and they're into some bad stuff. JT and my father fight a lot about it. Dad says they're nothing but a bunch of lazy, no count, arrogant—"

The tone of Khamille's voice roused the sleeping woman. She lifted her head and squinted our way.

"It's okay," I reassured the woman. "We're not dangerous." The woman's head dropped back onto the counter and I settled on the stool beside Khamille. "Phew. I hope my nose does what it usually does at work. You know? Stops working so I don't care anymore?"

Her half-smile made me feel a little better. I knew Khamille was not a coward. She stood up to my friends tonight without a hair out of place. The fact that she wanted to lay low meant this Trace was not one to fool with. I had to respect her decision.

The crossing took the usual twenty-five minutes, but it felt like forever. I twirled on the little round bench in front of the mirror and poked at my hair, lifting it with my fingers. Twice, I tried to ask Khamille about this guy and she silenced me with a single shake of her head. When the engines cut, signaling we were approaching the dock, we stood up and peeked out of the ladies room like two kids playing hide and seek. Khamille was still jittery. She hung back.

"We have to get off the boat," I said. "Unless you'd rather ride back and forth all night." I nodded toward our fragrant friend, still sleeping peacefully. "With her."

Khamille seemed to consider it, then blew out a breath. "Let's go."

We stepped out just as the boat settled into the dock, and surged forward with the small crowd pouring up the ramps. Night had fallen for real now, and the terminal felt sinister, a crowded cave we just had to get through. Khamille kept a close eye on the people ahead as we disembarked. She needed to go to one bus ramp and I needed another, but they were both in the same general direction, down another set of stairs to the street level.

"The buses usually meet the boat, so if we're lucky we shouldn't have to wait," I said.

"Good. That's good."

We hurried down the steps and were just about to split up to our separate bus ramps when we heard a deep voice call out, "Khami."

Khamille swore softly, but her next words sounded more like a muffled prayer.

"Come on," I said, pulling her toward the bus ramps.

"Khamille!" the voice boomed again, closer now. We broke into a run, but that only led to the heavy thud of footsteps behind us. They grew nearer.

"Yo. Don't you hear me calling you, girl?" A hand reached out and grabbed the back of Khamille's shirt and we both stopped. We had no choice.

He didn't look like someone to fear. He was dressed neatly in a light blue sweatshirt and jeans, with white Jordans that looked brand new. He seemed older than us, in his early twenties, light-skinned, maybe Hispanic, maybe Black, I couldn't tell. His curly hair was slicked back off his face except for a dramatic wave coaxed to swoop down and nearly hide one eye. The only hint of anything sinister was a tattoo of a snake that crawled from the bottom of his sleeve to the end of his middle finger.

But his looks didn't matter; I could feel the fear pouring off Khamille. I looked around for a cop or somebody who might help but the crowd had thinned and those who were left moved along like typical New Yorkers, eyes front and focused on their own business.

"Hey, Trace." Khamille made it sound as if she'd just now noticed him, even though we'd spent the crossing in the ladies room avoiding him.

Trace licked his lips and smiled to reveal a row of pearly white teeth.

"K, what are you doing out this late?" He took one step forward and wrapped his hand around Khamille's arm. I tried not to stare at that tattoo but my eyes kept going back to it. "Who's your friend?"

"No one. We gotta go, Trace."

"She doesn't look like no one. I'm sure she has a name." He removed his hand from Khamille's arm and faced me. "Do you? Have a name?"

I wasn't sure what else to do so I told him.

"Lilli," he repeated. "That's a beautiful name. Beautiful."

And now I could feel it too. The way he looked at me, the way he pronounced Lilli, soft and drawn out. The way he repeated the word beautiful. Everything about it made me feel like I was being drawn into a dark and dangerous place that Trace owned and controlled.

"We have a bus to catch," Khamille said.

"Yeah?" he said. "Cool. We can ride home together."

Not a good plan, I knew, but I had no idea how to get us both to the right bus ramps without Trace following. The terminal was nearly deserted now, most of the disembarking passengers having connected with their other transit. I could feel my insides starting to quiver.

"I'm going to Lilli's actually," Khamille said, like that had always been our plan. "We have to work in the morning and her house is closer."

"That's right," I agreed. It was good lie because it kept us together. We weren't more than fifty paces from the door to the bus line that would carry us to Stella's. But if we missed the bus that was waiting for this boat to unload it'd be a long wait for the next one. A long and dangerous wait.

Trace had a plan of his own. "Maybe I'll ride along with you. Keep you safe, a'right?"

"We're fine," Khamille said. She took a slow half-step toward me and I felt her fingers lace through mine. Whatever happened now we were in it together.

"You sure about that?" he asked. "Lots of trouble in this city these days. Helps to have somebody to look out for you."

"Nobody's gonna bother us." She lifted her chin and fixed him with a steely gaze. "And I mean nobody."

She squeezed my hand as a quick warning before she whirled around and headed for the bus ramps. I steered her toward the correct ramp and let adrenaline carry us hand in hand to the swinging doors. Once through them we broke into run, pounding up the ramp toward— thank God— the smell of the idling bus engine.

Heavy footsteps followed as we raced toward the bus but now at least we had a driver and a few passengers to witness whatever happened. We climbed on board. Khamille flashed her transit pass while I tossed a token into the fare box.

"Don't wait for him," Khamille told the driver, jerking her thumb toward the ramp where Trace ran. "Please?"

He stole a glance in his side mirror and yanked the handle to bang the door shut. "Righty-oh and away we go."

As we roared away, Trace pounded the door, shouting. The driver ignored him.

A few of the other passengers watched us drop into two seats close to the driver. But once we settled in they went back to looking out the window or reading their papers. My legs felt like jelly and our breathing didn't return to normal until we'd rounded the corner onto Bay Street and were safely away from the terminal.

"You did great," I said when I could finally talk again. "Standing up to him like that."

She closed her eyes and swallowed hard. "Thanks. It's the only way. He can smell weakness. I know he looks like a regular dude but—he's not. Last year? He— he really hurt a friend of mine who tried to get between us."

"Us? You mean you and he were—?"

She pushed my shoulder with hers. "Do I look crazy? Of course, there is no us, there never was. Trace and JT came up together in school. Trace always thought he was so smooth. That it was fine for him to be all up in everybody's business. He's in with the wrong people now. He is the wrong people. My dad? He's all over JT to lose Trace. I wish he would too but— he's a hard one to lose."

"So what happened? Last year?"

She squeezed her eyes closed again and shook her head. "I don't want to talk about it. This guy —this friend," she seemed unsure how much she wanted to tell me. "He got in the middle and tried to tell Trace to back off and Trace, he— it was nasty."

"I believe it. I could—like—feel it. You know?"

She nodded.

"Are you okay?" I asked.

She rested her hand on my arm and nodded again. "You?"

"Yeah." I was definitely relieved to be away from Trace. And there seemed no other way to escape except for me and Khamille to get on the same bus. But now that bus was headed for Stella's. And the last she knew I was going to a movie with an Italian girl named Camille. And now with no warning I was coming home—not exactly early—with Khamille, who was definitely not Italian and who might end up staying the night as our guest. I was pretty sure that wasn't going to go over too well.

"Um, Khamille?" I began. "You know I told you about my aunt. Stella? Where I'm staying? I need to warn you. She's not—" How much to explain? "She isn't always a sweetheart."

"Yeah, you said. You think she'll be mad we're out so late?"

"For sure." Given what I knew about how she regarded Ty and his mother it would be a small miracle if that was all she was mad about.

"My parents wouldn't be happy either. I'll need to call them."

"Maybe they can come pick you up?"

"Nah. For starters we don't have a car. And my dad's at work so he's not even home."

"Don't worry." I hoped I sounded convincing. "We have plenty of room. You can stay over."

"For real?" She rested her hands in her lap and studied the half-moons of her fingernails. "I never stayed at a white person's house before."

"Well, I'm pretty sure you're Stella's first African-American guest. And don't get your hopes up. The house is nothing special."

I felt a little queasy as we watched the rundown shops of Bay Street roll past. I reminded myself that Khamille was a strong, confident person. A courageous person. She had handled everyone tonight from Val and Jenny to my dad and Trace. I had reason to hope she could handle my aunt.

I only hoped Stella could handle Khamille.

Stuart: The Farewell

Of all the lies we allow, even encourage, in our world, the one we tell young men who are going off to war is among the cruelest. The lie that they are tough. That they can get through anything. We tell them all they need do is put away their fears and leave their courage on display, and that will save their lives.

It is a big, fat, desperately self-serving lie, and we repeat it over and over and over, century upon century in nation after nation.

I swallowed that lie whole. We all did. When we left for basic, we were gullible young men anxious to prove our worth. If any of us had a lick of sense we'd have been doubt-filled and terrified, but once we were trained, off we went, our fears packed away like warm sweaters at the first sign of spring.

The Army and everyone else encouraged our charade. An honest drill sergeant might have prepared us for the coming sacrifice. "If you want to survive what you're about to witness," he might have hollered, "you must peel away your softness and replace it with steel."

No one, of course, was ever that truthful, not that we would have listened. We scoffed at the very idea of softness. We thought we were strong and smart. Actually we were nothing but incredibly, achingly naive.

Stella wrote me every day of the ten weeks I trained in basic. The optimism in her letters could have floated the Hindenburg across the Atlantic and back, with fuel to spare. Both of us reeked of bravado on the outside but privately we prayed for the miracle that would end the war before we were to be separated.

And Stella and I did get a kind of miracle, at least we thought so at the time.

I was headed for Europe through the Port of New York, which happened to be my home town. So on a sweltering Wednesday in August, I called my mother to tell her Stuart McGee would need a hero's sendoff. She cried, as she did for all news, good or bad, and promised that she and Stella would be home to greet me.

The next day at four-thirty in the afternoon I marched up my front walk, looking mighty sharp in my uniform and cap. Mama threw open the door, and her arms, and cried. Of course.

"You're naught but skin and bones, Stuart," she said. The sound of the long Irish "u" in my name tripped off her tongue and scratched around in search of any remaining softness buried in my steely-soldier self. "Is this what the Army does, starves our young men before they go off to war?"

"Ma, I'm fine," I said, wrapping firm arms carefully around her. "Never been healthier."

My mother stepped back skeptically, clearing the path for Stella's welcoming hug. I could see the tears pooling in her beautiful eyes. I could sense her willing herself to stay strong. I gathered her in and she dissolved against me, seeking the comfort and peace we had longed for in our letters. I melted a bit, in her arms. I fought to defend that cold, jagged core the Army had nurtured, but I felt myself starting to falter.

"Look how brave and handsome you've become," Stella said. I'm sure she noticed more, much more, but she spoke only of things she was encouraged to see. We were patriots, sure, but we were also idiots, the way we followed the damned rules that kept us marching along the straight trail to our doom.

Friends stopped in, and family, to say farewell to their brave boy. Stella's little brother Harry and our young friend Joe both admired my uniform, their envy palpable. Stella sat at my side in a house full of noise and bluster, and it was mid-evening before we were finally alone. I took up my buddy on his offer of a car, and Stella and I drove to the beach.

We sat in the car for a while, heads and hands touching as we listened to the waves break. I pulled her close in the damp air and drank in the scent of her hair and her skin, desperate to store it in my own pores so it might travel with me across the ocean. After a bit we stepped from the car and walked along the sand to a quiet spot sheltered from the road by beach grass.

"Marry me," I said, brandishing that shiny brass carousel ring.

She giggled, slipping three fingers into the oversized ring, then gazed into my eyes and breathed, "Yes, oh yes."

We kissed and kissed, each kiss reaching deeper and more dangerously down into those hard-edged recesses within.

"Tonight," I said. "Now. Let's go find a judge, someone, anyone to do the job."

"There's no one at this hour," she said.

"There must be." Spontaneous weddings were a sign of the times, there had to be a way.

"No, Stuart, I…" She backed away, and I saw fear in her eyes.

"What?"

"It's Da," she said. "He would—"

"Would what?"

She shook the thought away, quickly found a new one. "He'd want a church wedding. He'd never recognize anything else."

"So we won't tell him," I said. "The priest can marry us later, after. In a church. But please. Let's go. Now." I tried to make my kisses more persuasive, but in truth they only succeeded in anchoring us both to that spot on the beach.

"Tomorrow," she said, pressing the ring into my palm. "Tomorrow morning, first thing. There'll be time before you go, won't there?"

"I think so," I said, and I believed it with all my heart. City Hall opened early, or we'd find us a priest to do the job. I was sure the rules could be relaxed. Tomorrow it would all be made right. Tonight had a different purpose. Tonight was all for love.

Never have there been such final hours, before or since. Having made our promise, we moved together like dancers who had practiced the steps in their minds for months, following each subtle movement to the next, and the next, and the next. The depth of our tenderness had no bounds, and needed none.

We parted just before midnight, our union forever sealed, with plans to meet early for a quick "I do" before my ship sailed at eleven. It sounded so easy, and I felt like the luckiest man alive to have had those marvelous hours with Stella. But as I crawled into bed at my mother's, I no longer felt like the man the Army had trained to send overseas. My core of steel was molten. The protective black ice of my heart had become a useless puddle.

At four a.m. the phone woke us. My orders had changed and I was due at the dock by seven. I gathered my things and waited for dawn.

At sunrise, just before I had to go, I called Stella. Her father hung up on me.

"Explain to her, Ma," I said, gathering my things, fighting to keep my feelings at bay. "I'll try to call her from the dock, but there might not be time. Tell her I'll write. Tell her—" I dug the brass ring out of my pocket and gave it to my mother. "Give her this. Tell her I love her."

"I'll tell her," Ma said, her tears a torrent. "Lord bless you, Stuart."

Stella and I had spent one joyous hour too many in the dark and wound up a few tragic hours short at sunrise.

Our fate was sealed. There was nothing to be done.

9 – Houseguest

"You stay outta trouble, y'hear?" the bus driver called as we hopped off in Rosebank. We waved our thanks, then turned toward Stella's block.

"Maybe she'll be asleep," Khamille said.

"Maybe." We walked quickly. No point putting off the inevitable.

Most of the houses were dark as we walked up Stella's block. If I had any flickering hope of sneaking in, one look at the light glowing in her window doused it. Stella was waiting up. I paused to calculate our best approach.

"You're nervous," Khamille said. "I can just catch a bus back to the ferry."

I didn't want her anywhere near there. "It's okay. Just let me do the talking."

Stella stood in the front window, the curtain pulled aside. I felt a short stab of guilt at the anxious look on her face. But the instant she spotted us she scowled and dropped the curtain. My guilt fled in a panic.

When we walked in she was in the sun porch, fingers drumming impatiently on the arms of her favorite gray chair.

"Hey, Aunt Stella," I said. "This is Khamille, my friend from work." My first strategy was to act normal, like we were just coming home from a movie ready for a snack. Milk and cookies, maybe. Nothing unusual.

Stella did not even pretend to smile at Khamille.

"Pleased to meet you, Miss Stella," Khamille said.

Where'd that Miss thing come from, I wondered. But it went over. Stella nodded like a queen who had been properly curtsied to.

"We had a little problem, Aunt Stel." I kept my voice light, trying for that perfect blend of nonchalance and contrite apology. "We waited and waited for Khamille's bus but it never came. I couldn't leave her there alone in that terminal. So I figured the safest thing would be come home together."

She frowned at me, then at Khamille, then at me again. "Have you any idea what time it is?"

I glanced at the clock. "It's past eleven. You're up kind of late, Aunt Stel. Were you watching a movie or something?"

Khamille winced. Okay, maybe that one was a little over the line. Stella did not grace me with a reply.

"I'm dying of thirst," I said, plunging ahead with a different tactic. Stella was always sympathetic to food needs. "Khamille, you want a Coke or something?"

"No, thank you." She looked like she wanted to drop through the floor.

"Young lady," Stella barked. "Khamille, is it?"

"Yes, ma'am."

"Where exactly do you live?"

I hadn't actually gotten around to asking Khamille this question myself. It didn't matter to me. Khamille gave Stella a street name I didn't recognize.

Stella mulled it over. "Is that near the projects?"

"Yes, ma'am. Actually, it's in the projects."

Stella's exasperated sigh was meant to convey that she knew I couldn't be trusted to associate with decent people. The projects — subsidized housing— were well known for trouble, especially in the minds of old-time Staten Islanders like Stella.

"Well, I have no intention of driving you there at this hour."

"No, ma'am. I don't expect you to. I can just get the bus back to the ferry and transfer."

"You cannot just do that," I said. "It's late, and you're alone. Why don't you just crash with us tonight?"

Stella's eyes became slits.

"If that's okay? I'll be out of your way real early," Khamille added quickly. "I have to be at Curtis in the morning."

I rushed to explain. "Khamille's a senior at Curtis High. She's taking AP college-level courses this summer. You already know we both work at the rides, right? Joe hired her. Two summers in a row." Even Stella couldn't dismiss these obvious signs of model citizenship. Could she?

Stella pursed her lips. "Lilli, come to the kitchen. I'll get you two a snack."

I knew this wasn't about snacks, but I gave Khamille a reassuring thumbs-up before following Stella through the dining room to the kitchen.

She stood beside the fridge, her hands on her ample hips, the overhead light splashing her wide, harsh shadow across the kitchen floor. The motor on the ancient kitchen clock hummed impatiently. "You showed very poor judgment bringing this girl home with you."

I nodded. I thought about explaining the real story, but decided that would only prove our poor judgment. In Stella's eyes it would seal Khamille's status as a low-life from the projects.

"What about that family next door?" she asked. "That boy and his mother?"

"You mean Ty and Darlene?"

"Yes. You all work together, don't you? Surely Khamille and Ty know each other?"

"Well, yeah, but—"

"Surely they would open their door for one of their own?"

I took a measured breath, remembering Joe's reference to "her kind." I pressed my lips together. How could I explain this to Stella? I understood why she thought staying at Ty's was the perfect solution for Khamille. Why would Darlene object to a surprise house guest at 11:30 p.m. as long as it was "one of their own"? But I knew it wasn't that simple, starting with the fact that Darlene bristled at the very mention of Khamille's name. Khamille brushed off my questions about her and Tyson. Something didn't add up, and until I understood more about Darlene's cold shoulder, I knew packing Khamille off to Ty's was simply not a plan.

"It's pretty late to bother Darlene, don't you think?" I hoped Stella would be reasonable.

"It certainly is. But that girl cannot stay here." I was sure her voice was loud enough for Khamille to hear in the living room. "Do I make myself clear?"

"Perfectly." I dropped my voice to a whisper. "Can you please keep your voice down."

"Do not tell me what to do in my own home," she said, more loudly still.

I stepped out of my aunt's shadow and faced her. It might be her house but she was being entirely unreasonable. I was determined to change her mind. Khamille was a perfectly polite, intelligent girl who hadn't done a thing wrong. In fact, she had proved herself to be a real friend tonight, defending me in front of Val and rescuing me from humiliation with Roger. Not to mention standing up to Trace so we both got away. I wasn't about to let Stella toss her out like an old shoe.

"Aunt Stella," I said. "You're being ridiculous."

"Excuse me?" she screeched.

"You heard me. Khamille is a perfectly nice person and you have no reason to say otherwise."

She bristled. "I never said otherwise." Her cheeks turned pink, with anger or shame, I didn't know.

"Then what's your problem? She's smart. Polite. There is no reason she can't stay in the other bed in my room. It's for one night, Aunt Stella. Just one night."

We stared each other down. If we'd been in an old western movie our hands would have been resting on our holsters ready to draw. I had no gun but I had been saving my best shot.

"Think about Aunt Helen. You know darned well what she would do. You know darned well that she would not have a problem with this."

She turned away, her lip beginning to quiver. "Helen," she said softly. "Helen, Helen, Helen. You spoiled this child her entire life. She is incorrigible. I tried to warn you. Months ago. You never listened. And now? Now I deal with the consequences."

"Aunt Stella. Please stop. There are no consequences. Khamille is my friend. And she's a good one."

She seemed to ignore me. She opened the fridge and scanned the shelves. After a moment she removed a carton of milk. She used slow, deliberate motions to take a jelly glass down from her cabinet, fill it, and replace the milk. Then she took a long sip, swallowed, and licked the milk mustache from her upper lip.

"The girl may stay."

Relief surged through me. "Thank you."

"Just for tonight," she added, in order to have the last word.

I had no further argument.

She strode out of the kitchen, clutching her milk glass. Khamille was pacing in front of the sofa, not even daring to sit until she had been invited.

"Young lady," Stella said. "You may stay the night. You'll share a room with Lilli."

"Of course. Thank you."

Stella turned to go up the steps.

"Um. Excuse me. Miss Stella?" Khamille's voice sounded uncharacteristically timid.

Stella paused without turning.

"I need to call my mom. If that's okay. She'll be worried."

Stella nodded. "Of course. Lilli will show you the phone. And I wish you the best of luck with your studies. Taking college level classes while still in high school? That is quite commendable. Perhaps your study habits will rub off on Lilli."

"Yes ma'am. Thank you," Khamille said. "Good night."

"Good night, Lilli Rose," Stella called, her voice almost lilting as she climbed the steps. "Don't forget to lock up."

Khamille and I watched her slow ascent with our mouths open.

"Did you put sugar in that glass of milk?" Khamille whispered. "I heard what she said. She definitely didn't want me here. Why'd she turn so sweet?"

"Guilt. I reminded her what Aunt Helen would have done. Her sister. She didn't like it but she knew I was right."

"Brilliant."

"Yeah." Mentioning Helen had been a stroke of genius. Stella for sure knew that Helen would have instantly put out the welcome mat for Khamille.

"But also—"

"What?" Khamille asked.

"I think she was actually worried about me. Worried that I might not come home. I think she was glad to see me safe."

"That makes sense."

"To you maybe. But not to me. It's all kind of—baffling." And I noticed something else. The word that stopped her arguments cold?

Friend.

With Helen gone Stella was completely alone now. Was it possible that Stella understood how badly I needed a friend?

I couldn't begin to explain all that to Khamille, not tonight anyway.

"Never mind," I said. "Come on, I'm pooped. Call your mother and let's get to bed."

10 - Pervert

That night I dreamed about my mother. In the dream, she wore a butter-colored sweater and brushed my hair with a silver hairbrush just like the one on Aunt Helen's bureau. She smiled over my shoulder into the mirror, and I smiled back as she gently stroked my hair. She hummed softly and leaned into my back. I could feel the vibration of her humming against the thumping of my own heart, and then she began to laugh. It was the carefree sound of a very young girl and I longed to laugh with her, to share that sense of pure joy that was missing in my own life. But when I opened my mouth the only sound I could make was a strangled scream.

The dream was so odd it jolted me awake. My mother. Smiling. Humming. Treating me with tenderness and laughing like a young girl. These were not actual memories. They were wishes, dreams, born of the strange day I had lived through yesterday.

I sat up in bed. It was seven-thirty and the bed across from me was already empty. Khamille wasn't kidding when she said she'd be out early. Last night, when she called her mother to explain the situation, there were a lot of "yes ma'ams" and "I wills" and "I won'ts" in response to a barrage of unintelligible sounds from the other end. Khamille told me everything was fine, but it didn't sound fine to me.

At least she had a mother to call. I would never say it out loud, because it wasn't her fault that she had parents who cared about her and all I had were jumbled memories and dead ancestors. But the irony and unfairness of it stung.

I could hear Stella on the phone downstairs, her voice its usual imperious screech. My quasi-lethal living ancestor. Probably regaling one of her friends with the sad tale of her wayward grand-niece and my riff-raff friends. Now that the old ladies had actually spent some time with me they'd probably believe anything she told them.

Well, so what. I put on my dorky red uniform and dried my hair, looking forward to spending the day with someone, anyone, else.

Over breakfast I explained that Khamille was already gone. Stella said she knew that and proceeded to tell me how tired I looked, implying that this was the result of returning home so very late.

"I feel fine," I said. Or I would, as soon as I got out of this house. "Eleven-thirty isn't really that late."

"It certainly isn't home early. Next time, if there is a next time, I will be more specific," she said, using her fork for emphasis, "And I will be very specific about what will happen if you don't heed my warnings."

"Fine," I said. "I better go. Don't want to be late for work." I was afraid the subject of Khamille was on the tip of her tongue and I really didn't want to hear it. Khamille had held up her end of the bargain. As far as I was concerned, the incident was over.

Ty was at the bus stop, bouncing to his Walkman.

"Thanks for giving me Khamille's number."

He shrugged. "You can keep it, far as I'm concerned."

"You're so much fun in the morning, Ty."

The bus slowed to a stop. We boarded but did not sit together. A few more people got on each time the bus stopped, and I noticed how they decided where to sit. This one lady—a white lady, like most of the people who rode this bus—glanced at the empty seat beside Ty, then quickly chose a different seat on the opposite side of the bus. Closer to the driver. Ty didn't pay her any mind. He just kept bopping to his Walkman and looking out the window.

When we got off together at the rides I could feel the lady's eyes watching us.

"You see that lady?" I asked Ty.

He pulled out his headphones. "Huh?"

"That white lady on the bus. Watching like you're some kind of criminal."

"So?"

"So, who does she think she is?" My heart pumped with fury on his behalf, newly fueled by my aunt's assumptions about Khamille last night.

Ty shrugged. "It's that Central Park thing."

I knew what he was referring to. Last April a woman jogger was beaten, raped, and left for dead. The papers were filled with stories about it and five black boys had been arrested for the crime.

"What's that got to do with you?"

"What do you think? Anybody who looks like those boys is automatically a suspect."

"That's crazy. We're both wearing an identical, dorky uniform, and

96

we're getting off at the rides. That ought to be a clue we're going to work, not going wilding." I used the word I read in the papers, the word they used to describe what happened that night in Central Park.

Ty made a disgusted sound. "Wilding? I never even heard of wilding. They just made that up. And you think it matters what I'm wearing? I get off at the same bus stop as you, and some nasty old white lady's sure as hell gonna notice."

I was incensed. "Well, it's not fair."

Another sound of disgust. "Speaking of clues," he said. "You let me know when you see something fair happen for somebody looks like me. I'd sure like to hear about that."

He didn't wait for me to answer, just stalked off to punch in. I followed him but not too closely. I figured he needed some space.

Khamille left a checklist for setting up and I ran down it, feeling proud about how fast I was learning. I was all ready for my first customer when I spotted Joe coming from the carousel. He wore his usual shirt and slacks, but they looked a bit more rumpled than usual. He gave the park the once-over, searching for anything amiss, and after that he made a beeline toward me.

"Morning, Joe. Everything okay?"

"Seems to be. All okay in there?"

I flashed him a thumbs up. "Ready to roll."

"Good, good." He seemed to have something more on his mind. He came right up to the counter and I noticed his toupee wasn't quite straight, like maybe he put it on in a hurry this morning.

"Uh—Lilli—I have some things to take care of right away. But later, come see me in the office. When Bev comes in."

"What's up?" He was acting weird, but I hadn't done anything wrong as far as I knew.

"Just stop by later. I gotta run. Damned carousel will be the death of me yet."

He was on the phone when I walked into his office a few hours later, his ever-present cigarette smoke spiraling up from the ashtray. He signaled me to sit in the chair next to his desk, and I listened as he tried to wind up his conversation.

"Yeah— yeah. I got about seventy or eighty, plus the carousel junkies. A hundred and fifty sounds right. Listen, find a way to stay under budget and still make sure there's plenty of food. I don't want it to look like some cheap-ass affair, okay? Okay. Okay. Call me tomorrow." He hung up the phone and pulled a hankie from his pocket to mop the sweat from his face.

"God da—" He stopped himself in the nick of time, as usual. "Caterer. Planning the party for the carousel opening. Thinks my pockets are lined with gold."

"Party?" I asked. "You mean the grand opening?"

"I mean the party, the night of July third. Didn't you hear? The Carousel Society, folks who helped finance the restoration, insisted on having a little private celebration the night before the opening. Which I get to organize and help pay for, of course."

"Who's invited?"

"The carousel people, plus all our employees, some friends and business associates. Sounded like a good idea, but it's turning into a pain in the—. Well, anyway, it's a lot of work."

"Sounds like it," I said. I assumed "carousel people" would include Jesse. "So, I'm invited?"

"Sure, sure." His arms made a wide, inclusive sweep. "All my employees."

A grin crept across my face. If this was the "grand opening" Jesse meant, it was even better than July Fourth, when I would have to work. At this party we might have time to actually talk. My mind instantly conjured all kinds of possibilities.

"I spoke to Stella and invited her too."

My fantasy went dark. "Did Stella say yes?"

Joe smoothed his hair. "Well, to tell you the truth, I'm not sure. We didn't have what you might call a rational conversation."

"Oh?" Why anyone would expect a rational conversation from Stella was beyond me, but I looked Joe in the eye. If this was why he needed to see me, I was ready.

He looked away and busied himself stomping out one butt and lighting another. Then he cleared his throat and began his explanation. "One of your aunt's friends called me last night to suggest that I invite Stella to the carousel opening."

"Roberta," I said, in case Joe thought I was completely in the dark.

He tilted his head in surprise. "Yeah, that's right. Roberta. Anyway, it sounded like a good idea—"

"Just like the party sounded like a good idea," I said. "Some good ideas are better than others."

Joe harrumphed, but he got my point. "So anyway, I called Stella first thing this morning, before I got too busy. I wanted to give her plenty of time to think about it, see? I was just trying to be polite."

He was taking great pains to explain, as if he knew I'd be upset when I heard the rest.

"So how did it go?"

"The party didn't really excite her," he said, to my immense relief. "She was too interested in telling me all about you and Khamille."

I rolled my eyes.

"I know, I know," he said, making a placating gesture with his hands. "I told her. Khamille's a good kid, nothing to worry about. But she gave me an earful anyway. Said it was my fault and I had to do something about it."

"She said what was your fault?"

"You know, the fact that you're out late at night, running around with—" Joe didn't elaborate. He didn't have to.

"Joe. Come on. We went to the city to see my dad." Kind of true. "We had some bus problems, and Khamille ended up at Stella's for the night. It was no big deal. It's not your fault and there's nothing to 'do' anything about."

Joe bit his lower lip. He knew I was right, but he still feared the wrath of Stella Whitaker.

"Look, Joe," I said, calmer. "You know my Aunt Stella. You know how she is."

Joe waved his arms. "Are you kidding? I know Stella better than anybody. I know her since I was a kid in school. I know her since—" he groped for words, "—since before she was the way she is."

I sat quietly, hoping he would go on. He didn't.

"What do you mean, before?"

"Nothing. Never mind." He picked up an invoice from his desk and studied it, avoiding my probing gaze.

"Joe," I said softly, "did you know her boyfriend? The one who died?"

Joe let the paper flutter from his hands, grabbed the cigarette from the ashtray and took a deep drag. "What are you talking about?"

I played this carefully. I didn't want him to realize how little I really knew. "We both know what I'm talking about."

The smoke poured from his nostrils, drifting into a halo above his head. "You know about Stu?"

Aha. Stu. The name in Helen's diary. Corroboration that he did actually exist.

I nodded. "They were talking about him at lunch the other day. Helen's canasta club."

"Hmmph. Old biddies."

"I know, right? They love to gossip. But Joe. You don't know how much this means to me. My family never talks about anything. I don't know a thing about my family history. I mean, it's my history too, right? They're my – my ancestors, right?" I could see I was starting to get through to him. "So, did you know this Stu?"

His nod began before his words. "Yeah. Yeah, I did." He flicked an ash toward the overflowing tray. "Stuart McGee was a hell of a nice guy."

McGee. Another nugget.

Joe stared off into space, wearing the same pained look I saw on Roberta yesterday, just nodding an absent answer. "That damned war took a lot of nice guys. But Stuart McGee was the best of the bunch."

I let him sit with his memories, hoping a few more details would float my way. But he just pulled on his cigarette and watched the smoke curl up between us. I wanted to gag but managed to hold back my cough. After a minute he ground the butt into the edge of his ashtray and leaned toward me.

"Listen," he said. "I'm telling you this for your own good. Don't ever try to talk to your aunt about Stu. The subject is off limits, you hear? Completely off limits."

"I figured that out already," I said. "But Joe. Seriously? Everything's off limits."

"Oh, come on—"

"I mean it. It's like living in a dark room. With my mouth taped shut."

"Your mouth is far from taped shut. It works fine, Lilli. Believe me."

"Okay, okay. Bad example, maybe. But some bad shit's happened in our family. Okay? Bad. And I don't even know how bad. Aunt Helen used to just wave her hands around and paint it all with butterflies and roses. You know how she was. And Stella? She just pushes all of us away. And my dad just pretends. It's like he erases every step behind him. Acts like nothing happened, like it will all just disappear as long as we don't leave a trail. We never talk about anything."

"Some things are best forgotten."

"But here's the thing, Joe. You never really forget. It doesn't go away. I have a past. My family has a past. It's in my blood. It's part of me. Don't I deserve to know about it?"

He pulled out his lighter and lit another cigarette, exhaling a long stream of smoke. "Kiddo," he said, "I wouldn't sweat it. When you get to be my age, you'll understand that the best thing to do with the crap in your past is hold your nose and run away as fast as you can."

I fumed with my arms folded. Joe was insulting me. Insulting my own powers of observation. Telling me to doubt my own gut instincts. He had no idea how much he was pissing me off by treating me the way everyone in my family did.

He shook his head. "How'd we get on this topic anyway? I didn't call you in to yell at you. I wanted to ask for a favor. I know Khamille's a good kid. She wouldn't be working here if I didn't know that. So if you want to be friends, that's great. Just don't plan on any more sleepovers at Stella's."

"But—"

"Please. As a favor to me?"

"Okay," I sighed. "Okay. But we both know there's no reason to agree. Stella and her ideas are wrong and old fashioned and—just wrong."

He didn't agree or disagree, and I left it at that. Clearly, I had a soft spot for Joe. I wasn't so sure I liked that.

When I got back to the snack bar Ty was squeezing mustard on a pair of hot dogs Bev had served up. Bev asked me some silly questions about my summer and how I liked the job. I could tell Ty was listening, even though he was chewing his food and staring across the park, pretending not to. When Bev finally went into the kitchen, Ty faced me.

"So, you and Khamille stepped out last night?" I could tell from his annoying superior tone that he already knew the answer.

"We took the ferry to the city. Yeah."

"Yeah, well I saw her leaving Stella's this morning. What was that all about?"

I stared at him. Hard. "Why should I tell you?"

He shrugged. "Don't make no difference if you do or you don't. I was just asking."

"We ran into someone Khamille didn't particularly want to ride home with. That's all."

Ty gave a low whistle and pursed his lips. "She's acquainted with a lot of people fit that description. Her brother knows even more. Some scary dudes."

"So I gathered."

"Really? And you understand the whole situation from one night out with Khamille?"

He was ticking me off now. "What's your point, Tyson? It's no secret you don't like Khamille."

"Who said I don't like Khamille?

"Come on. You give her the brush off all the time. You didn't want to go out with us the other night. And your mother can't even stand to hear Khamille's name. What's the story, Ty?"

Ty stared at me then, as if trying to decide how much to say. "It's not your concern," he said, the same line Darlene had used when I tried to press her for details.

He turned and scanned the park again, signaling the end of our discussion. His smugness infuriated me. Why couldn't people just say what was on their minds instead of playing "hide and secret" all the time?

"Mmm, mmm," he said, squinting. "Looks like our friend is back again."

My heart lurched, and my eyes roved in the direction he was looking, hoping to see Jesse. All I saw was a paunchy balding man munching popcorn.

"What friend?" I asked. "What are you talking about?"

"That man over there. I must have seen him five, maybe six times around here in the past week. Just sitting like that, eating or drinking."

"So?" I asked. "I waited on him the other day. What's the big deal? The guy likes to hang out at the rides."

Ty looked at me as if my brain was cement. "Look around you, girl. This look like a place where a grown man would just hang out? A normal grown man?"

I took another look. The man sat in a narrow band of shade thrown by the shadow of a ticket booth behind him. He wore khaki-colored shorts and a red pullover shirt with a collar and some kind of logo over his heart. Aside from the long black socks that reached nearly to his chubby white knees, he looked pretty ordinary. He seemed to be enjoying people-watching as he sipped his soda and took in the sights.

"He actually looks kind of lonely. Maybe he just likes being around people."

"Yeah, and maybe he's a pervert."

"What?"

Ty nodded with certainty. "Some kind of child molester just waiting to grab him a good one."

Bev popped out of the kitchen, suddenly interested. "What? Where?"

"Honestly, Ty," I snapped. "Where do you come up with these things?"

"I'm a very observant person."

"Observant? Don't be ridiculous. You're being paranoid. You can't decide anything just from looking at a person."

Ty let a small laugh escape. "We had this talk already. About the lady on the bus? People like her decide things about me all the time just by looking at me. Take one look and jump to all kinds of conclusions."

I felt a blush creep up my neck. He was right. Of course. Stella and the lady on the bus had both done just that. But that didn't make it right. "That's not how I decide things."

He tilted his head and gave a little shrug of dismissal. So smug I wanted to smack him.

Bev was already hopping on the bandwagon with Ty. "I don't know, Lilli. That guy does look a little weird. Look at those socks."

"We should tell Joe," Ty said.

Bev nodded solemnly.

I stormed out of the snack bar, letting the door bang behind me, and went around front next to Ty. "Tell Joe what? That he should call the cops and have this guy arrested because his socks are funny?"

Ty's snicker only fanned my anger.

"Bev, cover for me."

"Where you going?" she asked.

"I'm going to have a few words with this dangerous pervert myself."

Ty and Bev didn't try to stop me, not that they could have. They watched me walk toward the man, who looked less and less dangerous the closer I got. He wore a wide-brimmed hat that shaded his eyes and pinkish freckled face. When he saw I was headed his way, he sat up straight and pulled in his gut, flashing a friendly smile, which was about the last thing my dad would have done in the same situation. This guy obviously had a lot more practice smiling than Dad, judging from the crinkly laugh-lines around his eyes. His eyes were a washed out light blue. No comparison to my Jesse's vivid blue eyes, but definitely this old guy's best feature.

"Good morning," he sang when I stopped in front of him. His voice was deep and sounded all wrong for his rosy cheeks and pale eyebrows. "Gonna be another scorcher, huh?"

"Sure feels like it. Is there anything I can help you with?" I tried to sound official.

His forehead creased. "Help me?"

Okay, so it was kind of a lame opening question. What was I going to do, offer to get him another Coke? Walk him to the men's room? I sat beside him.

"Look. Let me get to the point. A couple of us have seen you hanging around here a lot lately, and we're wondering what's going on."

"Going on?" His blue eyes looked sincere, innocent.

"Yeah." How was I going to explain? "Let's just say, we don't see a lot of guys your age in the park."

He cocked his head. "My age?"

I actually couldn't tell how old this guy was. He seemed around my father's age, maybe a little older. But his age wasn't really the question, was it?

"I mean, we don't see a lot of guys at the rides without kids," I said.

"Without kids?"

"Yeah, without kids." He was making me crazy with this repeating-the-question stuff. "Let me be blunt. People who don't have a good reason to come here usually don't, okay? If you don't have a kid, or a grandkid, or a niece or nephew, and nobody's dragging you to the rides, why would you want to be here?"

"Why would I—?" He started to giggle then, a childish high-pitched sound, then let loose with a laugh that jiggled his stomach like Saint Nick. When he got hold of himself again he took out a hankie and removed his hat to mop his bald spot. The little hair he had left was a faded rusty red, same as the eyebrows, and he smoothed it back before he replaced his hat.

"I'm sorry," he said. "But I find your frankness refreshing."

"That's not what people usually say about it, but thanks." I waited for him to go on. He didn't. "What's your name?"

"It's Florio. Florio Giovanucci." He giggled again. "I know, I don't look Italian, right? My ancestors are from Northern Italy. My mother always told me they mated with their fair-haired cousins across the Alps."

True, he didn't look Italian, but I didn't really need to hear about the mating habits of his ancestors. "So. Why are you here?"

"Why am I here?" He paused. "I'm here because I— have an— interest— in the carousel."

Me too, I thought, Jesse's gorgeous blue eyes and soft mane suddenly flooding my mind. I forced myself to concentrate. "Are you one of those carousel people?"

"Carousel people?"

"From the Carousel Society? The ones who helped pay for the restoration?"

"No, no. I never heard of the Carousel Society. I'd like to know more, actually, now that I —well." He cut off his thought. "Let's just say I'd like to learn more about the carousel's history."

"You oughta talk to Joe."

"Joe?"

"Joe Alonzo. He owns this place. Been around for years. I bet he could help you."

He nodded and seemed to consider telling me more. He dug into his pocket then and pulled something out, clutching it tightly in his fist. When he opened his hand I saw he held a big, shiny ring. And I mean big, around three inches in diameter, much too big for anyone's actual finger. It wasn't gold, even though the sun glinted off it. The finish was darker, kind of burnished. Gently, as if the ring were made of glass, he picked it up and held it toward me, holding back enough so I understood he wasn't about to hand over his prize possession.

"Nice," I said, because he clearly expected a compliment. From the look on his face, I expected him to launch into some sad tale of a broken romance, which I wasn't that excited to hear.

"I think it's a carousel ring," he said.

Now I was interested. I reached toward the ring, remembering what Jesse had told me the day we met, about grabbing the brass ring on the carousel. "From this carousel?"

He shrugged. "I'm not sure. I don't have much to go on, but I think it could be." He held the ring under my nose, keeping a firm grip.

I squinted, trying to see if there was any writing inside. I put my hand on his to steady the ring and was beginning to focus when heavy footsteps thudded toward us.

"What's going on here?" Ty asked, his voice menacing.

The man yanked back the ring and put it in his pocket. "Going on?" The man folded his arms across his chest.

Great. I was just getting somewhere and now the man was back in parrot mode. Ty ignored my efforts to wave him off.

"You heard me," Ty challenged, stretching himself to look taller and more menacing than he actually was. Though come to think of it, this man might have been scared of Tyson just on his looks alone. I was beginning to understand how that worked. "Old guy like you hanging around the park all alone. What's going on?"

"Why, nothing. I was just leaving, actually."

"No, wait," I protested. "I wanted to—"

Ty's face twisted into a threatening grimace.

The man leaped up. "It was very nice chatting with you, miss."

"Lilli. My name is Lilli. Hey, don't run off—"

"No, no, please. This fellow's right. What's an old guy like me doing hanging around an amusement park anyway?" He carefully brushed off the back of his shorts. "It's silly, really."

"But—"

He backed away, waving, and after a few feet he turned and walked briskly toward the exit.

"Hey," I called after him. "Come back again and talk to Joe."

Florio turned and gave me a wave then quickened his pace and hurried toward the front gate. I turned on Ty, scowling. "Thanks, bonehead."

"What? The guy had his hands on you, he was getting ready to make his move."

We stood nose to nose. "He was showing me a ring that he thinks might be from the old carousel. I was trying to see if it had an inscription."

"And you fell for that? Man, he sucked you right in."

I made a disgusted sound and strode toward the snack bar.

"Next thing you know he'd be offering you free candy and a ride in his car," he yelled.

I ignored him.

"Least you could do is say thanks."

I turned, continuing to walk backwards toward the snack bar. "Thanks," I snarled. "For nothing."

Stuart: The Problem

They warned us to be tough, to stay strong, to never give in. It didn't matter. Just a few weeks after I landed in France, I was killed in action. No need to recount the details. Watch a film or read a book about any war. The characters and circumstances may change but the ending remains the same.

Back home, I was hailed as a hero. They held a beautiful Catholic funeral, a high mass with pomp and ceremony, hymns and incense, prayers and tears. They played Taps and folded a flag to present to my mother. The tears flowed forth like a leaky garden hose, spilling from every eye but my Stella's.

She stood between my mother and Helen, dressed in a simple black dress, her beautiful face veiled in lace. Helen, always so ready to support her, watched anxiously as the soldiers lowered me into the cold ground. Stella never wavered, not at the church, not at the graveside, not even later at the house.

"Sure, her heart is breaking," said one woman.

"When the shock wears off she's bound to fall apart," said another. Tongues clucked and heads bobbed, doubting Stella's remarkable poise as she listened with a Mona Lisa smile to their inanities about me being in God's arms and free from harm.

"Remember the good times," they advised. Stella nodded. She would try. Oh, she would try. But how was she supposed to hold onto the image of the face she loved knowing it was forever lost? How to keep the memory of that last kiss without the slap of truth that prevented the next one? Our love had been real, beyond doubt. How could Stella ever dare open her heart again?

As the weeks passed, Helen kept a watchful eye on her sister. Her step was a bit slower, it was true, but she went to work and kept up appearances. After supper she would settle with a book in the old gray armchair, though perhaps Helen alone noticed how the bookmark seemed stuck on the same page for days on end. Often Stella nodded off in the chair, and Helen gently slid the book from her sister's hands and led her off to bed.

Well, who could blame the poor thing? For feeling tired, for having no interest in anything? Helen believed her sister's loss had temporarily doused her spark. But she would heal, Stella would; she'd shine again. Helen prayed for faith as she devoted her days to her family—an oblivious father, a brother chafing for the freedom of manhood, and a sister paralyzed with loss.

Poor Helen. She had no idea it would take more than prayers and faith to heal what ailed our Stella.

Another month passed. Stella continued her show of strength and Helen waited patiently for some sign of healing tears or even emancipating anger. None came. Instead, Stella grew quieter, more distant, insisting she was fine when she obviously was not.

By the third month after our final night together, Stella sat in her chair after supper, the book unopened on her lap. She stared out into the dark fall evening, contemplating a future that grew more bleak with each passing day. And still she told no one.

At the start of the fourth month, Stella paid a visit to my mother. It began as all the visits they had shared since my death, Stella listening with a polite sense of duty as my mother prattled about my boyhood. They shared an unspoken bond of grief, my mother's trimmed in tears, Stella's silent and stoic, and took comfort in each other. But this night, without a word of warning, Stella fell into a sobbing heap.

Ma rushed to her side, enveloped her with soft arms. "I know, my dear. I know." She rocked Stella gently.

Stella's sobs increased. "No," she cried, her head shaking. "No, you don't understand."

My mother clucked her tongue. "Ah, sure I do. Indeed I do. It's impossible. Unbearable. Some days I feel as if I can't—"

"No," Stella interrupted sharply. She raised her head and gazed tearfully at my mother. "I'm going to have a baby."

My mother's stunned gaze locked onto hers, then fixed on to the small bump concealed by Stella's loose-fitting dress. "Mother of God," she breathed.

"Oh Mrs. M.," she wailed. "Whatever am I to do?"

This wasn't a problem my mother had expected to face. But it was not one with which she was entirely unfamiliar. In the small Irish town of her girlhood, babies often came unbidden. She knew how much I loved Stella. She would never consider shunning the girl, as was the custom in the old days. But she also knew at this stage, nothing short of a miracle would change a blessed thing about the situation. There was only the waiting left, and a suitable place to be found for it.

"Who else knows?" my mother asked.

"No one."

"Good. The less said, the better. I'll speak to Father Anthony tomorrow—"

"Father Anthony?"

"Now don't go worrying. He'll breathe nary a word. But he'll know what to do, and help to arrange it."

Stella dried her tears. "My sister—"

My mother gave a nod. "Helen will need to know. But your father—"

Stella's eyes widened. "No. Oh, no. He mustn't."

My mother's arms wrapped once again around her. "He shan't know. Helen and I will see to that. Now don't get yourself worked up, we'll get through this together. We shall."

And so a plan was laid. Stella was fit enough to work the rest of the month. After that, she would move to a convent north of the city, "awaiting her time in an atmosphere of ample opportunity for contemplation of her sin," as the Mother Superior so deftly put it. My dear mother, bless her soul, chose not to share this gem with Stella.

There was brief talk of keeping the child, but Father Anthony insisted that was impossible. "It will always have a black mark against it," he warned. "It's best to give it a decent home with decent parents. And you can move on with your life."

Stella couldn't imagine moving on with any sort of life. But she was smart, as I've said. And nothing if not practical. And as she couldn't imagine loving, much less marrying, anyone else ever, keeping her job was important. An independent future required an independent income. She needed to ensure that Warton Hicks, her supervisor, would grant her leave and allow her to return when ready.

With Helen as her loyal accomplice, Stella used her last month at work to demonstrate her mounting grief, allowing her interest in both job and friends to wane. Occasionally, quite deliberately, she'd lose control of her emotions in front of people who were known to talk. And then Stella made a polite request for a leave to recover from the loss of her fiancé.

She had every cause to believe it would be granted. Surely, no reasonable man would refuse such a reasonable request.

But Warton Hicks was not at all a reasonable man. He was a selfish, greedy worm in an ill-fitting gray tweed suit. His beady eyes peered out from thick lenses, watching for trouble in his kingdom on the fifth floor of the insurance company, a kingdom that was his only because a mysterious health problem had barred him from the military. He made the most of the lack of competition, Warton Hicks did.

Stella didn't know it, but Hicks had been watching her for a very long time. He promoted her to head the typing pool, enjoying the way her dark eyes danced when he broke the news. She was a hard worker, Stella was. But that wasn't the only reason he liked having her around.

In the last few months, since her soldier boy had died in the war, Hicks had observed something else, something disturbing, about Stella. This sudden request for a leave confirmed his suspicions. The girl was in trouble, and he would be damned if she'd get away scot free.

When Stella requested a six-month leave, he gave every appearance of sympathy. Of course, under the circumstances, there was no other choice. Of course, he would have the papers drawn up immediately. She would be missed, of course, but if she would be so kind as to show Miss Bailey what was what, at the end of the week her leave could commence.

"It will take until Friday to get the final approvals," he told her. "I have a late meeting that afternoon, but if you would be good enough to stay a bit past five we can wrap things up by the end of the day."

"Of course, Mr. Hicks," she said. "Of course." Whatever it took to be free, to escape the eyes that came closer each day to seeing the truth. Stella passed her last week barely daring to consider even the next minute of her uncertain future.

On Friday, just before six, Hicks summoned her. She walked past the rows of empty desks to his big corner office.

The papers were ready, yes. But there was one more matter to be dealt with. Hicks rose, went to the door, turned the lock, flashed a wicked smile. He knew, he said, just exactly why she needed this leave, and how important it was to her. And he was perfectly willing to cooperate, as long as she would cooperate too.

He laughed then, the laugh of a man whose conquest is assured, and went about his business. It was quick and cruel, far from the tender act Stella and I had shared on that last night. This man was a different species entirely, and when he was done, he snatched up the leave papers from his desk and threw them onto the floor beside her.

"Pull yourself together," he snarled, "and close the door behind you when you leave."

I wish I could fully explain how this all works, me being able to see my Stella after I was gone to the far side of the veil that divides the living from the dead. But I don't exactly understand it myself. Had I been mortal still,

I would have slugged that man from here to the moon and back. But I had no power to intervene.

I watched, helpless, as her heart shut down for good.

Too stunned to weep, Stella retrieved the papers and ran a shaky finger across that evil man's hunched and crooked signature. Then she collected her things, swung his office door as wide as it would go, and left.

11 – Snapshots

When Joe called Stella on Thursday morning to invite her to the carousel party, he lit the fuse in a chain of etiquette explosions that blew my entire weekend. The first bomb went off when Stella decided to say yes to Joe's invitation to the party, mostly to keep an eye on me, I'm sure. Accepting his invitation obliged her to invite him for dinner on Friday night, an invitation which Joe felt equally obliged to accept. Then my dad called out of the blue, inviting himself and my brother Mike's family for a visit on Sunday. I was scheduled to work on Saturday afternoon and evening, so there went the weekend, boom, boom, boom, like a string of July 4th firecrackers.

Maybe it was just as well. The distractions at home might keep me from spending too much time in a floating funk state, imagining conversations with Jesse, rehashing everything he said that day we met, counting the minutes until July third when I would see him again. Lord only knows what fantasies I'd invent with too much time on my hands.

When I walked in after work on Friday evening, my aunt's house was filled with a garlic and tomato smell rarely found in her spice-less Irish kitchen. I thought I actually heard her humming to herself as I walked into the dining room, but if I had, she stopped abruptly when I reached the kitchen.

Stella was peeling a cucumber at the kitchen sink, and I knew right away that Joe's visit was considered an occasion. She was decked out in a big flowered apron with pink trim, and a rose-colored skirt peeked out from under the apron in place of her usual housedress. Her dark waves were carefully lacquered in place, and her lips were a deep cherry red that resembled those old pictures in Helen's treasure box.

I thought about complimenting her but knew it would make us both uncomfortable, so I decided to compliment the food instead. "Mmmm," I said, lifting up the lid of a pot for a good, long whiff. "What's cooking?"

She reached across and tapped my arm with the peeler. "You're letting out the flavor. It's a marinara sauce. You know how Joe loves his pasta."

"Smells great," I said. "When do we eat?"

She eyed the old kitchen clock. "Joe will be here at six-thirty. We'll probably sit down around seven."

I walked to the fridge. The way my stomach felt, ten minutes was too long, never mind an hour and a half. I lifted the plastic wrap covering a plate of cheese and snagged myself a few hunks.

"Don't ruin your appetite," she warned.

"Don't worry about it," I replied, and went upstairs to change.

At 6:40 there was no sign of Joe. Ten minutes is your average traffic delay anywhere in New York, but even so, Stella stomped around the kitchen with one eye on the clock, fussing over things that were already done.

I pointed to the bottle of Chianti on the counter. "Why don't you pop this cork instead of yours?"

She pretended to ignore me, but I noticed she took my advice, and a few minutes later, the doorbell rang.

Stella was a little cool at first, but all was forgiven when Joe revealed a grocery-store bouquet of summer flowers.

"Beautiful blooms for a beautiful lady," he said, presenting them with a flourish.

"Aren't you sweet," Stella said, burying her blush in the blossoms. "Let's get them in water before they start to look as wilted as I feel."

I stared after her, wondering if I was in the right house, but Joe just laughed like nothing was amiss. He slipped his black jacket off and draped it over a chair while Stella swept off to the kitchen.

"Phew, this humidity is a killer." He peeled his damp shirt from his back and tried unsuccessfully to fan himself with the fabric. "Hey, kiddo." He came at me with that I'm-gonna-pinch-your-cheeks look, but at the last second he backed off, smoothed his hair, and delivered a sucker-punch to my arm instead.

"We were really busy today," I said. "Guess the kids are already bored with summer vacation, huh?"

Joe settled onto the sofa and dug into the cheese and crackers on the coffee table in front of him. "Happens every year just before the Fourth. I dunno, people get into a summertime mindset or something. Determined to have fun. Schuits me," he lisped, his mouth full of cracker.

Stella came back and presented Joe with a glass of wine. She eyed his coat on the chair, and without a word, snatched it up and whipped it onto a hanger in the hall closet. I'd have earned a "chairs-are-not-closets" lecture, but Joe was clearly entitled to special privileges.

"Looks like it's gonna be a good year," Joe continued. "Especially with the carousel opening. Did I tell you a reporter from the Advance is coming tomorrow afternoon?"

Stella sat and sipped her wine. "I think you've mentioned that every time I've spoken with you in the last two weeks."

"Stel, go easy on me, would ya? You know I'm only trying to convince you to let them interview you."

"Well, stop trying. There's nothing to say, and even if there was, nobody wants to hear an old lady say it."

"You're not old," he said.

She snorted. "I'm nearly ten years older than you, and you're no youngster. I've made my position clear and I'm through discussing it."

Joe looked at me and lifted one shoulder. "Your aunt is a little stubborn sometimes."

"You're kidding. My aunt? Stubborn?"

Stella set her wine glass on a coaster. "Don't encourage that child to be any more disrespectful than she is."

Joe laughed. "Sorry, sorry. But geez, Stel, I don't see why you keep saying no. You remember the place in its heyday, back before the war."

"And I choose to keep those memories to myself," she said, closing the subject. "I need to check the spaghetti." She got up and went toward the kitchen.

"Make sure it's al dente," Joe called, totally undaunted by her negative vibe. "Don't do the Irish thing and cook it till it's mush."

"Thank you, Mr. Alonzo," she called back. "But I believe I was cooking when you were still in knickers."

"Yeah, but were you any good?"

She didn't answer. Joe snickered and kept munching crackers like he was in a pie-eating contest.

"So, can I be interviewed?" I asked.

He stopped chewing, thought, chewed some more, then washed down his crackers with a big swig of wine. "You're pretty new," he said. "And they can only talk to a couple of people." He put down his glass and thought some more, finally rubbing his hands together. "I'll tell you what. They're sending a photographer, and since you'll be working the ticket booth at the carousel, maybe you can be in a couple of shots."

"I can?" I practically leaped out of my chair. "Really?"

"Sure, sure," Joe said. "It's actually a great idea. A fresh young face. Might remind the teenagers how much fun the rides are. Just remember a photographer takes a hundred pictures and uses maybe one or two. So don't get your hopes up."

"I won't." I wasn't worried. I was sure the look on my face when I was anywhere near that carousel would be so incredible they'd just have to print my picture. And when Jesse saw it, one look would tell him in an instant that we were meant to be together, and when we met again everything would happen just the way I'd been dreaming. I could hardly believe how perfect this plan was.

"Show up around noon tomorrow, okay? And hey— I'll tell you who I'd like to interview," Joe added. "That guy you were telling me about. The one with the ring?"

"Florio?" I had made a point of telling Joe about Florio and his brass ring as soon as I could, before Ty got a chance to convince Joe of the man's true perverted nature.

"Yeah, yeah, Florio. What a name, huh? You be sure and tell me if you see him again, huh? Now there's a PR story I'd love to get my hands on."

Stella called us to the table then. All through dinner I wasn't sure what was more amazing: Joe's playful teasing banter with my aunt, or the fact that she let him get away with it. She actually laughed a couple of times, and blushed again when he praised her marinara, which was a little bland, to be honest. The wine flowed like water, and as they squeezed the last drop into their glasses, it dawned on me that I could take advantage of this unusually festive mood to do some of the digging Khamille was urging me to do. Ask some questions and get some answers.

When Stella went to start the coffee, I leaned toward Joe. "Hey, Joe. Did you ever see my Aunt Helen's yearbook?"

"Why no, I don't believe I have. I'm a good bit younger than your aunts, you know. And you saw what happens when I remind someone about that," he added.

"I did. Anyway, we found the yearbook when we were cleaning out Helen's stuff. Some old photo albums, too."

Joe smoothed his hair and glanced over his shoulder into the kitchen. "What did Stella have to say about it?" We were on shaky ground here, and we both knew it.

"She let me look at the yearbook," I said. Okay, so it was one page, for two minutes, but he didn't need details. "But that's all. So far."

Joe shifted in his chair. "You heard what I said yesterday." He wagged a warning finger. "Don't go stirring the god da— Don't poke around in things you don't—"

Just then, Stella paraded in with a crystal plate loaded with Italian pastries. She was definitely humming now, some song I never heard. Joe grinned at the sight of her and the pastries and began to sing along.

"Oh, ma-ma, get that boy for me," he sang, loud and not exactly in tune with Stella. "Oh ma-ma, how happy we will be, oh ma-ma," he forgot the words and filled in with la-la-la's, then Stella joined him for the finale, "The butcher boy, the butcher boy, the butcher boy for me!"

They both laughed and I found myself laughing too, not at the silly song, but at the sight of Stella singing it. It was almost like when Helen was alive – feeling part of a family that sometimes laughed and sang and actually enjoyed being together. I wanted it to last forever, but I had enough experience with Dad to know the wine could turn at any moment. Three glasses might be just enough to keep them all glowing and warm and agreeable for the rest of the night. Or we might be one sip from the spark that would blow us into a stunned and sulky silence. If there was any way to accurately predict which way things would go, I had never been able to find it.

Still, this was about the happiest I'd ever seen my aunt, so even though I knew it was risky, I had to grab this chance. As they plowed into the pastries, I excused myself and slipped upstairs to Stella's room. The box stood in the corner, crammed in beside her dresser. I poked around and pulled out an old brown photo album and a newer-looking blue one. I had no idea what was in either one, but I might never have a better opportunity to find out. I suspected Stella wouldn't refuse me in front of Joe, and once she said yes, I was sure Joe would spill some facts about these pictures that Stella would keep locked up tight.

I hurried back to the table. "Hey Aunt Stel," I said, all innocence. "Wouldn't it be fun to look at these old albums of Aunt Helen's tonight?"

Stella's last fork-load of Napoleon stopped in mid-air, and she tilted her head with a mildly puzzled look, very different from her normal knife-edged glare of instant disapproval. She looked at the books and gently rested her fork on her plate, dabbing her mouth with a napkin.

Joe, bless him, saw his chance to help and jumped in. "That would be fun, wouldn't it? Kids are always so curious about the past. There might even be some pictures of Lilli in there, when she was little. Remember what a cute little tyke she was?"

I rolled my eyes.

Stella reached toward the photo albums. She fingered the blue one. "I was looking at this one the other day," she said. The corners of her mouth actually seemed to be toying with the idea of smiling, whether it was the Chianti or the memories, I had no clue. "And you know, I had forgotten, but Lilli was actually cute when she was little."

My jaw dropped and I had to hurry to snap it shut. Joe winked at me and picked up the brown album.

"Let's take our coffee to the living room," he said, "and have a little look-see."

We settled on the sofa, me sandwiched between Stella and Joe. Stella plopped the blue album on my lap, even though I was pretty sure the brown one had the older, more interesting pictures. I was not about to complain, so I eagerly flipped open the blue one.

The first few pages were small black and white shots of a skinny boy in shorts. In most of them he stood beside my Aunt Helen, her arm draped around him with that easy loving presence she always had.

"Who's the kid?" I asked

"What, you don't recognize your dear old Dad?" Joe asked.

"My father?" I lifted the page to my face as Stella laughed. I had never seen a picture of him this young. "He looks like a little dork."

"He was," Joe said. "He moved straight from high school into a job at the bank."

"Your father was a very responsible young man," Stella said. "He still is."

The compliment brought me up short, but I didn't have much time to think about it. The page turned and my throat caught. Dad was posed next to a young, awesome-looking woman. Her long brown hair tumbled over her shoulders and the two of them leaned into each other like they didn't have a care in the world. No one needed to explain this one to me. I knew the woman was my mother, even though I couldn't recall her ever looking that carefree.

Stella made a sad little tsking sound before saying, "You have her smile."

"I do?" Maybe I would have known that if my mom had smiled more. I tried to process what I was seeing, my parents, young and in love. Their faces pressed into my brain like footprints in wet cement.

"How did they meet?" I asked.

"Both worked at the bank, as I recall," Stella said. "They were very young. It was a whirlwind employee cafeteria romance."

I turned the page to more happy photos of my parents. In one, my mom wore a silly hat made of bows stuck onto a paper plate, and on the same page there were more shots of her smiling for the camera as she unwrapped presents.

"They don't give bridal showers like that anymore," Stella said.

"Nowadays they just move in together and expect you to send a check."

"Stel, you old cynic," Joe chided. "I went to a lovely shower for my niece last year. Big deal, at a restaurant. They invite the men now, too. Very civilized, if you ask me."

"Which I didn't," Stella replied. She poked me in the ribs as a signal to turn the page.

It didn't take a genius to guess the next big photo opportunity was my parents' wedding. Mom in a big poofy veil and long white dress, Dad in a white tux with black piping on the lapels. This very photo sat for years in a gold frame on a shelf in my living room. In fact, this was one of the pictures I hoped to find the night Khamille and I stopped at Dad's. I thought it was lost forever. It felt like a miracle to see it in front of me again.

"Your mother sure was a beautiful girl," Joe said.

I stared at the picture. It was true, she was beautiful, and on this day her smile was open and uncensored, and even my dad looked happy. Seeing them like that made me want to crawl into the page, trying to understand, trying to feel what they must have felt on that day. Love? Longing? Blind optimism? Were they totally clueless about the hard times ahead, or just pretending not to see them? The carefully posed picture didn't reveal anything that felt close to real. Nothing close to the truth I longed for.

I ran a finger over the picture. "They look so happy."

"They were," Joe said. "I think so, anyway."

Stella leaned toward me just a little, a move almost too small to notice. But it was there. "I think your mother tried hard to be happy. It wasn't always easy."

A vague memory floated up, my mother swinging me high into the air, laughing and twirling and saying my name. At first the flash made my heart race with joy, but the racing feeling soon turned anxious and uneasy. I felt a balloon start to inflate in my chest. It felt hard to breathe. I turned the page. Fast.

"Awwww," I said, trying to restore a light mood. "Isn't he cute?" My brother Mike, in a classic pose on a blue blanket, flashed his toothless smile and his bare little butt.

"I can't believe Helen kept that shot," Stella said. "Why do people do that to innocent babies who don't have sense enough to be modest?"

"Modest, schmodest," Joe laughed. "It's a baby's behind. Who cares?"

I kept turning, past pictures of Mike's first day at school, Aunt Helen with him and his new bicycle, a Little League shot. My mom and dad were in a few pictures taken on special occasions, but the smiles were more strained, and it was clear that Mike had become the new focus of Aunt

Helen's attention. I kept turning, knowing what was coming and not sure I was ready to see it.

Finally, there I was: my mother next to Mike on the sofa, and me a faceless pink bundle cradled in his six-year-old big-brother arms. He had a dopey, baffled grin on his face, and she looked exhausted. I once heard someone refer to me as a bonus baby, a nice way of saying I hadn't exactly been planned. Add that to the list of the zillion things you weren't supposed to discuss.

When I looked at the next page I couldn't help giggling. I mean, that tiny, drooling, bald-headed, toothless little twerp in the diaper was actually me.

"I was cute," I said. "Wasn't I?"

"Mmmmm," my aunt teased, her voice doubtful.

It was my turn to poke her in the ribs.

"You were a little doll," Joe said as I paged ahead. "The first time Helen brought you to the park, you couldn't have been more than three. Pink corduroys, big brown eyes, pigtails flying. You didn't have much of a vocabulary but you made sure we understood. You had to ride on every ride. Every one." He laughed. "Helen had the patience of a saint to deal with you."

"That she did," Stella agreed.

My First Communion picture made me shiver— eight years old, posed like a tiny bride between my parents, Dad looking off to the left, Mom's smile wooden from the drugs she was full of by then. Story of my life in a three by five. Mom wasn't in any of the other pictures, and I knew that was because if Helen took a picture, I was visiting them while Mom was away. *She needs the rest.* I remembered that phrase, how it confused me. There were long stretches when my mother seemed to sleep all the time. But she never could get enough rest.

When I got to the pictures of me in junior high, I closed the book. "OK, enough of that," I said, swapping the blue book for the brown one on Joe's lap. "Let's look at this one now."

I could feel Stella stiffen but I plunged ahead. The first pages were dotted with small black and whites, glued to the pages with special black holders that slipped under the corners. "Joe, you have to tell me who these people are, because Aunt Stel won't."

"Who said I won't?" she huffed. "Let's see. There's my brother Stan, your grandfather. And this is me and your Aunt Helen when we were little."

I pulled the book closer to my face. "This looks like it was taken the same day as the one on Aunt Helen's dresser."

"Maybe so," Stella said.

I leaned away from my aunt and took a good look at her profile, then turned back to the photo. The soft, fleshy curve of her nose was the same, but her eyes seemed to have lost their brightness. Maybe that just happened when you got old. Maybe it happens to all kids. Or maybe not.

The sound of Joe's sniffling interrupted my thoughts. "Helen was such a good soul," he said, his voice cracking.

A small quivery sound escaped from my aunt, then she cleared her throat and drained her coffee cup in one long gulp. "Joe," she said, her cup clicking loudly as it hit the saucer, "don't start, now."

"It's true," he protested. "Look at these girls, Lilli. What a pair of American Beauties, huh?"

I nodded, turning the page. I didn't mind Joe's tears, but the threat of Stella turning into a sniveling mess panicked me. "Is this your mother?" I asked, pointing to a picture of the girls posed next to a frail looking woman. She had pale skin and her hair was pulled back from her face in a way that made her look far too thin.

Stella nodded, a dreamy look in her eyes "Now there was a good soul."

I opened my mouth to ask her more, but something stopped me. I know how I feel when people ask me about my mother. There aren't enough words to explain what goes on inside when I think of her, so what is there to say? She's gone, and that's that. My aunt's mother had been dead a whole lot longer than mine. I decided to shut my mouth and give her a chance to say whatever she wanted, or, if she preferred, to wallow in her own muddled memories.

The next several pages were blank, but I could see the little marks where pictures had once been glued by their corners. I looked up at Joe, puzzled. He and Stella were exchanging a look, both refusing to catch my eye.

"The war years," he explained. "Who wants to remember?"

That sounded fishy to me. I could see they had been carefully excised from the album, and even as I wondered if they might be stored someplace else, I realized I'd lost my chance at having Joe accidentally identify any of Helen and Stella's old friends, including the mysterious Stu. I felt cheated.

"That's my father," Stella said, changing the subject by pointing to a small black and white of a man leaning on a car. "You can't tell in this photo but he had bright red hair, till most of it fell out."

"Never did lose the temper that went with it," Joe said.

A flash of Stella's eyes warned him off. "That's his '48 Ford he's leaning on."

Again I pulled the album closer, but the picture was so small it was hard to see much of his face. Maybe he was a redhead, but he looked mostly bald and about as round as Stella was today. His arm was stretched across the car roof with obvious pride in his new possession, but he wasn't smiling.

"Hmmph," Joe said. "If he'd cared for his family half as much as he cared for his damned Ford—"

Stella cleared her throat in warning.

"What?" I said, looking from one to the other. "What does that mean?"

"Never mind," Joe said.

I stared at the picture again.

"Lethal."

The word slipped from my lips before I had a chance to stop it.

"What?" Stella asked. "What did you say?"

"Lethal. That's what Roberta called him. Lethal."

Joe cleared his throat loudly and looked away.

Stella grabbed the book and closed it sharply. "It's high time Roberta learned to zip those loose lips of hers."

I reached toward the books. "Wait, I want to see the rest, I wasn't—"

"We've seen quite enough for tonight. Too much, I'm afraid."

Stella set the books on the coffee table and pushed them beyond my reach. My most pathetic pleading look only earned me a what-can-you-do shrug of sympathy from Joe. The mood was broken. Stella gathered the coffee cups, and Joe jumped up to help, exchanging harmless small talk about the wonderful evening. I eyed the albums one last time, but I knew it was hopeless. I took my cue, said good night, and drifted upstairs.

I fell asleep with my mind on fire with memories, the flames stoked by those old photos. I tried playing the radio on my Walkman, and it soon lulled me to sleep, but it led me to more strange dreams. I could see my mother waltzing with my father, laughing and laughing as they danced. I heard her call my name, but then she danced away and left me behind, and suddenly the soft music was replaced by the garish sound of the carousel's band organ.

I sat up in bed and realized I was fully dressed in someone else's clothes. Old fashioned clothes, the kind I'd seen in Aunt Helen's pictures. I reached up, surprised to find a soft hat pinned to my hair, but I simply straightened it and began to float across my room, feeling elegant and airy.

When I looked down I saw a soldier sitting on the other bed. He stood as I drifted nearer. He was tall, not dashingly handsome but attractive and well-built. He swept me into his arms and began to twirl me around and around to the music. His shirt felt stiff and scratchy against my face, but as he held me close in his strong arms I felt surprisingly safe.

Suddenly we were on bright-colored carousel horses, and I could feel the up and down motion and hear the sound of the mechanism. The soldier transformed into Jesse, inviting me to abandon my horse and squeeze onto the saddle behind him. But before I could jump off, Jesse became the soldier again and my mother reappeared, looking as young and beautiful as she had been on her wedding day. She and the soldier touched hands and laughed, a light, tinkling, seemingly endless laugh that echoed around and around my head.

I reached for my mother but my hands became claws and I desperately pawed at the air, unable to reach her. She was on one carousel horse and I was on another, and we went up and down, up and down, always the same measured distance apart, and no matter how I tried I could never catch up to the horse my mother rode.

My eyes flew open. Jesse. My mother. The soldier. The carousel sounds. All instantly, abruptly gone as I came to consciousness. I had fallen asleep with my clothes on, but I knew right away they were my own clothes, not some retro outfit from the 1940's. My Walkman was still in my ears, still playing the piano music that probably set me off on the dream of my parents dancing.

I sat up and yanked off my headphones, annoyed at the radio station for playing that junk in the middle of the night. As my eyes adjusted to the dark I saw a shadowy figure perched on a chair beside my bed. I shook my head, afraid I was still dreaming, but the figure remained.

"Aunt Stel?" I asked, my voice filled with disbelief.

The chair creaked as she leaned forward. "You were crying," she whispered. "In your sleep."

"No," I insisted, reaching to touch my own face. She was right, it was moist. I licked my finger and tasted salt, and my mother's face came floating back. "I had a dream— My mother. And a soldier. On the carousel. I couldn't—"

"Shhhh. It's just a dream. It isn't real." Stella's hand hovered above my arm. Her hand came down tentatively and patted me, then stroked gently. "It will fade. Go back to sleep."

She stood and leaned over me, straightening the tangled sheet I had wrapped around my feet in my fitful dream state. As she pulled up the sheet her hands rested on my shoulders for just an instant, but she didn't say another word before she turned and walked out.

I curled into a little ball and dried my face with the hem of the sheet, then drew a long, deep breath. I knew I was wide awake. But at the same time, I was sure I must be dreaming.

12 – Poses

The pre-July 4 frenzy Joe talked about kicked in for real on Saturday. By the time I showed up around noon, the place was more crowded than I had ever seen it. The video arcade was pinging and dinging in full-tilt, and all the rides were running, the sounds of their motors mixed with the excited squeals of the kids. It all filled me with a weird sense of belonging the minute I walked through those tacky front gates.

I passed Khamille and Bev, both going ninety miles an hour to meet the noon rush. I waved at them but kept walking toward the office to meet Joe. The usual opera music blared from the radio, but he wasn't at his desk. Since Joe said the reporter would be here at noon, I decided to check the carousel.

Big sheets of plywood still hid the newly restored ride from the public eye. As I poked my head through the door I heard laughter and voices. Joe gestured toward the band organ while a guy in glasses scribbled notes. The photographer circled them, camera clicking as he shot the carousel horses from the front, side, rear, even underneath.

I raked my fingers through my hair and cleared my throat.

Joe looked up. "Well, well, here's our photogenic ingenue now." He guided me toward the photographer and rested a hand on my shoulder. "Tony, this is Lilli, one of my girls. I thought you might want to take a few shots with her."

"She your daughter?" the reporter asked, tapping his pad with his pen.

"No, no," Joe said, "she works here. She'll be taking tickets at the opening on July Fourth."

The reporter didn't look impressed. "I'll need your full name," he said, pen poised.

While I gave it to him, making sure he spelled it right, I could feel Tony the photographer sizing me up like a store-window mannequin. I sported my dorky red uniform, but he couldn't blame me for that. He squinted and gave a small nod, then turned back to the horses. I guess I'd do.

"You were explaining about the music," the reporter prompted, and Joe resumed his non-stop narrative. He explained what Jesse had already told me, that they wouldn't actually use the band organ for music all the time, just on special occasions. I listened intently, hoping to pick up a few new facts that might impress Jesse when I saw him.

After a few minutes, Tony tapped my shoulder. "How about we shoot you with this one?" he suggested, nodding toward one of the horses.

The horse's head was cocked at an odd angle, its bared teeth garish and frightening. Two horses down was the one Jesse had restored, with its soft brown eyes and bright blue saddle. "Do you mind if we use this one instead?"

Tony shrugged. "A horse is a horse."

That showed how much he knew about it. I stood next to Jesse's horse, trying to look my best in spite of the fact that Tony was instructing me to twist my body and pose my arms like I actually was a store-window mannequin. He finally backed off, leaving my hand resting awkwardly on the horse's mane. I closed my eyes for an instant, drew a long, slow breath and felt Jesse's energy tingle through my fingertips. Then I turned toward the camera and blasted Tony's lens with my best smile.

"Good, good, great, good," said Tony with each successive click of the shutter. "Now if you wouldn't mind getting on it, please."

"Sure." I hopped up and settled my butt into the saddle, grabbing the pole with both hands.

Tony crossed in front, where he had a full view of me and the horse. "Lean to the right and smile."

Just then, a miracle: Jesse walked through the plywood door. My stomach sank into the horse's saddle but I'm pretty sure my smile was now fit for the cover of Vogue.

"Terrific! Great," Tony said, clicking like mad. Jesse stepped onto the carousel and stood grinning a few feet behind Tony. "Now lean left. Perfect. Great. Thanks."

Tony stepped out of the way and fiddled with his camera. I sat tall in the saddle of that beautiful horse, running my hand over its glossy painted mane.

"Hey." Jesse approached the horse. "Lilli, am I right?"

"That's me," I said.

"I see you're riding my favorite. What's with the photo shoot?"

"Story for the Staten Island paper," I said. "Grand opening and all. Hey Tony? This is Jesse. He's one of the people who worked on the restoration."

"Oh yeah?" He could not have seemed less interested.

"Maybe you can take our photo together?"

"Sure. Why not?"

Jesse stood next to the horse while Tony aimed and focused the lens. "Pretend you're showing her something. Make it look interesting."

I put on my most intelligent face even though inside I felt like jelly. Jesse pointed to the decorative harness on the horse's neck. Tony clicked a few times and mumbled his thanks.

"You need to give your name to the reporter," he told Jesse, "else we can't use the photo." He crossed toward the band organ, which Joe was still explaining to the reporter.

"I didn't expect to see you before the opening," I managed to say.

"A little last-minute work on the chariot," he said. "Apparently the mermaid needs a bra. I was thinking seashells?"

I felt myself blush, but Joe chose that instant to demo the music, filling the place with the tinny sounds of the recorded band organ.

"See you," Jesse shouted. He waved and went off to do the job he came to do.

I needed to get off the horse but I wasn't sure my knees would support me. I closed my eyes and let the tinny music fill my head. My mind was a jumble of images from last night's strange dream, my mother's smile and that soldier in uniform, all mixed up with images of Jesse's eyes and smile and hair. I felt myself floating, falling, spinning, even though the carousel wasn't moving. I closed my eyes and clung to that horse and let myself just sink. Even when the music stopped abruptly, I couldn't move.

"You okay, kiddo?"

Joe's voice called me back. My eyes wrenched open. I gulped for air. My lungs felt ready to burst, like I'd been swimming under water and holding my breath.

"I'm fine," I said, because what else could I tell Joe that would make any sense?

"She's a beauty, isn't she?" Joe spread his arms wide, admiring his brand new baby, this old carousel.

"She's fantastic, Joe," I said. I felt a little shaky as I clambered off the horse. "I can't wait till it opens."

"Me neither, kiddo. Listen, remember what I said, don't be disappointed if your picture's not on page one, okay?"

"Okay," I said, not a bit worried. I knew that smile was a winner. "I'm gonna just hang out till it's time to punch in."

I wandered out to the rides and settled myself on a bench across from the Ferris wheel, next to a woman feeding an ice cream cone to a little girl in a stroller. The kid was lapping up the sweet stuff as fast as her little tongue could move, and her mother cooed at her, totally oblivious to the smears of chocolate goo covering her face and the bib of her overalls. It hit me how powerful this mother-child thing could be, if you were lucky enough to get the right mother.

I was toying with getting an ice cream cone myself when I spotted a familiar figure in shorts and black socks in front of the kiddie helicopter ride.

"Florio!" I called.

He turned, squinting into the sun.

"Over here," I waved.

He smiled when he recognized me. He hurried over after a quick glance at the helicopter ride. "Lilli, right?"

I nodded. This time, I wanted to be careful not to scare him off by asking too many questions.

"I can't talk long. My grandson's with me. He's on the copters."

"Grandson?"

"Bobby. He's almost four. Independent little cuss, insisted on riding alone."

"It's perfectly safe," I said, eyeing the ride as it made its slow rounds, bumping up no more than eight feet off the ground. Bobby waved to his grandpa each time he passed. "I'm sure he's strapped in tight."

"Made sure of that myself," he said. "You can see, I decided to take your advice and stop hanging around the place without a decoy."

I blushed. "I never suggested that, Florio."

"Well, even so," he said. He removed his cap, smoothed what was left of his hair and resettled the cap on his freckled bald spot. "It's a good idea. Bobby's having a ball."

"I'm glad," I said. I sidled into the subject I really wanted to broach. "Hey, you know that ring you were showing me the other day? I talked to Joe about it—"

His lips tightened. "I wish you hadn't. I probably shouldn't have showed it to you."

"Hey, it's okay, I only told Joe." Why was he so nervous all of a sudden? "He was very interested. He wants to see it. As a matter of fact, Joe's over at the carousel right now, with a reporter from the Advance."

"The Advance?" Florio looked around anxiously, as if we had planted hidden cameras behind him. That made me wonder again if he really did have something to hide.

"They're doing a story on the carousel. Why don't you go over? Show him the ring. If you play your cards right they'll interview you. You could be in the paper."

Florio shook his head. "No. No, I don't think so."

"Why not? Listen, Joe can tell you if that ring's real or not. You get your story and he gets his. It's a fair deal. Come on, Florio, why not take your shot at fifteen minutes of fame?"

He gave a short laugh and looked toward the carousel, but when he glanced at the helicopter ride again it was slowing down to unload. "I need to run. I'll stop by and see Joe some other time."

"Today's the deadline for the story," I warned.

"I understand. I appreciate the offer, but—" He ran off to his grandson without finishing his sentence, but clearly he meant no.

There was something odd about that guy. I knew he wasn't the pervert Ty thought he was, but he did seem to be hiding something. One day he was dying to show me that ring, the next he acted like it was a big secret. I watched as his grandson bounced out of the ride like a coiled spring, giggling as Florio scooped him up. That part of his story was true, of that I had no doubt. A blind man could see their bond from three blocks away.

"So he's back again?" Ty circled around from behind and slouched beside me on the bench. His sneaker tapped restlessly as we watched Florio's grandson pull him toward the next ride.

"You got a problem with that? Tyson Davis, Private Eye?"

"I got a problem with him grabbing little boys off the helicopter ride."

"It's his grandson."

"Can he prove it?"

I smacked Ty on the arm but he just laughed.

"Lighten up. That old woman you live with stole your sense of humor."

"Maybe I don't think you're so funny." I was actually relieved to see Ty wasn't serious but I didn't want him thinking I'd forgiven him so easily.

"You're fun to mess with," he said. "You're like a firecracker. Don't take much. Just light it, toss, and boom."

"Oh yeah?" I reached my hands up toward his throat and he dodged back with a laugh.

"Now you're just proving my point," he said.

The park was busy. A man with two little blonde girls in tow stopped to stare at us. Ty backed away from me.

"Everything okay here?" the man asked. He took a step closer, and I noticed he pushed his two little girls behind him. "Miss? You okay?"

"Totally," I said.

"We work here," Ty said. "Uniforms?" His hands indicated our identical t-shirts and shorts. "We're friends. Just, you know. Goofing around."

I nodded my agreement, too shocked to say more.

"Okay then," the man said. He drew himself up taller and lifted an index finger at Ty in gentle, but definite, warning. "You behave. Hear me?" He took the girls' hands and headed toward the snack bar.

"What the hell?" I sputtered. "He's got a hell of a nerve. I mean— what the hell?"

Ty's fists were balled at his sides but he stood his ground several feet away from me. "Remember what I said? When you were so sure I was wrong about the pervert? This is how it is, my friend. People decide things just because of how it looks. Happens all the time. Truth doesn't really matter all that much."

"But— that just sucks." The man and his little girls were now waiting in line to board the mini roller coaster. "The guy's just a jerk. Making assumptions. He should be—"

Ty shook his head. "Let it go, Lilli. It's not the first time and it's not gonna be the last. There's nothing me or you can do to fix it today." He started to walk away, then turned back again and pointed his finger at me.

"But you might want to work on that temper of yours. You know who you take after, don't you?" As he walked away his gait did a fair imitation of my Aunt Stella's slow, plodding steps. My own fists balled up then but I didn't yell or chase after him.

I didn't want to give anyone else a chance to jump to the wrong conclusion.

I punched in at two, and Bev took off her apron the second she saw me headed for the snack bar.

"Check out time," she sang, obvious joy in her voice. "Khamille's in till five, then you're on your own for the evening. Khamille's on early tomorrow, and I'm in for the afternoon, so I guess you must be off. Is that right?"

"Right. My family's coming to visit," I said, rolling my eyes for emphasis.

"Yeah, I know the feeling, honey," Bev said. "But family's important. You'll see that someday. How many brothers and sisters you got?"

I started to answer, but Khamille thrust one hip between us.

"Excuse me, ladies?" she said. Her arms were laden with three dogs and a few sodas. "When social hour's over maybe you could help serve our customers?"

"They'll wait," Bev said with a light wave.

"They might," Khamille said, her jaw firm.

"Take a chill pill, will you?" I strapped on my apron. "I'm coming."

"So's July Fourth."

As if I didn't know that. Khamille delivered the dogs and drinks and made change for the customer.

"You see your dream boy was here?" she asked.

I nodded. "We got our picture taken on the carousel. For the paper. If they run it." I sighed. "I wonder if Joe can get me a copy of the picture even if they don't run it?"

"Who-ee, you are a goner."

I wanted to argue but what was the point? She was right.

Khamille and I quickly served the rest of the waiting customers. It was a relief to be busy, and we had flurry after flurry of business until a little after four, when most normal people started to think about taking their kids home to feed them some decent food. We used that slow time to refill the drink bubblers and check supplies, and chatted as we worked.

"So, tomorrow's family day?" Khamille asked.

I groaned. "My dad, my brother, his wife, their two kids. Stella's cooking already."

"And how is our favorite auntie?"

"She's okay. Better than usual, actually. Last night Joe came over for dinner."

"Mmmm, mmmm. Sucking up to the boss, huh?"

"I told you they're old friends," I said defensively.

"Sure, sure," Khamille said, pouring herself a jumbo pink punch to sip while she worked.

"Anyway, they had fun. They drank a bottle of Chianti and got tipsy."

"Did he stay over?"

I'm sure my face looked horrified. "What? Of course not. What kind of question is that?"

Khamille took a long pull on her straw. "Logical question. He was tipsy, they're old friends. I was just wondering what kind of old friends. And don't look so shocked, Miss Priss. Some of the things people say about Joe, might be good if people knew he slept with a woman. Even that woman."

I hadn't heard those rumors about Joe, but I was certain there was nothing behind any talk of him and Stella. "Forget about that. It didn't happen. That woman's never slept with anybody."

Khamille put her hands on her hips and stared me down. "Don't be too sure about that."

I snorted at the very idea.

"I am serious. To hear my mama tell it, most of the sorriest, tiredest looking old women in my family got that way living hard when they were young."

"Well not my Aunt Stella, okay?" I felt my anger rising. Khamille met Stella once and thought she knew her better than I did. It ticked me off.

The straw in her cup sucked noisy air and she wiggled it in her ice chips. "You ask me, there's a whole lot more to Miss Stella than you can see from the wash on her line."

I folded my arms and turned my back to the counter, refusing to continue this conversation. Khamille faced the opposite direction, resting her chin in her hands and gazing out at the park. I could see her out of the corner of my eye, checking her watch every minute or so as she waited for five o'clock to roll around.

After a few minutes I decided staying mad wasn't worth it. "Khamille, do you remember your dreams?"

"You mean the ones I have at night? Sometimes. Once I dreamed Denzel Washington was my science teacher, and he was teaching Khamille the facts of life. Ooooh, he was a good teacher."

"Like bad good?"

"So bad."

We giggled and spent a few minutes listing possible lesson plans for that class: basic anatomy, with required hands-on lab; the impact of scent on the ability to concentrate; and life-altering mouth-to-mouth techniques. When we quit howling and grew quiet again, I told Khamille about looking at pictures with Stella and Joe, and about my strange dream. As she listened she fiddled with her straw, her long fingers twisting it into a knot.

"What do you think it means?" I asked her.

She pursed her lips. "The Jesse part makes sense. I mean he basically rents a room up in your—" she tapped her head. "Am I right?"

I shrugged. I didn't want to tell her how right she was.

"And seeing all those pictures reminded you about your mother. Who was already on your mind from the other night in the city. So that part makes sense too."

"I guess."

"That soldier though." She shook her head. "Sometimes dreams come from inside us, but sometimes—" She waved an arm above her head, tinkling her gold bangles. "The ancestors —"

"Please, not the ancestors again."

"Lilli, you can ignore Khamille if you choose to. But you cannot

131

ignore the ancestors. You rattled their cage when you found that stuff of your Aunt Helen's and started asking questions. You can deny it. But they're up there. They have some say. I believe that."

"Well, I don't." But even as I said it wondered. I was thinking a lot about my ancestors. That was new for me. I barely allowed myself to think about Aunt Helen or my own mother, never mind the people who came before them. My past, my entire family's past, felt like a minefield to be avoided at all costs, a place overflowing with twisted and potentially harmful memories. "Honestly? When I let myself think about my mother I tell myself she's better off where she is. At least she's peaceful. Maybe happy. No more worries. My mom, she was so unhappy. My whole life, she was unhappy. I try not to think too much about it, but then sometimes—"

"Sometimes you wake up feeling like you know something's missing and you don't know what it is."

"Yeah." There it was again, my thoughts coming out of Khamille's mouth. How does she do that? "It's like I'm being pulled toward something I've been trying to ignore."

"And the more you try to ignore it the worse it gets. Like a toothache you can't keep your tongue from touching."

"Exactly. It's exhausting. Wearing me out." She nodded, waiting for me to go on. I wasn't sure how to explain all the complicated feelings I had about my mother. "Sometimes I think what I really miss is the idea of a mother. Not the person my mother actually was, but the mother she was supposed to be. It's like there's some fantasy person I should have had but never did. Does that make sense?"

"Oh, yeah. Perfect sense. It's why you miss your auntie so much. And maybe why Miss Stella isn't exactly a substitute."

I hadn't told Khamille the strangest part of last night. That was the moment I woke to find Stella at my side, stroking me, soothing me back to sleep. I had no words to explain that. But before I could even try to explain, Khamille glanced at her watch and jumped.

"It's after five. Quitting time." She took off her apron and slid her backpack over one shoulder, then rested her hand on my back. "What was your mother's name?"

"Celia."

"Celia. That's a pretty name. Listen, don't let a little old dream shake you up."

The edges of my mouth turned up slightly. "I won't."

"I'll see you at the party on the third. And more important, that Jesse boy's gonna see you too." She opened the door of the snack bar with a sweeping motion. "And won't you both be surprised when Khamille shows up with her favorite science teacher."

"In your dreams," I called after her.

"Look who's talking," she called back. Then she waved and headed for the front gate.

Stuart: The Wait

On the cold December day my Stella arrived at the convent, the trees on the high-fenced grounds were bleak and bare. The starkness suited her mood and a sense of peace settled in. For the next few months, these grounds and this rambling old building, with its sparse and formal furnishings, were to be her safe haven. Far more important than the beds or the food, the place was far away from the normal bustle of life so the nun's guests--women with excellent reason to avoid running into friends-- could be assured of their privacy.

The nuns allowed Stella to wander freely in their self-contained world, and she soon grew to appreciate the soothing nature of strict schedules and predictable hours. The loud but dependable bells that summoned them to prayer. The simple but plentiful meals. The singing of psalms and hymns. Although one or the other of the sisters did occasionally refer obliquely to the magnitude of Stella's sin, it was by way of suggesting that they were praying for forgiveness. She had no quarrel with that. She spent a good deal of time praying for the same thing herself.

Helen had supported the story they invented for their father, a sudden business trip to audit another insurance company in Chicago. It was unheard of to send a woman alone on such a mission, as anyone should know. But they did a convincing job of it, those desperate girls, explaining how the war had changed things, how the lack of men was opening doors for capable women like Stella. And it was certainly true that the lack of one man in particular had forced Stella through this narrow door, one could hardly argue with that.

If Paddy Whitaker was a more attentive father, his mind would have quickly been sown with doubt. But for once the girls were glad he paid them little mind and rarely talked at length to anyone. The old man seemed to accept their story with the same grudging contempt he had for everything.

Once, and only once, Stella's kid brother Harry asked about her, repeating a remark he'd heard. Their father was out of earshot, thank God, and the tongue-lashing Helen delivered was so swift and out of character, Harry never mentioned it again.

Most Saturday afternoons Helen rode the train north to visit Stella. In good weather they walked together on the convent grounds. When it was cold or rainy they sat in the parlor to catch up. Helen liked to talk plainly of the coming event, to compliment her sister's growing belly and speculate on the wonder of the healthy child to come. But Stella would have none of it. Helen quickly learned that the only baby talk Stella would tolerate was a factual recitation of the number of weeks until she could go home again.

Birthing this child was a chore to be completed. Nothing more. And after that final Friday in Warton Hicks' office, Stella was more determined than ever to put this darkness behind her. It would not ruin her life. It would not jeopardize her job. She aimed to return stronger and more capable than ever. And for this strategy to succeed, she must keep both feet on solid ground, and avoid sinking into the quicksand of maternal emotions.

A short list of things that must be banished for her plan to succeed: any memory of her child's face, of its tiny fingers or toes, the sound of its first cries, and, alas, for me, the slightest brush of remembrance of Stuart McGee.

When Stella left for the convent, she carried no pictures, no letters, no rings or reminders, nothing to complicate her resolve to live out the rest of her days without the entanglements of love: real, imagined, or recalled. Anything else was simply too terrifying, too much of a risk to contemplate. And who could blame the woman? Our love had been a rose that bloomed and bloomed and suddenly—nothing but thorns. Not just emptiness but pain, real pain. Any sane person would have done the same as she, closed up tight and vowed never to let anyone close enough to hurt that much again.

Spring arrived. The trees on the convent grounds burst into glorious blossom. The old doctor who visited weekly announced in late April that her time was fast approaching. On May the sixth, just before lunch, she felt the first urgent signal of the baby's arrival. The sisters summoned the doctor and Helen, according to the pre-arranged plan. Then they took up their vigil, alternately praying to God and giggling with anticipation.

As Stella braced herself for the task ahead, Helen scrambled to put things right before she left the house. She scanned the icebox one last time: a casserole large enough to last three days if it had to, bread, some coffee, milk, a few eggs, an apple cobbler.

Helen had tried to warn Harry that she might have to leave suddenly, hoping he knew enough to ply Da with nicotine and beer in her absence. She knew there would be the devil's due when she got home, but it could not be helped. Harry was nearly grown now, and their father was perfectly capable. They could survive a few days on their own. Stella, on the other hand, needed Helen.

But caring for Stella wasn't Helen's only motive. Unlike her sister, Helen never ceased to envision the sweet-faced child about to be born. She wanted her chance to hold it close and somehow convey to the baby how very much it was loved.

Helen finished her note to Harry and grabbed the Macy's bag containing a change of clothes and her personal things. She was nearly out the door when a sudden thought gripped her. This child had a father, too. He should be part of this day.

She dropped the bag and raced up the steps to her sister's room, pausing in front of the dresser. She wasn't sure what she sought, but she had to find something. She opened the jewelry box and rifled the chains and bangles, tsking in irritation when nothing suitable surfaced. She yanked open the dresser drawer and spied a small green quilted stationery box. She closed her eyes, picturing Stella tenderly handling this box last summer when I was away, in the days before I was thrust from memory.

Helen flipped open the box. Her throat tightened at the sight of a neatly pressed lace-edged hankie that bore their mother's monogram. No time for emotion, she thought, plowing past it. Below were pictures of Stella and me, and the SkeeBall tickets we'd collected for our future, and an envelope with my last letter home. Fighting back tears, Helen probed until she found what she was after. She hesitated for a second, wondering if Stella would miss this talisman, but decided it was worth the risk. She tucked it into her change purse and with one last, guilty, prayerful glance at the house, she hurried to her sister's side.

13 - Q and A

On Sunday, I stayed in bed until nine hoping Stella would forget about church. Part of me knew that was like expecting squirrels to forget about nuts, but I figured it was worth a shot. I lounged around reading a magazine article about Princess Di for nearly an hour after I woke. Stella huffed past my bedroom every so often, and each time I heard her coming I ditched the magazine and did my open-mouthed heavy-breathing I'm-still-asleep act. After the third or fourth time, I opened one eye to peek after I was sure she was gone.

"Ah-ha." She stabbed a finger at me from my doorway.

My eye shut but it was too late. I stretched and yawned an enormous, casual yawn. "Mmmm," I said sleepily. "What time is it?"

"Time to get up," Stella said. "And plenty of time to make ten o'clock mass." She crossed to the other bed in my room and fluffed an already perfect pillow.

"Are you going too?" I asked, between fluffings.

"I went last night." She pounded the second innocent pillow into submission and smoothed the bedspread. "But that has nothing to do with you."

I sat up and scratched my head, barely containing my relief that at least we wouldn't be forming a worship team. "Okay. I'm up."

She nodded. "Your father and Mike will be here at two. I'll need some help after church."

"Sure," I said. Church, kitchen drudgery, and a visit from my family. So far, this had all the makings of a terrific Sunday.

"And I have a deli list. You can stop on the way home from church."

I nodded. Good food and lots of it, the one thing we could count on when anyone visited Stella.

I showered quickly and dressed in my acid-washed jeans and a peach colored t-shirt, then went down and sliced a bagel to shove into the toaster. Stella was peeling steaming potatoes for potato salad. As I waited for the bagel, she looked pointedly at the clock, then at the toaster, then back at the clock.

"What?" I asked. I still had plenty of time.

"A little late to be eating, isn't it?"

I realized my sin. Eating too close to communion, a mortal transgression.

"So I'm not going to communion," I said. "Since when is it a sin to skip communion?"

"It's not a sin," she said, turning her attention back to the mountain of potatoes. "But if I were you, I'd look for help wherever I could get it."

I tore into my bagel, chewing ferociously, and seven minutes later I was out the door with a deli list and twenty dollars safely nestled in my pocket. Maybe she was just edgy because she was having company, but that didn't mean I had to sit there and be her punching bag.

I meant to go to church, I really did. I headed for St. Mary's but when I caught a glimpse of the people climbing the church steps, looking so earnest and eager, I couldn't bring myself to join them. The sunlight suddenly seemed so inviting, I knew I'd only daydream my way through mass. Besides, skipping church didn't hurt anyone but me. Aunt Helen would have understood, and I think God does too. Even if Stella doesn't.

An hour wasn't long enough to do anything major, but I knew the shoreline was just a few blocks below Bay Street so I decided to head that way. I passed a high-rise under construction, its sign advertising new condos with "Ocean View." A few blocks later I was at the barricade that marked the end of Hylan Boulevard. A patch of grass denoted a small park, and I followed a twisted path down to a narrow strip of beach to my left. The gray harbor was dotted with barges and scows. Brooklyn lay across the bay, the Verrazano Bridge to my right and the Manhattan skyline in the distance to my left.

I picked up a rock and tossed it into the gentle surf, earning a scowl from the old man whose fishing line dangled in the water. Go to church, I thought, but I held my tongue. I brushed off a big flat rock and settled on it, enjoying the warm sun on my face and the soothing sound of the softly lapping waves. I fixed my gaze on Brooklyn. Jesse was over there somewhere, in his house, maybe still in his bed. I closed my eyes and conjured his face in my mind for about the hundredth time since the day we met.

Just two more days until he'd be real again and I wouldn't need to imagine or dream about him. I suddenly found it hard to sit still, and rose to pace the beach. I dug a small gray shell out of the sand and went down to the water's edge to rinse it. The sand was still firm from high tide, and I squatted down with the shell in my hand. J-E-S-S-E, I wrote, and right under that, L-I-L-L-I. There. Even though the tide would wash it smooth later, I liked seeing those names together in the sand.

A slight breeze ruffled my hair. Breathing deeply, I closed my eyes and thought about praying. I always had a hard time doing that while sitting in a stuffy old church, but it felt easier out here in the open. I didn't like to pray for anything too specific, because I observed too often that God liked to pull a fast one just to keep me on my toes. I kept it really general. I hoped Aunt Helen was happy, wherever she was, and my mother too. And maybe for Khamille's sake, a quick hello to the ancestors I had never actually met. And I wanted Jesse to come to the party on the third, and I hoped today with the family would be calm. If any of those things got through to whoever was listening up there that would be enough.

I opened my eyes and checked the time. Half past. If I wanted to beat the after-church deli rush, I needed to get moving. The small gray shell safely tucked into my pocket, I picked my way back up the path to the street.

By four that afternoon, I had walked my nephew Patrick on a half-dozen treasure hunts up and down my aunt's block. He found the usual stuff a three-year-old sees— bugs, grass, leaves, candy wrappers, old chewing gum— stopping to carefully examine each. Patrick used to love to hold my hand, but today he refused to touch me in spite of my brother's warning to hang on. I didn't force him. The kid had just survived a meal with Stella, with her constant nagging to mind the manners he hadn't even learned yet, so I figured he deserved a break.

We reached the corner again and turned back toward the house. My brother Mike had come out to the front yard and was fiddling with something on the lawn.

"What's Daddy doing?" Patrick asked.

Mike was uncoiling a length of green hose. "He's setting up the sprinkler," I replied.

Patrick recognized this as a clear signal for fun on a hot afternoon, and immediately began to dance in circles. My sister-in-law Dette came out holding their baby, Amy. Patrick began to circle Mike, cavorting like a zoo monkey at the prospect of going under the sprinkler. I didn't blame the kid; I could recall the thrill of it myself on hot days like this.

"Let's go put on your swimsuit," Dette said. Patrick clambered up the steps and Dette followed him into the house.

"Great idea," I said to Mike. "Now the kid won't die of boredom."

He flopped next to me on the stoop, using his t-shirt sleeve to wipe the sweat from his face. "Dette convinced Aunt Stel it wouldn't ruin the lawn."

"Good for her." Dette had a lot more patience with my great aunt than the rest of us did. My sister-in-law seemed to know instinctively what not to say and how to smooth over Stella's sharpest comments. She had no trouble conversing with Stella for hours, like she was doing today, somehow appearing to agree with the old woman even when I knew darn well she didn't. The thing is, Dette got a clean start when she married Mike, while the rest of us had to overcome years of nasty remarks and resentments built up like yellowed floor wax.

"Dad looks good," Mike said. "Don't you think?"

I shrugged. He looked about the same to me, tired and sad. "Probably glad to have me out of his hair for the summer."

"Who wouldn't be?" Mike teased.

I punched him in the arm. He laughed.

"Actually, Dad said it was kind of quiet without you. I think he misses you."

"He didn't tell me that."

"Yeah, well. You know how he is."

Did I ever. I picked at my nail polish. The stripes from my canasta club outing were starting to wear off. I'd need to paint them again before the party on July 3.

"You know, he was actually planning this visit even before Joe called the other day," Mike said.

"Joe?" The hair on the back of my neck rose. "Joe called Dad?"

"Don't get all bent. Seems like Joe called Dad and suggested it might be time for him to visit his Aunt Stella. Said you were getting to be a handful for her to manage alone."

"When was this?" I demanded.

He shrugged. "I dunno, Thursday maybe? Friday?"

The day after the Khamille incident. I gritted my teeth as my insides churned.

"I'm a handful for her to manage? Somebody should try managing her."

I fumed for a minute, but decided not to blame Joe. He didn't understand my family dynamics. Didn't know my father and I barely spoke, or that a visit wouldn't change a thing. Joe called my father because he was scared of my aunt, just like everyone else. He wanted to make her happy. As if anyone could do that. In the right light, the whole thing was kind of funny. Pathetic, but funny.

"So, Squirt," Mike said, ruffling my hair. "How are you managing with Aunt Stel?"

"Great. Terrific. It's Disneyland. What do you think?" I sighed. "At least I like my job at the rides." I told him about making friends with Khamille, and about the carousel and the party on the third.

"And Stella's really going to this shindig?" he asked, his skepticism obvious.

"She says she is. Joe can talk her into anything."

"Really? Joe? He looks so— harmless."

"You wouldn't believe how she is with him. It's like— it's almost like watching another person. A regular, normal person."

"I'd have to see it to believe it."

"I've seen it, and I'm not sure I believe it myself."

Patrick barreled out and Mike turned on the sprinkler. The kid ran right in, squealing as the cold water sprayed his back and his belly. He ran out, laughing so hard I wondered how he was even breathing, then turned to run in again, fearless and screeching loud enough to wake the dead. He made me smile but at the same time I felt that strange tightness growing in my own chest.

"Hey Mike," I asked, without looking at him. "Was I ever a kid?"

Mike smirked and drew back. "What kind of knucklehead question is that? Were you a kid? Of course you were a kid. What a knucklehead."

Of course Mike would say that. Obviously I knew that I once was Patrick's size and age. But that pure unfettered joy, that absolute trust that someone— maybe your mother— would have a dry towel and a snack ready whenever you decided you were too cold to take it anymore. Someone who would stand ready to bundle you into a giant warm hug. Of that, I had no memory. It was like watching a movie about childhood in some foreign place, like Patrick was a refugee from a land I'd never been. Or maybe I was the actual refugee.

"You used to love going in the sprinkler," Mike offered. "Don't you remember?"

"Not really," I sat beside him on the stoop. "Tell me."

"When you were about Pat's age. Aunt Helen used to put it on for us. Or Mom, sometimes."

"Mom?"

"Sometimes. Sometimes Aunt Helen would go under the water with us in her shorts, running back and forth, the three of us screaming like banshees. Stella was completely scandalized."

I had no trouble believing that part. But when I dredged my memory for an image of Helen laughing in the sprinkler with me and Mike: nothing. It's funny how your memories are a mixture of the stories you're told and the things your actual senses saw and heard and felt. I didn't think Mike would lie to me or invent a story. I had some sense of how it felt to have that cold water hit your bare skin on a hot day. But I had not a shred of memory that involved my mom helping or even watching, and if there had been actual joy involved in any of that, the memory was long lost. It made me sad to realize that.

"Hey Mike, can I ask you something else?"

He shrugged "I guess."

"Did I ever have a lunchbox?"

"A lunchbox?" He shook his head. "A lunchbox. Geez, you're full of ridiculous questions today. I think the old lady's getting to you, Squirt."

I closed my fingers around his forearm just to get his attention. "Try and remember, Mike. Did I have a lunchbox?"

He looked into my eyes and saw I was serious. "Yeah. Pretty sure you did. Big Bird or somebody, I don't know. Why?"

"And did Mom used to make my lunch?"

My brother flinched. He turned his gaze on Patrick. "I dunno. Sometimes. Once in a while. Not too often. Why?"

"Because I don't remember. I'm starting to forget everything about her, Mike. And I don't want to." I told him, then, about Aunt Helen's photo album.

"Have you ever seen the pictures, Mike? You should have a look. Mom and Dad. So happy. Their wedding? Big, happy smiles, both of them."

"Yeah, so?" He shrugged. "Everybody looks happy at their wedding."

"I know that, dummy. It's just that— well, I don't remember her ever being happy."

"She was happy sometimes. She used to laugh at the TV, remember? All in the Family? Mork and Mindy? She had a kind of a giggle laugh. Goofy, like a kid, when she really got going. Gasping for air, you remember?"

I tried. The memory of her watching TV on the sofa was pretty clear, and I tried to summon the sound of her laughter and remembered my dream, where she'd been laughing and brushing my hair. At first that memory was a comfort. My mother laughing. It was real. That was good, right?

But right away my stomach clenched. The more I remembered her laughter the more I remembered it was not a sound to be trusted. In an instant, what felt like fun could spin out into hysteria, a genuine laugh morphing into a high-pitched scream. It happened without warning. Then, just as suddenly, she would stop, stare into space. Reach for a glass or a pill or both. I closed my eyes and I could see her on the sofa in our living room, her eyes squeezed shut, tears leaking out. The memory seeped through me like a cold fog.

I brushed Mike's arm with my fingers and he shivered slightly despite the muggy air. "I'm not talking about laughing at a stupid TV show, Mike. I'm talking about being happy. Was she really happy, Mike? Ever? Do you remember her being happy?"

He looked into my eyes for a second then turned away. He nodded once. "Sure. Yeah. She was happy sometimes."

"When, Mike? When? Because I don't remember anything even close to that about her. And since Aunt Helen died, I've got to deal with my memories of Mom all by myself."

Mike swallowed, his Adam's apple straining with the effort. "You're not alone, Lilli," he managed to say. "You're not an orphan."

"I know. But I might as well be. Because nobody wants to talk about it. About anything."

"Hmmph. You got that right. Let me tell you, Squirt. I'm okay with your questions but this topic is completely off limits with Dad. Off limits, O.L., absolutely, don't even try it. You hear me?"

"I know that, Mike. I do have a brain."

"Well, okay then. As long as you plan to use it." Patrick ran up to Mike and shook off like a wet dog. "You're starting to turn blue," Mike teased. Patrick denied it and tried to scamper off, but Mike picked him up and swung him over the sprinkler. The boy giggled as the water tickled his toes. He set Patrick down again and patted his bottom. "That's my boy."

He turned to me. "Keep an eye on him. I'll be right back."

In the few minutes Mike was gone, Patrick managed to tease me into the sprinkler and my hair was dripping slightly when Mike returned with a long-neck beer. The family antidote to my line of questioning. Mike noticed Patrick was starting to shiver for real now so he shut down the sprinkler, ignoring the boy's protests as he bundled him into a towel and sent him in to Dette for dry clothes. Then he twisted the top off the bottle and settled next to me.

"You want to know when Mom was happy?" He took a sip. "I'll tell you the truth. The happiest I ever saw her was the day she brought you home from the hospital."

"When I was born?"

"When you were born. I was six. First grade. You were a little screamer in pink with the ugliest squished up face I ever saw, and Ma was cooing all over the place. My little flower, she said. My beautiful Lilli Rose."

"Wait, wait, slow down." I wanted to savor every word. "She actually said that?"

"Oh yeah, it was sickening."

I punched him.

"She said she named you Lilli Rose because one flower just wasn't enough, that's how beautiful you were."

I thought my chest would explode. I closed my eyes and remembered the photo I had seen the other night. Myself in that little pink blanket with Mike and Mom holding me. I tried to imagine what it felt like to be bathed in the rays of love that poured from my mother. Her beautiful Lilli Rose, named for two flowers, not one. I was trying hard to build a foundation on shifting sands, and I wanted to keep trying.

"She never told you that?"

"Course not. So. What else?"

"Sheesh, you're just like Aunt Stel sometimes, you know that? Never satisfied."

"What else?"

"What else, what else." Mike looked into the distance, trying to remember. "Well, she dressed you up like a baby doll, in pink dresses and booties and little hats."

"Little hats?"

"Yeah, to cover your ugly little bald head."

Another punch.

"Well, you were like a billiard ball, Squirt, for a long time. Not that this is much improvement." He ruffled my hair. "She put you in pink so people would know you were a girl. Let's see— she used to walk you around the park, and push you in the baby swing. And of course we came to visit the aunts. Once I remember we went to the rides with Mom and Dad."

"We did? Did we ride on the carousel?"

He shrugged again. "Who remembers? I hated those baby rides. I was bored out of my mind by third grade. Stupid helicopters and that dopey roller coaster. At least now Joe has some video games."

I didn't elaborate on how Joe felt about the video arcade. I was lost in thought, imagining that I had actually ridden the carousel with my mother. I tried to remember for sure, but I had been to the rides so many times with Aunt Helen, I was all mixed up about who was holding me. Senses and stories, all blended into one big mess.

"What else?" I demanded.

He shook his head. "Honestly? That's about it. Sorry. Things went downhill pretty fast once they got rolling."

I stared at the sidewalk, trying to piece together these new scraps of memory. I knew the gist of the rest of the story. Why did I crave the details?

"Mom was pretty sick, wasn't she, Mike?"

He nodded. "She was depressed a lot. Bi-polar, they call it now. Fancy name. Not like Dad or anybody in our family ever called it anything, not in so many words." Mike ground his beer bottle into the palm of his hand.

"Like if it didn't have a name it might just go away. Only it never did. Did it?"

Mike shook his head. "She wasn't so bad when you were first born but the older you got—"

"So it was my fault," I said.

"What? No. No, of course not." He paused. "It was nobody's fault. It just happened. She took meds, or she was supposed to anyway."

"Did it help?"

"Sometimes. When she took it. Sometimes she took it and it still didn't help. I don't know. She never talked about it to me. Neither did Dad. It's complicated."

A question nagged at me, the big one I didn't want to ask, but had to. The week my mom died I had been sent to Aunt Helen's because things were so bad, and nobody ever told me what happened. I mean, exactly what happened.

"Mike. Did she— did she just die in the hospital— Or did she— did she take something, like, on purpose?"

Mike tipped the beer and drained it, staring at a point way off in the distance. "You mean did she kill herself?"

I winced, hearing him say it so plainly.

He gestured toward me with the bottle. "See that look on your face? That. That's why we don't talk about it. You were only a kid. A kid, Lilli. What were we supposed to tell you?"

"The truth?" I suggested. "Mike. Please. I'm not a kid anymore,."

He grunted in dismissal. "Listen, Squirt, when it comes to this stuff, we're all kids. Okay, so this is what they told me. Told us, okay? She had some kind of complication with her meds and it affected her heart. Her heart gave out. That's it. End of story."

I pushed my lips together and puffed out my cheeks, forcing the air out slowly.

"It's not like we're hiding some big secret," he added.

"Everything feels like a secret. This whole family lives behind a giant door with a padlock the size of the moon, Mike."

"Yeah, well get used to it. You can't divorce your family. You're one of us, till death do us part." Mike stood up to go inside. "Anyway, talking about Mom won't bring her back. And Squirt?" He aimed a finger toward me. "Don't forget what I told you. Do not bring this subject up with Dad, or you will be very sorry."

"O.L.," I muttered. "Right."

I reached into my pocket and pulled out the shell I found on the beach, turning it over in my hand. It was a perfect, smooth gray oval, but when I looked closely I noticed one edge was chipped, and there were markings etched into the finish where the shell had been battered by the ocean.

I closed my hand over the shell and shut my eyes, trying to focus on what Mike had said. My mother had a sickness. I didn't make her that way. She died from complications, not because she couldn't stand living with us anymore. I was her flower, and her love had once been as real as this shell in my hand, even if it was just as battered and imperfect. It was good to know that. I longed to know more, to have more. But at least this was something.

I stood up and went inside, clutching the shell in my fist. Dette and Stella's non-stop chit-chat floated in from the kitchen, punctuated by my aunt's occasional corrective orders to Patrick. My father was on the sofa watching a ball game, and I sat next to him.

"So," I said, leaning on him a little, craving a closeness we didn't quite share, "you miss me yet?"

He picked up his scotch glass, swallowed, wiped his mouth with the back of his hand, then looked at me curiously. "Sometimes. It's kinda quiet."

"I thought you liked it quiet."

"Sometimes I do."

"Well," I said. "I miss you."

Dad looked at his loafers, cleared his throat, then looked back at the TV. "It was nice to see you the other night. With your—um, friend."

"Khamille."

"Right. Stella called me, you know. She—"

"Don't listen to Stella, okay? You know how she is. Khamille's really nice. She's a good friend."

He chewed the inside of his cheek. "Do you miss your other friends? From school?"

"I thought I would but—well, I don't. Not really."

"But you miss me, huh?" he asked, looking at me as if I had just informed him I was planning a career as a supermodel. "Is this some ploy to get me to take you home today?"

146

"No. I like my job, and I'm making new friends." I thought about Jesse, but decided I wasn't quite ready to talk to Dad about it. I might never be ready for that. "So I'm actually okay."

"Good. That's good."

"But I do miss you," I said again.

I was deliberately repeating the words I wanted him to hear. Mike was right, there was nothing I could do to bring my mother back, or Aunt Helen, either. But Dad was still here and so was Stella, with all their warts and wrinkles. And if I had to put up with them, they had to put up with me, too. Till death do us part. I leaned over and kissed Dad on the cheek, ignoring the shocked look on his face and the fact that his body went stiff as a board.

"Are you on drugs?" he said.

I laughed. "No. Forget it, never mind." I stood up and waltzed toward the kitchen. It was as if my brother's stories about my mom had lit one tiny light on a long, deserted street. And even though it still felt dark and lonely, and everywhere I looked there were roadblocks and warning signs, I knew, no matter what anyone said, that I would keep walking.

14 – Celebration

Thank God, the next day was Monday, July 3, the day of the carousel party. I was scheduled to work, which was a blessing, because I doubt I could have made it through one more day of waiting. From my post at the snack bar, I watched Joe run past at least a half-dozen times within an hour, smoothing his hair so frantically I feared he might tear the rug right off his head. On my break, I headed toward the carousel to see what the heck was going on.

A wall of plywood still blocked the carousel from view, but she was all glittery and gorgeous and ready to be revealed. All around her, however, was total chaos. A party supply truck just arrived and the workers were unloading chairs and tables and setting them up according to Joe's instructions. Or trying to, anyway. The way he was wringing his hands and barking orders, it seemed nobody was doing what he wanted. When he caught my eye, he ran toward me, his hands covering his face.

"My hot-shot caterer was right on time with the setups," Joe said, pacing like a caged animal. "But the fly-by-night party place was late with the tables and chairs so there was no place to set 'em up. The caterer stood around for an hour, giving me that this-is-gonna-cost-you look, but what was I supposed to do? Is it my fault the damned party place was late?"

The fact that he wasn't filtering his swear words to protect my delicate ears told me how upset he was. "Of course not," I agreed. Not that I really knew, but Joe looked like a man who desperately needed someone to agree with him.

"Whose stupid idea was this, anyway?" Joe whined.

I was pretty sure the party had been his idea, but maybe this wasn't the best moment to remind him. "I know. Crazy, right?"

"Totally looney tunes." He pressed his palms against his temples so hard I was worried he might squeeze his brains right out the top of his head. Then he banged his forehead with his palm. "Wow, kiddo, I almost forgot. I bet you haven't seen this yet." He pulled me over to where his jacket and papers were piled. "I got an early copy of the Advance. Check it out."

He handed me the Lifestyle section and I broke out in a huge grin. There I was, right smack in the middle of the page, leaning to one side of the pole on Jesse's horse. My hair looked a little screwy but otherwise it wasn't a bad picture.

"Above the fold," Joe said, explaining that the placement of the picture represented the very best in free publicity. "They had the sense to put me a little lower. What do you think, do I look okay?"

I glanced down at the photo of him peering out of one of the carousel chariots. His face was clear and so was the decorative work on the side of the cart, but his body was a mere shadowy lump on the seat.

"You look fine," I said. "Like a proud father."

That made him grin. He pointed to the third photo on the page. "News guys dredged this one up. They got everything filed away someplace down there. From 1937, it says. Not much of a picture but it gives you the idea of how things used to be."

I stared at the photo of the crowded boardwalk, overflowing with people in strange clothes. I knew Joe was secretly hoping for that kind of crowd at his grand opening tomorrow. "Maybe it will be like that again," I said.

"From your mouth to God's ears," he said, pointing his praying hands skyward. "The article's pretty good, so I can only hope—"

Someone hit the button to test the band organ, cutting him off. The deafening noise rattled what remained of the plywood shell, and we simultaneously used our fingers to plug our ears. I couldn't hear Joe's reaction but I could read lips and it wasn't pretty.

"Hey, kiddo," he said, leaning into my ear, "be a doll and bring me a great big Coke, would ya?"

I nodded and skipped off.

"With a splash of rum!" he screamed after me, his fingers still in his ears.

The afternoon rush kept me busy for a while, and just before my shift ended at two, Tyson strolled through the front gate, wearing his uniform.

"You working all afternoon?" he asked, leaning on the snack bar like he owned it.

I shook my head. "Khamille. Joe scheduled me early so I'll be free to come with Stella tonight."

"Who-ee, every bone in my body is green with envy."

"I'll be fine." I hoped I was right. "Hey, did you see the paper yet? There's an article about the carousel. My picture's right there in the middle, next to Joe's."

Ty's lips formed a stiff little smile. "Haven't seen it. Probably won't."

"Why not?"

"I don't read that rag, as a rule. Plus, I should have seen it coming. It's my second year here, and you're a newbie, but you're the one gets her picture on page one."

"Ty, Joe didn't mean to—"

"Don't explain. It's nothing new. I'm the guy who helps tear down the plywood gift wrap on the carousel this afternoon and lug it into storage. Sweep up the place for the party. That's the kind of job Joe thinks of when he thinks of me."

"Oh, come on, Ty. All that means is, Joe knows you're young and strong and he can depend on you.

"Right. I'm young and strong and also good-looking." He batted his long-lashed brown eyes. "They could have put me in the paper, don't you think? Right next to you, maybe. Somehow Joe didn't think of that. I'm not connected like you." He shrugged. "It doesn't matter. I just do what Joe asks."

"So do I," I insisted, but clearly he didn't agree.

"I gotta go punch in." Ty started to walk away but turned back, as if considering whether to ask me something else. "Hey, is Khamille going to the party?"

I narrowed my eyes suspiciously. "What do you care?"

"I don't. Just asking."

Right, I thought. I was getting a little tired of his who-cares act around Khamille when it was obvious he did care more than he let on. "She'll be here. She mentioned something about maybe bringing a date." I smiled, unable to resist a little dig.

"Might have one myself," he boasted.

"Me too," I said.

"Oh, that's right, Mr. Merry-go round will be here. Can't wait to hear what your aunt has to say when she gets a look at his ponytail."

"Stella doesn't run my life," I said.

Ty laughed. "Whatever you need to tell yourself." He walked off with a little wave.

"She doesn't!" I called after him.

I was kicking the wall in frustration when I realized Khamille had come through the back door and overheard that last remark. She watched me, hands on her hips, grinning her wide smile.

"Who you trying to convince?" she asked. "Me? Him? Or yourself?"

I got off after the lunch rush and was back home before three. The party was scheduled to start at six, and the first disagreement Stella and I had that afternoon was about what it actually means when a party is scheduled to start at six.

"Obviously, it means you arrive at six," Stella said, peering into the hall mirror to inspect each hair-sprayed wave of her new hairdo. "So we will leave at 5:45."

As anxious as I was to get there tonight, I obviously had more experience with modern party protocol than she did. "When a party starts at six," I explained, as patiently as I could, "you leave the house at six fifteen or so, and you take your time driving over."

"Who taught you that?" She kept patting her bouffant, as if the curls might actually move without a hurricane-force wind gusting through the hallway. "That's just plain rude."

"No it's not. Only losers get to a party on time. Really. The cool people wander in at least a half hour late looking like they decided at the last minute to fit it into their schedule."

"Ridiculous. I won't hear of it. And in case you've forgotten, I'm the driver."

She had me there.

"So I suggest you be ready to leave with this loser at five forty-five." She turned toward me. "Besides," she added. "Don't think I'm planning to spend the entire evening watching people riding some silly carousel. This whole thing is completely overblown. I'm only going to satisfy Joe, as you well know, and the sooner I get there, the sooner I can leave."

"Of course," I said. I guess that was why she got a "wash and set" for the second time this week and was now headed off to her room to primp for an hour before we left.

"By the way," she said, turning on the stairs. "I saw the Advance article. They did a decent job. Rather a nice shot of you, I thought."

"Thanks," I stammered, staring open-mouthed as she walked up the steps. Was she trying to keep me off balance, bossing me around one minute, complimenting me the next? If so, it seemed to be working.

As soon as she disappeared I grabbed the paper and read the article closely. It was mostly about the history of the carousel and how it was restored. They quoted someone from the Carousel Society and mentioned that they were sponsoring an invitation-only unveiling tonight. There was no photo of Jesse, and his name was not listed, but Stella and Joe were right; it was a great story. After I read it, I was more excited about the opening than ever.

My second disagreement with Stella came less than a half hour later when we collided in the hallway on our way to the shower in the house's single bathroom. I lost again, reminded firmly that it was her house. I stomped back to my room to wait her out. The last thing I needed was more time to sit and think. I already knew what I was wearing— my royal blue mini (his favorite color) with a black tank top, casual, comfortable, but nothing too shocking. I just wanted to get ready and go.

When I bounced down the stairs at five forty-four I landed in my third fight with my aunt. This one was about "appropriate jewelry," and I won by reminding her that we'd be late if I took the time to change even one single earring. It took me less than a minute to derail her, and I was sure within another week I'd have this woman wrapped around my finger. If we didn't kill each other first.

On the way to the rides, it dawned on me that Stella might be picking fights because she was nervous. I hated to admit this, even to myself, but the reason I suspected it? I do the same thing.

"When's the last time you went to a party?" I asked.

"Sunday, when your father and brother came."

"No, I mean a real party. Like this one."

She pursed her lips, thinking. "Mike's wedding?"

Four years ago. I considered that and decided yes, weddings definitely counted as parties. "This will be more fun than a wedding," I said. "Weddings are boring. Church, hors d'oeuvres, first dance, dinner, more dancing, cake, bouquet, garter, and good night. Duller than dull."

"I couldn't agree more."

Uh-oh, this was getting scary. Stella agreeing with me again.

"But I don't believe this party will be any more fun than your average wedding," she added.

"Sure it will," I said. It will be for me, anyway. "Try and relax, Aunt Stel. I know you're probably nervous and all, but—"

"Nervous?" She gave a short laugh. "Why would I be nervous?"

Because you don't get out much? Because you haven't been to this amusement park in a hundred years? "I don't know," I said. "I just thought you might be, that's all."

"Perhaps you're the one who's nervous."

"No," I said quickly. Actually, my heart thudded louder and louder as the blocks between us and the rides melted away, but I wasn't saying a word to her. "Why should I be?"

"No reason," she said.

We were both full of it and we both knew it. We were on edge for very different reasons and we were both too stubborn to admit it. People teased me about being just like Stella. I didn't want it to be true. But I was beginning to wonder.

She swung the car into the parking lot and shut the engine off.

"You look very nice, by the way," I said. "That's a pretty dress."

She sat up a little straighter in her seat and smoothed the floral-print skirt. "Thank you. I'm hoping there's a breeze off the ocean so I don't pass out from the heat."

"Me too," I agreed, though the cause of our overheating would be completely different.

The walk from the parking lot was agonizingly slow, with Stella carefully picking her way along the uneven gravel surface. I forced myself to stay at her side. I knew Joe expected me to deliver her safely.

"The carousel's back there," I pointed as we finally passed through the front gate.

"I know where the carousel is. I spent a lot of time here in my younger days, you know. Of course the whole place has changed considerably." She looked around with a frown. "Just like the rest of this island. So many changes and none for the better."

"Come on, Aunt Stel, lighten up. Wait until you see the carousel. It's going to blow you away."

As we walked past the snack bar, I spotted Khamille.

"Joe split the night shift," she said. "Bev goes early, I go late. So we both get to go to the party."

Stella had stopped but was staring off at the carousel. Or maybe she was just avoiding eye contact with Khamille, but she seemed to be listening to the big-band music that blared from the party.

"Evening, Miss Stella," Khamille said. "Guess they're playing your song, huh?"

Stella turned sharply toward Khamille. "I do not have a song."

"You oughta think about getting one. Music keeps a heart light." Khamille winked and smiled a disarming smile at Stella. "See you later, Lilli. Have fun."

The plywood barrier was gone, replaced with velvet ropes and metal stanchions provided by the party rental place, so the carousel was exposed but still separated from the general public. A printed sign on a gold stand proclaimed, "Invited Guests Only! Carousel Open to the Public July 4th. See you then!" A wide ribbon was wrapped around the carousel, ending in a giant bow fastened to one of the chariots on the outer edge of the machine. On one side of the carousel Joe had set up two rows of chairs in a big semi-circle, and on the other side the caterer had set out the food and drinks, with a few tables and chairs so folks could sit to eat. There was room between the chairs and the actual carousel for people to stand and mingle. So far, the few dozen party-goers who had gathered were milling around, sipping from red plastic cups as they circled the carousel admiring the brightly colored animals.

We stopped at the stanchions to register with the guy who was checking a list of names, and we were barely in before Joe swept down on us.

"Here's my two favorite girls," he said, his arms spread wide.

He wrapped Stella in a bear hug and smacked her cheek with a noisy kiss. I hung back, hoping he'd skip that with me. He was dressed in a flashy ringmaster suit: a short, tight-fitting red jacket with tails, stretch riding pants, and black boots. If I was his fashion consultant, I would not have recommended Spandex in good conscience but the overall effect was impressive.

"Where on earth did you get that ridiculous get-up?" Stella asked, standing back for a better look.

Joe spun like a runway model, the jacket tails flying as he turned. "You like? The carousel people got it at some rental place in Brooklyn. Sharp, huh?"

"Way sharp," I agreed. Stella did not comment.

He fanned himself. "And hot as hell."

"So, are the carousel people here yet?" I asked.

"Some are. The official ribbon cutting's at seven. Come on," he took Stella's arm. "Let me introduce you around."

I sighed with relief as he shuttled Stella away, then scanned the crowd. No Jesse yet. Of course he would never arrive on time. Bev waved from one of the tables and I went over to sit with her.

"Quite a crowd," I said, watching people stream into the party.

"I don't know half of them," Bev said. She was trying to cut a sausage with a plastic knife. The sausage was winning.

"Me neither." But I'd know the one I wanted when I saw him. Outside the ropes curious people stopped to stare. Some moved on when they realized it was a private affair, but others craned their necks, oohing and ahhing at the new carousel. I felt important, sitting inside where those outsiders wished they could be.

"The food isn't bad," Bev said. "You should go get some."

I had no appetite, but that didn't stop Bev from jabbering about the sausage and peppers and the baked ziti and how it was way better than anything we served at the snack bar. I was half-listening when I spotted someone I hadn't expected to see. "Be right back," I said, then darted through the crowd and slipped outside the barricades again.

"Florio!" I called.

He turned toward my voice. When he saw me, he looked away, then took off his cap and fumbled with it, staring at the ground.

"Are you coming to the party?" I asked when I caught up to him.

"Me? No. I read about it in the paper. Saw your picture. Very nice, by the way. Anyway, I just thought—" He crumpled his cap into a ball. "Oh hell, I don't know what I thought."

This guy was a mystery, all right. He seemed friendly enough, but there had to be a reason he was here again, hanging around the rides like a lone alley cat at a dumpster. "If you want to get a better look, I'll get you in."

"No, I couldn't ask you to—"

I'd already made up my mind. "Come on, I want you to meet Joe." I tugged his arm before he could think too much. "One more guest won't hurt."

Florio smoothed his thinning hair and slapped his cap onto his head as we made our way to the barricade. "Lilli Whitaker," I told the guard. "And this is a friend of Joe's, Florio—" I faltered, forgetting his weird Italian name.

"Giovanucci," Florio jumped in.

The man scanned his list, frowning. "How do you spell that?"

"G-i-o-v," Florio began to spell slowly.

The man ran his finger halfway down the page, shaking his head. He eyed the couple waiting to get in behind us and shook his head again.

"Friends of Joe," I repeated, smiling. "I work here?" The gatekeeper paused only a second more before waving us through.

"See?" I said to Florio. "Cake. Now let's find Joe."

Florio stared open-mouthed at the carousel.

"Pretty stupendous, isn't it?" I asked.

He closed his eyes then, and took a big deep breath. I began to wonder if maybe this guy did have some kind of weird fetish for carousel ponies. Or maybe he was just as blown away as I was by all those dazzling colors.

"I want to get a closer look," he said. "Do you mind?"

"Be my guest." Florio waded into the crowd and I took an empty chair at the end of a table to resume my casual, but persistent, vigil. A few other guests were chowing down at the other end of the table, and I smiled and nodded just to be polite. I was making a mighty effort to stay calm and reasonable when a thought occurred to me that I hadn't considered: what if Jesse decided not to come?

Sure, Joe said all the carousel people were invited, but Jesse said he'd be back for the opening. What if he meant tomorrow's opening, on the Fourth of July? That actually made sense. Jesse probably didn't even like parties. He was an artist, after all. Maybe his artist's soul craved solitude. Maybe all this music and noise was too crass, too common for him. This wasn't his scene. I grew more and more certain he'd steer clear of the whole thing.

Having convinced myself, I settled back in my chair, feeling more relaxed. It was disappointing, but it only meant I'd have to wait until tomorrow to connect with him again. Tomorrow wasn't that far off. Tomorrow, when I saw Jesse again, we could—

My thoughts skidded to a halt when I spied him at the barricade, flashing his blinding smile at the guard checking the list of names. Jesse's hair was drawn back as usual and he wore a loose-fitting denim shirt, sleeves rolled up to the elbow, with tight jeans whitened from long wear. My heart rapped against my ribs and the sound of my own blood rushing in my ears nearly drowned out the raucous music and conversation around me. I gripped the chair seat to prevent myself from jumping up and down to catch his attention, or worse still, just flinging myself at him. Be cool, I commanded myself. Do not race over. Wait until he comes to you.

That sort of worked, but not entirely. I didn't run over but I did stand up and place myself between the front gate and the carousel. I reached up to spike my hair, then struck the closest thing I could muster to a relaxed pose. My gaze turned toward the carousel but I did not allow those velvet entrance ropes to escape my peripheral vision. I was all set to turn, casually, to greet Jesse as soon as he crossed into the party zone.

But then my peripheral vision caught sight of a bright red blob hovering next to Jesse. A slight head turn revealed that the blob was actually a sleeveless red mini-dress clinging to the body of a girl about his age. I watched as the two of them shared a laugh with the list-checker before they crossed– together—to this side of the velvet ropes.

There was no way to hide, now that I had deliberately placed myself in plain, impossible-to-miss sight. I silently prayed for a giant sinkhole to swallow me, but instead God chose this moment to answer my earlier prayer: please let Jesse notice me.

"Lilli?"

I turned my flushed face toward them. The girl stood close – way too close – to Jesse. She wore matching red heels and her mass of black curls skimmed her bare shoulders.

"Jesse." I tried to breathe before I spoke, but my voice still sounded like sneakers on a wet gym floor. "You made it!"

"Wouldn't miss it." He made a sweeping gesture toward the carousel. "This puts the grand in grand opening, doesn't it?"

"It's amazing," the girl said. She gave Jesse a little squeeze, her face lit with a total adoration that felt sickeningly familiar.

"Oh, sorry," Jesse said. "I'm so rude. Lilli, this is Christine. Chris, this is Lilli. One of the kids who works in the park."

Her teeth bared into a smile and she waggled her red fingernails and said, "Hiya."

"You'll be at the carousel, starting tomorrow. Am I right?" he asked.

He was right. Of course, he was right. But my brain had seized when he uttered the word *kid*. It felt like I had been slapped. I nodded to answer his question, but I'm sure my attempt at a smile looked like something that belonged on a Halloween fright mask.

"Ribbon cutting's at seven," he said with a wink. "Can't wait for that first ride. Come on, Chris. I'll show you my favorite horse."

Chris giggled and did a scrunchy thing that pulled her bare shoulders toward her ears. Then she slid those red-tipped fingers into Jesse's hand and they flounced off toward the carousel.

My eyes squeezed shut. I couldn't bear to watch. A few minutes ago, I'd been dying to see Jesse. Now, all I wanted to do was die.

15 – Swoon

I counted to ten slowly.

Twice.

It did not help.

All around me Joe's guests continued eating and drinking, laughing and shouting over each other as the noise level gradually increased. The party was really getting underway, but I felt like a balloon had just exploded in my face.

This was not how things were supposed to go. But isn't it how things always went?

In an instant, my mood had swung from joy to despair and was now flipping toward furious. I was mad at Christine just for being here. Mad at Jesse for calling me a damned kid. Mad at Khamille for getting my hopes up, convincing me that Jesse really did like me. But mostly? I was mad at myself. How could I have been so dumb? Believing that this time would be different, that a really good guy could be mine. When did things ever go my way? When did anything I ever wanted actually land in my lap?

Never. That's when.

Ty strolled over, his plate heaped with food. "Mind if I sit here?"

I pinched my lips together and shrugged.

"Nice turnout," he said.

I shrugged again. He sat, then lifted his head to follow my gaze, which, sadly, was still one hundred percent trained on Jesse and Chris. He had one arm draped around her waist while the other one gestured at those gorgeous painted ponies. Her black curls bounced as she nodded agreement with whatever he was explaining.

"Uh-oh," Ty said.

"Who cares," I snapped.

Ty looked from me to them and back again. "Seriously? That right there? That is not good news for you."

"So he brought a friend. So what? No big deal."

"If you say so." He turned his attention to his plate of food. He took a big forkful of baked ziti, tilted his head back and forth judging its taste as he chewed and swallowed. "This is pretty good. You should try it."

"I'm not hungry."

"Maybe not for food," he said.

I seethed and gave him what I hoped was a menacing look. He surprised me by refusing to take the bait. He rested his fork on the edge of his paper plate and looked me right in the eye.

"I'm not trying to be mean," he said. "Just trying to make light, you know?"

"Well I'm definitely not in the mood for jokes."

"I get it. I do. I been there. I know. It hurts."

Empathy was the last thing I expected from Tyson. But as soon as he spoke I felt better. Not great, but better. Like somebody here was on my side. I sank into the chair and felt my anger valve release a little pressure.

"Thanks. I appreciate that."

He nodded and picked up his fork, scanning the crowd as he ate. Everyone was busy admiring the carousel and folks who seemed to know Jesse were patting him on the back, congratulating him. Christine remained glued to his side as they circled the machine, apparently intent on seeing all the highlights. Every cell in my body longed to be the one beside him, learning more about the restoration, praising his color choices and the meticulous detail of his work. I was desperate for a chance to make him forget that little red dress. To think of me as more than a kid who worked here. I just needed to figure out how to make that happen.

I had almost convinced myself to get up and at least give it a try when Ty spoke again. "Who invited the pervert to the party?"

He indicated Florio, who was carefully inspecting one of the chariots on the carousel. He looked a bit lost.

"I did." I waved to catch his attention. He worked his way through the crowd toward where Ty and I were sitting, near the food. "Did you find Joe?" I asked Florio.

Ty snickered before Florio could reply. "Hard to miss him, in that lion-tamer get-up."

I shot him a look. "Joe's just having fun. It's a party. Lighten up." I turned toward Florio. "Well?"

"He looks really busy. Getting ready for the ribbon cutting."

It was six forty-five, just fifteen minutes from the big moment. I wondered vaguely where Joe had left Stella. It was weird she wasn't circling the buffet. Was she missing me? I knew I should go find her and sit with her, maybe offer to get her some food. Although that was the last place I wanted to be.

"Why you looking for Joe?" Ty asked.

Florio looked uneasy, though I had no idea why he should.

"I have something to show him," Florio replied.

Ty gave him a hard look. I elbowed him to make him stop. "I'll be sure to introduce you to Joe after the ceremony, if that's okay."

"Fine." Florio stared at the carousel. He seemed mesmerized. "They did a terrific job on that thing."

"They sure did," I agreed. Jesse and Chris had wandered back to this side of the carousel. Suddenly my mind flashed on an idea so great, so obvious, I couldn't believe I hadn't thought of it sooner. "Florio, you've got the ring on you, right?"

He nodded. "Of course. To show Joe, like you said."

"Right. Listen, I have an idea. Come with me, okay? I want you to show it to another expert."

I flashed a quick smile at Ty, pretty sure he knew what I had in mind. He rolled his eyes but stayed put as I led Florio through the crowd, slowing down when we got within a few feet of Jesse. I pointed toward a carousel horse.

"I just love the saddle on this blue one, don't you?" I said, a little louder than necessary. "The color is almost blinding." I kept my head turned toward the carousel, continuing my high-volume commentary as I sidled toward Jesse, acting as if I wasn't watching where I was headed. "And this one here is just —" I faked a stumble and bumped right into Christine, who squeaked like a surprised mouse.

"Oh, I'm so sorry!" I reached out to steady her. "I was so entranced with the carousel I didn't even see—" I looked up, wading into the deep blue pools of Jesse's eyes. I flashed my best smile.

Jesse smiled back. "Hello again."

We stood eye to eye, an equal match, with Christine between us. It was all I could do to keep from pushing her aside and dragging Jesse off somewhere. Florio hung back. He had already been a nervous wreck, and now his face telegraphed that he wasn't sure what the heck was happening.

"The carousel looks totally awesome," I said. Christine smiled at me then looked up at Jesse. I hoped she was wondering the same thing about me that I wondered about her. I reached toward Florio. "Jesse, Chris-- this is my friend Florio. Florio, Jesse helped restore the carousel. He knows a lot about them. I bet you could ask him about your ring."

"Ring?" Jesse asked, eyes glinting.

Florio dug into his pocket and produced the brass ring. "I suspect it's from this carousel."

"Oh, wow," Christine said. "Look at that, Jess."

Florio held the ring toward Jesse, willing to show it to him but obviously not about to hand it over. Jesse leaned down to get a better look.

"Where did you get this? A collector?" Jesse asked.

"I—" Florio began, but then paused and cleared his throat. "It belonged to my mother, actually. She gave it to me just before she passed. Last month."

"Oh, sorry," Jesse said, his eyes softening.

"Thanks. She was very ill, so it was a blessing when she went." He was saying all the right words but I could see how the memory made it hard for him to speak. I knew that feeling. "Anyway, she had this ring. It was tied to a piece of ribbon, and— well, she told me she thought it came from here but she was never sure. Naturally, I'd like to find out more."

"Geez, Florio, you never told me all that about your mother," I said. "You should have talked to Joe sooner, the reporter would have loved that story."

"Speaking of reporters," Jesse said, "I see they ran your photo in the paper. On my favorite horse, no less. Great shot."

Christine's brow furrowed, a movement I enjoyed immensely.

"Thanks." I felt my confidence struggling to regain its footing. "Joe might be able to get copies of the photos they didn't use. That one of both of us. Remember?"

Jesse nodded. Christine pouted. "That'd be cool," he said.

"Anyway, Florio, how come you didn't talk to the reporter the other day?"

"Ah, reporters," Florio said, waving his hand in dismissal. "I don't want the whole world to know about this. It's personal, you know? Just something I'm trying to piece together." He held the ring out to Jesse again. "So, do you think it's the genuine article?"

Jesse examined the ring again. It was over an inch in diameter, far too big for anyone's finger. It shone like it had been recently polished. "Does it have any identifying marks?" Jesse asked. Florio shook his head. "Hmm. Well, it looks like the real deal. Joe would know best if it's from this carousel. Or someone else in the Society. You should show it to them."

As if on cue, Joe's voice suddenly cut through the crowd. "May I have your attention, ladies and gentlemen!" The mic screeched with feedback and everyone winced. I scanned the two rows of chairs behind us and spotted Stella, safely settled in the first row. She was watching Joe and didn't seem to be looking for me. The people who were standing, like us, flowed around the chairs and pressed toward Joe to better hear the announcements. As we all tightened to make room I was grateful to be hemmed in near Jesse rather than Stella.

Joe thanked everyone for coming then introduced the president of the Carousel Society, who read a short history of the carousel and bragged about how hard they'd worked to fundraise and restore the machine. If Florio did turn out to have some kind of kinky carousel thing he was at the right party, that was for sure. The president seemed even more excited about the restoration than I was about rubbing shoulders with Jesse, and believe me, sparks shot through me every time that happened.

When the president finally finished he passed the mic back to Joe, who brandished a big pair of ceremonial scissors.

"Ladies and gentlemen, here's to many more happy rides on the beautifully restored South Beach Carousel!" Cameras clicked as the scissors snipped and the giant ribbon fell to the ground to cheers and applause. "There'll be free rides all evening, so don't feel pressured to rush on board. There's plenty of time for everyone to ride. And welcome aboard!"

When Joe stepped down from the carousel people scrambled forward, all anxious to be on that first go-round. I glanced at Jesse but he didn't move.

"I want to watch," he told Christine. "Just once."

"Me too," Christine and I said simultaneously. Our eyes locked and we flashed one another big, fake smiles. But the president of the Society came over to Christine and offered a hand, inviting her to board, and she laughed and followed him to one of the chariots.

"He's her uncle," Jesse explained.

Fine with me that she was out of the way. I stood between Jesse and Florio watching every seat and horse fill. When the band organ blared, a ripple of spontaneous delight surged through the crowd. Then the big bell sounded and everyone applauded again as the carousel lurched into motion.

The colors and bright lights pulled my gaze in ten directions at once. My arms became gooseflesh as the old machine sped up, carrying its riders round and round in front of us. Some rode the stationary horses on the outer rim and others were moving up and down with slow mechanical precision. Most of the riders were adults, but they waved like excited kids as they passed. We laughed and waved back with silly grins pasted to our faces.

"Was it worth all the work?" I shouted to Jesse.

He nodded vigorously. "Absolutely. It's amazing."

"I don't care what you guys do," I shouted. "I'm on the next ride. I can't wait any longer."

I turned around and saw Stella, still seated in the first row of chairs. The crowd between us had thinned and she was now in my direct line of vision, not four feet behind me. I was close enough now to see how her butt overflowed the seat of her wooden folding chair. Her ear was cocked toward the music. Her eyes were shut, but if she was asleep, I wanted to be in her dream. Her head bobbed slightly to the beat, her body swayed just a little, and her lips curved into a small but undeniable smile. Maybe she did have a song after all, and this was it. It was odd to see her in that kind of trance, looking — dare I say it? Happy. I wasn't about to snap her out of it. If the carousel put Aunt Stella in a good mood, nobody stood to benefit more than I did.

The carousel began to slow, and the sound of its motor grew gradually softer. As the machine glided to a stop, Stella's eyes fluttered open and she shuddered slightly, clearly struggling to come back to reality. She squinted toward me and her mouth turned down slightly, a look I decided meant that she'd spotted me.

Jesse began to walk toward the carousel.

"Let's go," I told Florio, intent on following Jesse. But suddenly, Tyson appeared at my side.

"Lilli!" he shouted.

Jesse stopped and turned slightly toward us, just in time to see Tyson throw his arms around my neck and smooch my cheek. I was too stunned to react, but over Tyson's shoulder I saw Stella's eyes go wide at the sight of her worst nightmare: the Black boy next door romancing her grand-niece.

"Girl, you look fabulous. Is that a new haircut?" Tyson asked loudly, taking both my hands in his.

"What the hell are you doing?" I hissed.

"Making our boy jealous," he whispered back. "And look, it's working. Just play along."

Florio stepped away from us, the way he always did when he smelled the first whiff of trouble. He backed toward the row of chairs and then pulled a one-eighty to face away from the carousel and towards the chairs. In the process he also opened Stella's view of me and Tyson, who now had me in a full-on bear hug, really hamming it up.

Stella blinked a few times and shook her head the way they do in cartoons when they've been conked by an anvil. Suddenly she slumped in her chair, her head lolling on her neck and her mouth falling open.

The man sitting next to her leaped up and tried to keep her from sliding to the ground. It was not a one-man job.

"Somebody help," the man said. Stella continued to slide. Florio rushed ahead then and together they lowered her to the ground as gently and discreetly as humanly possible. Her face was as pale as the concrete she was now sprawled on. The man made a vain attempt to arrange her skirt so it covered the essentials, but I could see the tops of her rolled-down stockings exposed just above her knee.

She didn't move. She looked dead. And if Stella was dead, I had killed her.

My hands flew to my face. "Joe," I screamed. "Where's Joe?" People turned to look at me. Florio backed away. In a flash, Joe appeared. He sized up the situation and knelt at Stella's side.

"Somebody bring some water. And call 911. Hurry!"

A few people scurried off, but I felt nailed to the ground. Every evil thought I'd ever had about my great aunt Stella converged in one big fireball until my head threatened to incinerate with guilt. As many times as I'd wished her out of my life or tried to do something to shock her, I never actually wished her dead. But this time, she saw me doing something she found so unsavory it might just have done her in.

Never mind that she was being ridiculous again. I could argue that point later, Right now I just wanted her to be okay.

"Please," I whispered. It was half prayer and half desperate plea to Stella herself, even though I knew she couldn't hear me. Please be okay. Please wake up.

An ambulance siren whined in the distance. The carousel music kept playing, its tinny sound a surreal soundtrack to the scene unfolding before me. I turned on the gathering crowd. Jesse and Christine stood side by side, their faces filled with concern. Bev and Ty stood beside them. It looked as if Ty was trying to explain to Bev what had happened. I wasn't sure he actually understood, but he soon would. In two big strides I swooped down on Ty, determined to let him know what I thought of him right now.

"Look what you did," I screamed.

"Me? I didn't do anything. She just keeled over. Like, bam."

"Yeah, right," I said. "You don't think the sight of us hugging had anything to do with it?"

Tyson's face registered complete shock at the notion. "Say what?"

Bev placed a hand on my arm. "Calm down, Lilli. Tyson didn't—"

I shook her off and shot dagger eyes at Tyson.

"I was just—" he began.

I turned away from him. I hid my face in my hands. "This can't be real. Tell me I'm dreaming."

Bev draped an arm around my shoulder. "Take it easy. The EMTs are coming. They'll know what to do."

I appreciated Bev's attempts at comfort but I was not convinced. My aunt Helen had died in an instant just a few weeks ago. If anything happened to Stella, no matter the circumstance, there'd be hell to pay with my father. Only a few people actually witnessed what had happened. Besides Jesse and Tyson, I knew there had been at least one other person who saw it all. I scanned the crowd and wasn't surprised to find that my new friend Florio was nowhere to be found.

Stuart: The Goodbye

Just before dawn on May 7, 1943, Stella gave birth to a son. She bore her labor with dignity and determination, supported by the convent's ancient doctor.

"A bonny boy," the old doctor declared. He held up the babe for her inspection, offered him to her arms. But not for one instant did her look soften or stray in his direction. She faced the wall, eyes closed, holding firm to her plan. She wanted nothing whatever to do with this child.

The doctor had seen such behavior before and did nothing to discourage it. He wrapped the baby snugly and carried him to the door where Helen waited with a few of the nuns. Their sure hands held him close, eager to ease his first harsh moments in this world. Helen stole a look at the small pink face, the searching eyes, and with some difficulty managed to tear herself away. Her place at this moment was with Stella.

At the bedside, Helen clutched her sister's hand. They shared silent tears, but exchanged no words. Soon enough Stella fell into a deep, exhausted sleep.

Helen closed the door quietly and crept down the hallway to the nursery. The doctor was gone. One of the nuns sat beside a crib where the baby now slept as peacefully as his mother.

"May God bless him," the nun said. "Precious angel that he is. Mother says they've found a home for him already."

Helen hid her shock as well as she could. She knew, of course, that the baby was to be adopted. But the reality stung. "So soon?" she asked.

"They'll be here this evening," the nun replied. "They're so excited. A good Catholic family, Mother says, from Brooklyn." She gazed at the child, who slept serenely. "You'll have a good home, little one."

Helen leaned over the crib, listening to the child's soft, even breath. His face was hidden by the blanket but the sparse fuzz that stuck out had strong hints of the same russet color that had once graced her own father's head. Sheer will kept her hands at her sides, prevented her reaching out to gather the boy up. Stella had the courage to release him. Helen had to be as brave, she knew, but it was not so easy now that this beautiful perfect child lay before her.

"May I hold him when he wakes?" she whispered. "Before he goes?"

"Of course, dear." The nun draped an arm around Helen's shoulder. "We're praying for you, and for your sister. May God's love keep you strong."

Helen stole a few hours of restless sleep, and when she awoke it was mid-afternoon. She splashed her face and smoothed her rumpled dress as best she could. Then she went to her sister.

Stella sat before the window, staring out at the bright afternoon. She had not asked to see the child, a decision Helen feared Stella would come to regret.

"It's a beautiful day," Helen said, hugging her sister. "How are you feeling, dear?"

A noncommittal shrug, indifferent.

"Did the doctor say when you could come home?" Helen asked.

"A few more days. I'm healthy as a horse, he says. A fine specimen. As if that matters."

"Of course it matters," Helen gasped. "It matters to all of us. And to you."

Another shrug. Helen's fists knotted and she drew a breath. Perhaps it was just too soon, she thought. With patience, time, and love, surely her sister would be more like herself again.

They chatted about nothing important, and in the early evening shared a simple meal. When they were done, one of the sisters cleared away the dishes. Another appeared at the door and said it was time to get the baby ready.

Stella yawned. "I can't keep my eyes open one more minute."

"I'll get you settled," said the nun. She nodded toward the door and encouraged Helen. "You go on, now."

Helen hated to leave Stella but she didn't want that boy to slip away without at least one familial hug. "Good night then, love." She kissed Stella on the cheek. "I'll be on my way early in the morning. I'll prepare Da for your homecoming. Call me the day before."

Helen fairly raced down the hall to the nursery. She joined the two nuns currently doting on the babe.

"Sure, he's God's little lamb," said the younger one, rocking him with a soothing side-to-side motion. "Aren't you? Hmmmm? God's tiny lamb."

"May I?" Helen asked. She gasped softly as the child was pressed into her arms. How warm he felt. How fragile. He mewed and gurgled, pursing his lips. Slowly, his eyes struggled open.

"Hello bright eyes," Helen cooed. As she spoke the boy turned his gaze toward her voice. Helen's heart raced as his small eyes probed hers—eyes of a familiar, unmistakable pale blue color. "Oh! He's looking right at me."

The older nun clicked her tongue. "I'm afraid not, dear. He's too young to see just yet."

Helen didn't want to argue but she was sure that wasn't true. She had seen at once that these eyes, so honest and innocent, were the very same color as the eyes of Stuart McGee. Helen felt them peering deeply into hers with a wisdom and clarity she would never forget. She stared back, drinking his love, filling her soul with his sweet innocence.

At the old nun's suggestion, Helen dressed her newborn nephew from diaper to cap, slowly, deliberately, taking special care with each item, burning him into her memory.

She was no sooner done when there came a soft knock at the door.

"It's time," Mother Superior announced.

The young nun smiled serenely, lifted the tiny bundle from Helen's arms, and headed for the door.

"Wait!"

Mother Superior frowned in the doorway. "It's time, dear." Her voice gentle but firm. "Nothing to be gained by waiting."

"No," Helen agreed. "But Mother. I have something for him. For luck."

"He shall have God's love. He'll need no more than that."

"Please. It's important. His father—"

"May he rest in peace," said the nuns, simultaneously crossing themselves.

Their eyes grew moist as Helen explained the significance of the gift she planned to bestow.

"What can it hurt, Mother?" the young nun urged.

Mother agreed and Helen wept freely as she lifted the ribbon over his downy fluff of hair and pressed the token under his bunting, close to his heart. Then she kissed the soft spot on his head and turned away forever.

On Stella's first evening home, Helen made a special dinner, as much to distract their father as to welcome her sister. Paddy Whitaker sat down to supper with no outward acknowledgment of his daughter's return. Helen chattered through the meal, praying the subject would not stray to Chicago or the work Stella had supposedly been doing for these last months. Harry had been warned to keep his curiosity in check, and the rest of them ate in silence as Helen prattled.

When Paddy finally wiped his mouth and stood he stared at Stella for a long minute.

"You've been eating well," he proclaimed.

"I have," she replied, not flinching under his gaze. "Chicago has some fine food."

"So I see. You look like a cow."

"Da!" Helen cried, her lip quavering at his warning look.

Harry suppressed a giggle, earning a kick in the ankle from Helen.

Stella lifted her chin. "A cow is a proud beast. Hardworking. Loyal."

Paddy snickered. He picked up his beer and headed for his easy chair. Life as they knew it resumed.

A few days after, something caught Helen's eye as she was putting out the trash. She dug down and discovered Stella's green satin box. Snapshots, letters, mementos, all destined for the dump.

"This is wrong," Helen said to the box. "All wrong."

She gathered the lot and hid it in the shoebox that already held her own diaries and poems. One day, she was sure, her sister would long for these things, would wish they had been saved. And Helen would have them.

The next year Stella's brother Stan married and soon produced a son. Oh, the fuss that was made for that scrawny child! Even Paddy Whitaker proclaimed him a fine little lad. Helen, who still burned with the memory of her lost nephew, quickly warmed to Baby Stan. The boy was somewhat sullen but Helen embraced him, cuddled him, and set out joyfully to spoil him rotten.

Stella did just the opposite. She refused to hold him, citing his smelly diapers and his tendency to spit up. As he grew into a curious toddler, she set impossible standards, doing her best to reinforce the fearful look that crept into his eyes as she approached. Her heart was closed for business. Nothing, no one, was worth the risk of opening it again to show love or even affection.

Stella kept very busy at her job. After her time at the convent she suggested to personnel that a fresh perspective was due. Jobs were plentiful, thank God, and she was assigned to a new department, away from the probing eyes of her former co-workers. More importantly, she was placed well beyond the reach of Warton Hicks.

That scoundrel no longer had power over her but she never forgot what he'd done. From a safe distance she kept an eye on him, quietly monitoring, waiting for him to stumble. He may have been sneaky but he wasn't actually very smart. It took three patient years but eventually Stella proved he was involved in a double-deal to line his own pockets. She crafted an anonymous letter to the board of directors. Though she would have loved to tell them a few other details about that horrid little man, what she did say had him investigated and sent packing.

Helen and Stella lived together from then on, their lives unfolding along parallel lines. Helen grew content with a small circle of friends and devotion to family, while Stella worked hard and hid behind those prickly quills she'd donned. Helen never questioned, never pushed; she respected her sister's decision. And she held their secret close, right until the end.

That is, until her end.

With Helen gone, Stella wanted nothing more than to be left alone for the rest of her days. But she is not alone. She has family close by, family with a roving, curious eye on her.

As for me? My part in the matter is, at long last, nearly done.

16 – Lectures

Just as the ambulance squealed into the parking lot, Stella came to with a vengeance. She shot an evil eye at the curious crowd, sending the less-hardy fleeing to safer ground. She boosted herself to one elbow and attempted to stand.

"Stay put," Joe warned. "The ambulance is coming. They need to check you out."

"Nonsense," she snapped. "I will not lie here on the ground. I'm perfectly fine." She glanced down then and realized her dress was hiked up. She immediately began a valiant, if vain, struggle to tug it back below her knees. Her arms were too weak to support her while she lifted her butt and her knees remained exposed. Joe removed his red ringmaster jacket and draped it over her.

"You there." Stella aimed a finger at Jesse, of all people. "Don't just stand there, help me up."

Jesse eyed Joe for instructions. None were forthcoming.

"Come on, young man," Stella barked. Joe helped Jesse hoist Stella into her chair. She looked shaken and pale, and she was breathing like a bull that just charged a matador. But at least she was upright. I surprised myself by rushing forward to throw both arms around her.

"You scared me to death," I whispered, and I meant it.

"For heaven's sake." She shook me loose and thrust the red jacket at Joe. "Give me some air."

I stepped back, a bit bruised by her brush off but relieved that she seemed to be her old self. She eyed the onlookers again, this time more intently, and I followed her gaze with mine. I expected her to be fixed on Tyson but she seemed to rove right past him. I wasn't sure what or who she was expecting. Maybe she just wanted everyone to look away now, because clearly she was fine. Just fine.

Jesse backed away from her and brushed my shoulder with his arm. A half hour ago the same movement would have sent me into orbit but Stella's faint had dropped me solidly back to Earth.

"Is that your grandma?" Jesse asked.

I shook my head. "Great aunt. And believe it or not she really is acting perfectly normal."

Normal or not, the paramedics insisted on taking her to the hospital.

"With someone her age we can't be too careful," they said, earning a wicked sneer from Stella. "She may have a concussion. Sometimes it's actually a stroke." They paid no attention to her protests. With Joe's encouragement they loaded her onto a gurney and wheeled her off.

Joe and I followed them to the ambulance, along with a small entourage of gawkers and friends. I kept an eye out for Florio but was forced to conclude that he wasn't the type to stick around in a crisis. I wondered once again if maybe he really did have something to hide.

I figured I'd ride to the hospital with Stella, but when I started to climb into the ambulance the paramedic held up his hand.

"Whoa, there. Nobody rides the bus but the patient."

"Well, I'm the only relative handy at the moment and I can't drive. So what do you suggest I do?"

The paramedic eyed the crowd. "There must be someone here who could take you to the hospital."

Joe wrung his hands. "I suppose I could go if I have to." He glanced nervously toward the carousel, which had started up again. "If there's no one else who can do it."

Jesse stepped forward. "I'll take her."

A half-dozen new emotions joined the throng already running relay races through me. "You will?"

He shrugged. "No biggie. Joe can't leave in the middle of the party. I can."

"What about Christine?" I blurted.

He smiled. "Chris knows plenty of people here. She'll be fine."

Before I had a chance to reply, the driver was giving Jesse directions and firing up the ambulance. I stuck my head in the back and told Stella I'd see her there. Thank God the paramedic slammed the ambulance door before she could issue any further orders.

Joe patted Jesse on the back and thanked him.

"No problem," Jesse said. "I'll be back in a flash."

Not if I can help it. I followed him to his light blue VW Beetle and hopped in beside him.

"Don't worry," he said. "She'll be okay." And even though my mind understood that he had no way of knowing whether that was true or not, every logical, sensible thought in my mind flitted away when Jesse's hand reached across the plaid fabric seat to give my arm a reassuring squeeze.

As we peeled out of the parking lot behind the screaming siren he cranked his window open and invited me to open mine.

"Chris said it smells like a turpentine factory in here," he said. "I don't notice it anymore."

"I don't notice it either," I said, which was kind of a fib. What I meant was, I didn't mind it. It was Jesse's car and Jesse's smell and I knew that even if that smell killed me on our way to the hospital, I'd die happy.

That night I was watching some lame show on TV trying to settle down enough to sleep when Stella's doorbell rang. I pushed aside the curtain on the front window to see Khamille and Ty. She waved at me, and I could swear I saw him drop her hand as soon as he realized I was watching. These two might be fooling someone, but they weren't fooling me.

They were the last two people I expected, and I swear I was never happier to see anyone. I tore open the door. "What are you guys doing here?"

"You drive off with Carousel Man and miss half the party and Khamille is just supposed to wait till tomorrow to find out what happened? No way. Uh-uh."

I closed the front door behind them and flopped onto the couch. "Make yourselves at home."

Ty stepped in and looked cautiously around. "Where is she?"

"They're keeping her overnight. Just for observation, they said. Her blood pressure was sky high, but she's going to be okay."

"That's good," Ty said. "I guess."

Khamille landed a light kick on his ankle, and he yelped.

"Show some respect," she said.

"Soon as she shows me some respect." He rubbed his ankle then sat cross-legged on the floor near the chair Khamille chose. "You can't pretend she'd be happy knowing we were both here right now."

"Miss Stella's not as bad as she seems," Khamille said.

"No," Ty snickered. "She's actually worse."

"Cut it out, please. Both of you. It's been a long night."

"Tell all," Khamille coaxed, tearing her attention from Ty to focus on me.

"I wish there was more to tell." I sighed. "Jesse was really sweet but he just dropped me at the emergency room and left." I closed my eyes, summoning the smell of his car, the touch of his hand on my arm.

"Look on your face tells me you're leaving out a few details, honey," Khamille teased.

I just smiled. "Anyhow, Stella was difficult. She kept saying she was fine and wanted to go home. But they wouldn't let her. I think they gave her something for her nerves because pretty soon she settled down and dozed."

"You should get some of those nerve meds," Ty said. "You could settle her down whenever you needed to."

Khamille kicked him again, but I noticed she was smiling this time. "I saw Jesse come back to the party. How come you didn't?"

"By the time they were done with everything I wasn't in the mood."

"Not in the mood? To spend time with those dreamy blue eyes?" Khamille scrunched her nose. "You sure they didn't slip you something at that hospital?"

"I'm sure. Jesse was fine— better than fine," I added, recalling his reassuring wave as the car door closed behind me. "I'll see him again. But for tonight, I'm pretty sure his mind was headed back to that little red dress."

"Little red dress?" Khamille asked.

I gave her a quick rundown of my evening before the ribbon cutting, how Jesse had arrived with Christine, how I'd figured out that he might be interested in seeing Florio's brass ring. "And he was interested. It was a great idea. So there we were, me and Jess and Florio—"

"And the red dress," Ty chimed in. "Let's not forget her."

I ignored him and continued. "And we were just about to board the carousel for our first ride, and this guy here," I jerked my head toward Ty, "decides that he has his own great idea. He's going to make Jesse jealous."

"Say what?" Khamille asked.

"Exactly. So Tyson Davis comes flying at me and locks me in a giant bear hug. I don't know what Jesse thought, because right then my great aunt Stella takes one look and boom. She practically dies of shock at the sight of it."

"For real?" Khamille turned to Tyson. "What were you thinking?"

"I was just trying to help. Lilli was a mess, she's leaving that part out. Sight of that girl with Jesse got her all riled up. I was trying to make her feel better. How did I know the old lady was even watching? Or that a little old hug would make her flip out?

Khamille looked from one of us to the other, trying to decide how she felt about all this.

"And besides, that weird dude just always weirds me out."

"What weird dude?" Khamille asked.

"That old guy. Florida."

"Florio," I corrected.

"Whatever. The pervert who's obsessed with that carousel. Him and his fake grandson, I don't trust them."

"Let it go, Tyson," I said. "Florio's harmless. A little strange, sure, but he's sweet."

"Well if you ask me he's just as responsible as me for spooking the old lady. Waving around that brass ring like it's got some kind of voodoo magic. Maybe he put a spell on your aunt, ever think of that?"

"No Lilli did not think of that," Khamille declared. "Because it's plain ridiculous."

Ty made a pfft sound and rolled over. "No more ridiculous than her fainting cause I was giving the girl a hug."

I replayed the scene in my mind, trying to recall exactly where Florio had been when everything unfolded. It was odd, how fast he disappeared. But even though Florio was right there when Stella fainted, I was pretty sure Tyson and I were the trigger. It was crazy that such a thing would upset her so much, but I knew it was entirely possible. Though why hadn't she mentioned it at the hospital? Maybe just saving her strength to lecture me later. I wasn't looking forward to arguing with her about the whole thing and how ridiculous she could be.

"Never mind Florio, and forget about Miss Stella. Let's talk Jesse." Khamille narrowed her eyes and assessed me. "You seem okay about that red dress, considering. What gives?"

"He said Christine was just a friend. Her uncle runs the Carousel Society, so of course she was there tonight. Jesse made a big point of saying he'd be around tomorrow. I figured, why race back and compete with her tonight? Tomorrow's another day."

"Good thinking," Khamille agreed.

"Thank you." I didn't add that Christine was only part of the reason I didn't go back to the party. I was exhausted, physically and emotionally. The sight of my aunt Stella stretched out on the ground, whatever the cause, had rattled me more than I could have anticipated. The sound of the sirens, watching them hustle her off on a stretcher. All of that brought back memories of my mother that I wasn't ready to deal with. And even though I had been locked in a power struggle with Stella since the day I arrived, I sure as hell did not intend to kill her. I didn't want her to die. I didn't like her very much, but when it came right down to it, my dad was right: she was family.

That word again. Family. I wondered if I might be starting to understand the subtleties of the word, with all its ups and downs.

"So she's really gonna be okay?" Khamille asked, as if she were reading my mind

"I think so. I hope so. Don't noise this around, especially to her. But I was scared when I saw her go down. I felt like it was my fault she was at the party to begin with. If anything bad happened..." I shook my head.

"She's gonna be fine," Tyson said. He casually moved himself around so his back was against the chair where Khamille sat. He leaned against her. She didn't stop him. Her hand moved to the chair seat and rested on his shoulder. He seemed more relaxed than I'd ever seen him and Khamille's smile seemed easy and genuine. I decided they looked good together.

"How'd you get home?" he asked.

"Stella gave me money for a taxi. I didn't even know you had taxis on Staten Island."

"We call it car service," Khamille said. "But yes. We have entered the modern age."

"Well it was news to me. And even in her dazed state Stella was alert enough to give me detailed instructions about tonight. Rule number one: no visitors."

"Uh-oh, time to go," Ty joked, pretending to begin a sprint toward the door.

Khamille's hand remained firmly on his shoulder preventing him from getting up. "We're not visitors, we're friends," she said. "And I've been here before. Even stayed the night once. Besides, what Miss Stella doesn't know can't hurt her."

Ty's head rolled back a little against her thigh. I was about to make some kind of remark about them suddenly being so tight, but before I could manage the doorbell rang.

"Don't answer that," Ty warned. "No visitors, remember?"

I peeked out the curtain then dropped it and took a step back, surprised by what I saw. "It's your mother, Ty. And she does not look happy."

Ty scrambled up from the floor, looking like he might throw up. I wasn't sure what to do.

"You can't just leave her standing there," Khamille said. "Open the door."

Ty tried backing away but Darlene for sure knew he was here. She took two long strides into the living room and planted her clunky nurse's shoes firmly on Stella's beige sculpted carpet. She wore dark blue scrubs and she folded her arms across her stomach, glaring at Ty as she tapped her fingers on her upper arms.

"Where is Miss Stella?" she demanded.

"She's in the hospital," I stammered.

"Say what?"

"She fainted, at the party down at the rides," Ty explained.

"Is she okay?" Darlene asked me.

"I think so. They kept her overnight."

"Where at?"

"St. Vincent's. She's okay. Really. She should be home in the morning."

"Uh-huh. And this," her arm swept toward Khamille, "this is how you respect her home while she's down?"

"Mama," Ty said through clenched teeth.

Darlene whirled on him. "Don't you mama me. We been all through this, Tyson. How many times you got to learn the same lesson? Once wasn't enough to teach you?"

Ty hung his head.

"We were checking on Lilli," Khamille said. "She went off to the hospital with Miss Stella and she didn't come back to work. We were worried so we came to check on her."

Darlene gave Khamille a look that would freeze freshly roasted chestnuts right on their flaming coals.

"That's the truth, Miss Dar," I said, adopting the respectful address Khamille had used with my aunt. It couldn't hurt. "They haven't been here more than a half hour. They were just checking on me. And all we're doing is sitting here. Just talking."

"Sometimes talking with the wrong person is all it takes. You can get in a heap of trouble. You haven't learned that? You're lucky." Her fingers closed on Ty's arm. "Say goodnight, now. You're going home."

I expected Khamille to speak up in her own defense but she didn't. She and Ty were both looking in every direction but Darlene's. They seemed to harbor some kind of vague guilt but I couldn't understand where it was coming from. "What do you mean, the wrong person? You mean me? Or Khamille?"

"You wouldn't understand," Darlene said.

I was about ready to pop. "I would if somebody explained. Can one of you please set me straight?"

Darlene's manicured fingers kept a tight hold on Ty's arm. He stared at the carpet. Darlene flashed her dark eyes at Khamille, then at me. She took a deep breath and blew it out very slowly. She seemed to be working as hard as I was to keep her temper from exploding.

"You want an explanation? Okay. I can explain. Let me tell you about last summer when these two were a serious item."

I looked at Khamille, unable to hide my surprise. Khamille stuck out her chin, doing an equally poor job of hiding her jumble of emotions.

Darlene went on. "Ty comes home and tells me he met a new girl, down at the rides. Pretty. Hard-working. Smart. Sure, she lives in the projects, but she's a nice girl, he tells me. Nice family, he tells me. Tells me I'll like her." She glanced at Khamille. "I had my doubts, but when I met her I thought maybe Ty was right. Khamille seems sensible, level-headed. So off goes my boy with his brand new friend."

Darlene's face clouded as she continued. "Two weeks later—not two years or two months, mind you. Two short weeks. Housing Authority cop brings Ty home all scuffed up. Been in a fight, the cop says. With some bad-boys down near the projects. Keep an eye on him, the cop says. You're lucky I'm a friend of the girl's family. A brother who cared enough to size up the problem and bring my boy home. He warned me. Warned us both. Stay away from there if you want to be safe."

"But Ma, I haven't been near there since—"

"That had better be true, Tyson Darnell Davis. And don't you bat those eyes at me, I ain't falling for that. I don't want to catch you there or near there or with anyone who lives anywhere close by. As far as I am concerned, that first time was the last time. The end. The end, you hear me? Boy don't have sense enough to know fair from foul, he loses his turn at bat."

"But that's not fair," I insisted. Ty gave a small shake of his head, but it was too late. Darlene turned on me.

"You think you know what's fair? You gonna tell me about it? A girl like you."

Something about the way she said the word *you* spoke volumes. It made me feel very young and very innocent and very, very— well, honestly, very white.

"You think I give a damn how this looks to you? If you worked as hard as I have all my life, maybe you could talk. If you raised your boy alone and worked while you took classes, then studied like hell for your LPN then got a job that still doesn't pay enough. If you had to nag this boy to study and stay in school and make a life for himself then maybe, just maybe, you could tell me what to do. You could say okay, Miss Dar. Don't worry. It's fine to hand this boy over to the first girl who shows up, no matter who she is. He'll be fine. If you were me, you could do that. But you are not me.

So please. Keep your mouth shut and let me keep my boy safe, like I been trying to do since he was a baby."

I opened my mouth to speak but shut it again when I realized I had nothing to say. I wasn't part of this story when it unfolded last year. Even today I was no more than a bystander. But Khamille? She was in the thick of it all the way around. She took a step toward Darlene.

"What happened last year was my fault," she said. "And I'm sorry for it. Real sorry. My brother JT, he— he's been hanging out with the wrong people. Tyson tried to do right by me and he got in the middle of something bad. That cop was right. Ty should stay away from there. From them."

Darlene grunted assent.

Our encounter with Trace came into my mind. His cool, seductive look, the way he said my name soft and slow. The way he called her Khami. The way Khamille stood up to him in order to escape. How he kicked the door as our bus pulled away. Trace was trouble, all right. Real serious trouble.

But I could see now that Khamille hadn't told me the whole truth that night. The friend she mentioned on the ride home, the one who got roughed up last year? She shouldn't have to say it straight out for me to know it was Tyson. Tyson. Now it was crystal clear to me why he refused to have anything to do with Khamille.

"My parents don't like it either," Khamille continued. "JT and my dad argue all the time. And my mom? She worries like—well, like a mom. Like you. The projects isn't all bad people, Miss Dar. It's full of people like my parents. Trying to survive and make a better life for their kids."

"You telling me?" Darlene asked. "I got out. Me and my son."

"I know that, ma'am. I know you worked hard to get where you're at. But you know, these past few years been – something else." She looked down at her white sneakers. Her face, which had been so relaxed and happy before Darlene knocked at the door, had turned ashen. When she looked up again her eyes were moist. "Crack. It's so cheap. Too easy. Like that," she snapped her fingers, "and a good person goes bad."

"Isn't that exactly my point?" Darlene asked.

Khamille's eyes met hers. "I don't blame you for thinking bad about me. Or my family. But Miss Dar? I'm not going to be one of those gone-bad people. No way. Not Khamille."

Darlene fell into Stella's armchair and rested her head in her hands. She pressed her thumbs against her cheeks while her fingertips massaged her temples, the way you do when you think your head is about to explode.

Ty slid around behind the chair and began to gently rub her back and shoulders with a movement that looked natural and well-practiced. No one spoke. I could hear the sound of everyone's breathing, soft and steady. The air buzzed with tension and yet here we were, together, just inhaling and exhaling. Waiting. All of us desperate to make things right. None of us knowing how.

After a few minutes Darlene reached up to still Tyson's hand. She sat up straight in the chair.

"Khamille," she said.

Khamille met her gaze head on. "Yes, ma'am?"

"I respect you. I do. I know you can't help where you come from or who your brother hangs out with. I know you don't mean to hurt anyone. But please. Understand. It's my job to keep my son safe. I cannot — I will not — lose him."

"I understand," Khamille said. "And with the same respect? I feel the same way."

"Hello?" Ty said. "I'm standing right here?"

"We see you," Khamille said.

"Hush up," Darlene added. Maybe Tyson couldn't see it, but I could tell this discussion wasn't really about him anymore. It had gotten way, way bigger.

"I intend to make something of my life," Khamille said. "Like you did, Miss Dar. All I'm asking for's a chance."

Darlene started to speak but pressed her lips tight and shook her head slightly. "I'll pray on it. I'm sorry, Khamille. That's the best I can do. Lilli? You tell your aunt I asked after her. Or maybe—" She shook her head. "Or maybe best not to mention we were here. Imagine the look on her face if she knew the three of us were holding a little meeting in her living room?" She chortled. "Lord. That woman. Just so you know, I do pray she's home and back to normal tomorrow, just like they said."

As soon as the front door clicked shut, Khamille's brave face collapsed. She punched the sofa with a balled fist, crying and spitting out a string of names—JT, Trace and a few other people I'd never heard her mention. I rubbed her back, the way I had seen Ty do with Darlene, and just let her cry it out. I had no idea what else to do.

When her sobs subsided we agreed it was too late for her to take a bus home alone.

"Car service?" I suggested.

She shook her head. "Honestly? No driver will go to the projects at this hour. Miss Dar's not entirely wrong about things. That's what makes it so hard." She stood up. "I gotta call my mom. Phone in the kitchen?"

From what I could hear of the muffled conversation, Khamille's mother interrogated her about where she was, why she was there, and when she would be home. It wasn't lost on me that my own mother would never have worried that much. For most of my life I could have fallen off the face of the earth and nobody would have missed me. Aunt Helen, maybe. But not my mom. I came from a supposedly "good" family in a "good" neighborhood, and here was Khamille, forced to defend her reputation just because she happened to live in the projects. A place too risky for Tyson's mom to let him hang out. And both she and Tyson had mothers who would jump in front of a speeding train to keep their kid safe.

It was all so sad, stupid, and unfair.

What was fair, anyway? Darlene was right. I had no idea anymore. Everything I thought I understood was turning upside-down before my eyes. The world was full of injustices that had never come close to touching me. I could barely grasp what they were, never mind figure out how to fix them. It all felt like a huge, impossible mess. The only positive thing I could think of doing was to be a good friend to Khamille. As good a friend as she was to me. It might not change a thing. But I was determined to do it.

When Khamille and I finally went to bed I was too exhausted to sleep. Every time I closed my eyes my head filled with the sights and sounds of this strange evening: the carousel music, Jesse's voice, his sculpted profile behind the steering wheel, his strong hand on my arm before we parted. I rolled over and smoothed the sheet, trying to relax, but my mental film clip just shifted from Jesse to the memory of Stella slumping in the chair, then stretched out on the ground. My fault, my fault. Mine and Tyson's. I wanted to be mad at him, to blame him for causing trouble, but in my heart I knew he meant no harm. He was trying to be my friend. He thought he was helping. It wasn't his fault or mine that Stella swooned at the very sight of us. And I knew if I confronted Stella, she would never tell me the truth about why she was shocked. The whole thing would become another secret that I didn't need to— wasn't allowed to— unlock.

I wanted to unlock it, though. I wanted Stella to understand that even if she was surprised to see me with Tyson, she had no cause for worry. This was not the "consequence" she feared, and even if it had been, so what? We were friends. We were just friends admiring the refurbished carousel, me and Tyson and Jesse and Florio.

Florio.

His face swam into view, his earnest expression as he held his ring out to Jesse. There was something about that guy. Not creepy, the way Tyson thought, but something vaguely "off." A little desperate. Searching, like me, for something he didn't quite understand. When my mind replayed those last few minutes in slow motion, I realized that Florio had been right there until Stella fainted, and then he was gone. Poof.

What if I had it all wrong? I couldn't shake the feeling that I was missing something important, a key or clue that would explain it all. Or at least lead me to ask Stella the right questions.

I threw back the sheet and switched on the lamp beside my bed. Khamille stirred but didn't wake. I opened the closet door and fumbled until I found Aunt Helen's battered old shoebox. I hadn't had any more time to study its contents but when it came to clues and keys, it was all I had. I night as well make use of my insomnia.

I flipped the box upside down and dumped its contents across my bed. Pictures scattered every which way, along with the diaries I had already abandoned as useless. What was I looking for? I turned the box upright and started to put it aside, but as I did I noticed a folded white envelope wedged in the bottom. Excited, I tugged it out

The edges of the envelope were smashed from its cramped-up years in the box. I smoothed it as best I could and drew a quick breath when I saw it was addressed to Stella Whitaker at this address. The letter inside was dated September 2, 1942, and was signed "Forever yours, Stuart."

At last we were getting somewhere. I scanned the letter, my eyes opening further and further with each word until it felt like my eyeballs would pop right out. This was a love letter, and we weren't talking holding hands and smooching in the balcony of the movie theater. This was serious. This verified everything Khamille suspected about my prudish aunt: when she was young, she and this Stuart had been totally, wildly in love and anticipating a wedding.

When I'd read it twice I refolded the letter and returned it to the envelope. Inside I found a small piece of note paper folded into quarters. It was covered with pencil scrawl. The writing wasn't a paragraph; it had line breaks like a poem. A love poem, I assumed, though the writing was so smudged it was nearly impossible to decipher.

I squinted at the title. It looked like "Blue Ribbon Boy." I could only make out a couple of other words— love, lamb, curls and what could be the phrase bonny wee babe. There was a hard-to-read line about eyes and heaven. The paper was dated at the bottom — 5-8-43 — and my mouth fell open when I read the signature: "With love forever, Aunt Helen."

Though the print was smudged and faded, I recognized the flowery script from Helen's notes and cards to me over the years. I wondered if it was some kind of prayer, with all that business about eyes and heaven. But why was it signed "Aunt Helen?" In 1943 Dad wasn't born yet, and even if it had been about my father, why would she have buried it in the bottom of a shoebox, in the same envelope as this steamy letter from Stuart McGee?

None of it made any sense.

I piled everything back in the box except the envelope with the letter and the poem or prayer or whatever it was. I replaced the box in its hiding place and considered my options. The best I could hope for if I asked Stella about any of this was stony silence, and it could go a whole lot worse than that. My father? He would tell me to mind my business. And if Joe knew anything he'd be too scared of Stella to tell me.

I climbed back into bed with my brother's warning ringing in my head. O.L. Off limits. But I couldn't help thinking that Helen left this stuff for someone to discover. That someone was me. At this instant I missed Aunt Helen with an ache that about tore me in two. I knew she would explain, if only I could ask her. But of course, I could not.

With a weary sigh I turned off the light. I needed sleep. I was way too tired to stay up puzzling over a riddle with no obvious solution.

I shut my eyes and let my body drift, closing off tonight's events from my consciousness. In that half-awake state just before I nodded off, something about a ribbon floated across my brain. I reached out and grabbed the thought, managing to hold it for an instant, but it fluttered past as sleep surrounded me. Tomorrow, I told myself. Tonight, sleep. Tomorrow, ribbons and brass rings and a way to ask the right people the right questions that would lead to an answer.

17 – Puzzles

It felt way too early when Khamille shook me awake.

"Phone's ringing."

With a moan I hurried to the phone in Stella's room and muttered a sleepy hello.

"Hey, kiddo," Joe said. "How is she?"

How could he be so perky at this hour? I gave him the word on Stella's condition according to the doctors.

"Holy smokes," he said. "I would have called last night but I didn't want to risk waking her. I never dreamed they'd actually keep her. This is serious."

"They said it was just for observation. Just a precaution. Joe, you heard her last night when they loaded her into the ambulance. Did she sound like the end was near?"

"I suppose you're right," he agreed. "But still—geez, the hospital. I'm not ready to lose Stella. I'm not even used to being without Helen yet."

Helen. At the mention of her name, the letter and poem lit up my brain like a flashbulb. I remembered thinking about Aunt Helen before I dozed off, wishing she was here to explain the poem, knowing she was out of reach and no amount of wishing could change that. But a second aftershock pulsed through me: I absolutely, positively had to talk to Florio as soon as I possibly could.

I struggled to recall the source of this insane notion, and then it hit me. Blue ribbon boy. Florio had mentioned a ribbon yesterday in connection with his ring. I might be grasping at straws but I was desperate to find some connection. If there was any connection to be found.

I suddenly realized Joe was talking to me.

"Is that okay, kiddo?" he was asking.

"Huh? Oh, sorry, Joe, my mind was wandering."

"Never mind, I'll call you back after I talk to Khamille and we'll work it out."

"Khamille? Uh— hang on, she's right here."

"Right there? What the—"

I ignored him and called her to the phone. Then I crawled back into bed. As I waited I pulled out the poem and tried again to decipher it. I pieced together a few more lines, but they still made no sense so I set it aside when I heard Khamille hanging up. She bounced back in and stretched out on the other bed wearing my tee-shirt and shorts.

"What'd he want?" I asked.

"I'm working your shift today."

I leaped up. "What?"

"He said if the rain keeps up he might not even need me all day. What's the big deal?"

"Khamille! How could you forget? Jesse? Those dreamy blue eyes?"

"Khamille did not forget any eyes of any color," she huffed. "But what about your old auntie? Do you want her to come home to an empty house after what she's been through? All tired and weak?"

"She's gonna be about as weak as a heavyweight champ." I knew there was nothing really wrong with Stella, but Khamille raised my guilt a hair. "I should probably call my father and let him know what's going on."

"Yes, you should. And you should definitely be here when she gets home."

"Khamille, I can't, I—"

"I got your back." She fussed with her hair in the mirror. "Don't worry. I'll call you the minute those blue eyes show up, and you can wander on down. If you're not actually working you'll be free to, you know— chat. Or whatever. You can't ask for a better deal than that."

I mulled that over. I wasn't pleased about the idea of being Aunt Stella's welcome wagon, especially since she'd probably be in rare form. But Khamille was right. I had to trust her.

"What's that?" She pointed to the envelope on the nightstand beside my bed.

"I'm not actually sure. It's something my Aunt Helen had tucked away. I found it last night after you were asleep. "

Khamille snatched the envelope. As she scanned the letter a long, low whistle escaped her lips.

"Mmmm-mmmm, what did I tell you about your auntie, huh? Khamille knows what she is seeing when she sees it, and don't you ever forget it."

"Lucky guess," I said, yanking the letter back.

She snorted. "Who was this Stuart anyway?"

I told Khamille what little I knew about Stuart and my aunt Stella.

"There's something else in that envelope," I added. Khamille pulled out the folded note paper covered in pencil scrawl and held it up. I nodded. "That's it. See what you can make of that."

Khamille pursed her lips, struggling to read the poem. "Blue Ribbon Boy," she read, then looked up. "Man, this is a mess, huh? Looks like they wrote it on a bumpy road. Or a subway train." She squinted and continued. "Oh, bonny wee babe, Last to us now."

"I think that's lost," I said, standing to read over her shoulder.

"Lost to us now, God's sweet lamb, with — something — smile."

"How are you reading that?" I asked.

"Practice. I have to read a lot of old documents in my classes. They're called primary sources."

"Excuse me," I said.

She twisted her lips and pushed the paper toward me. "Maybe you should just read it yourself?"

"No, no. Please. Keep going."

She cleared her throat. "The memory of thy sweet face, Thy russet curls, Forever etched on my heart."

"Go on," I urged.

She read slowly, squinting as she made out the words. "I release thee to a life of joy. Thy father's eyes smile down from heaven, and in his stead, the last brass ring—"

"What?" I grabbed the paper from her hand. There it was, plain as day. A detail I had missed last night.

And in his stead, the last brass ring.

We stumbled through the rest until we pieced it together.

"A remnant of happier days. May you always know you were born of truest love."

I fell back on the bed, my knees unwilling to hold me. It couldn't be. Could it?

"Khamille, you know that guy who's been hanging around the park?"

"The pervert?"

I rolled my eyes. "His name is Florio and he's actually a pretty nice guy."

"Most perverts are, till you get to know them."

"I wouldn't know."

"Lucky you."

"Okay, okay, I get it. But I have a funny feeling about this guy."

"So does Tyson. You won't listen."

"I'm serious, Khamille. Last night— when my aunt collapsed? Florio was there too. I thought Stella fainted when she saw Tyson hugging me. But there's another possibility. She might have been looking at Florio."

"He is pretty scary."

When I didn't laugh, Khamille understood that I wasn't kidding.

"So what's the connection?" she asked.

"He has a ring. A brass ring. He told me last night his mother gave it to him when she died. It was tied to a piece of ribbon."

"A blue ribbon?"

"I don't know. A ribbon. A ring on a ribbon. And now this." I waved the poem at her. "Maybe his mother was a friend of Aunt Helen's? Or maybe—"

"Maybe what?"

I didn't actually know the answer to that. It was all just a hunch, an instinct I could not ignore. "I have a feeling he's connected to me somehow. It's like—you know those ancestors you're always talking about? It's like they want me to figure this out."

Khamille's eyes opened wide and her eyebrows reached for her scalp. "Am I hearing things? Lilli's 'bout to listen to the ancestors?"

"I know, I know. Right?" I put the poem back into the envelope. "Listen. If you see Florio today, will you let me know? I really need to talk to him."

She sighed heavily. "I'll be spending my day as your spy. Wish I had some binoculars."

"You don't need them. Your eyes are the best." I hugged her. "Is Ty working today?"

She shrugged. "Don't know, don't care."

So we were back to that. I couldn't blame her, after last night. "Maybe it will work out." I told her what time Ty usually caught the bus and let it go at that. I had my own problems to solve.

I tackled the challenge of calling my father by dialing Mike instead. He listened carefully, wrote down Stella's phone number at the hospital, and offered to call Dad, sparing me a deluge of why-didn't-you-call-sooners. I had just hung up when the phone rang again.

"What are you up to?" The voice on the far end didn't sound particularly weak.

"Hi, Aunt Stella, I was just going to call you." I hoped the lie sounded convincing. "How are you?"

"I'll be better when I get out of this miserable place. I tossed and turned all night. Not one wink of sleep."

I didn't mention that my last glimpse of her, she was out cold. "Me neither. I was worried about you. Are you coming home today?"

"Of course I am. There's nothing in the world wrong with me, as I tried to tell those fools who brought me here. Joe is coming at noon, the minute that blasted doctor signs me out."

"Joe?"

"Yes, Joe. Unless you have another suggestion?"

"No, no, it's just that it is the fourth of July and all, and I figured he was—well, never mind." I could imagine the conversation that had brought this about. Joe, on a busy holiday, taking a break to spring Stella from the hospital. "When I get to be your age, I hope I have a couple of old friends like Joe."

"Hmmph. It's the least he can do and he knows it, considering the whole thing is his fault. Insisting I go to that silly party. That carousel made me so dizzy I couldn't stand up."

Oh, so it was the carousel's fault. I knew she'd have a simple excuse. But her ruse didn't make sense to me. "You were sitting down when you fainted."

"That is not the point. The point is, the carousel was obscenely loud and drove me to distraction."

I decided not to argue. "I didn't even get to ride it."

"You work there, Lilli Rose. I'm sure you'll get your opportunity." With that she rattled off a short list for the deli and some chores I was to do before she arrived. I jotted them down and finally managed to hang up after convincing her I'd handle it all.

It was nearly ten so I had a few hours to do her bidding. I fished around for the phone book, flipped it open to the G's and ran my finger down the page. Giovanelli, Giovaniello, Giovannini, Giovannoni, I finally stopped at what I hoped was the right spelling. There were three listings for F. Giovanucci and one for Fiorello, but no Florio. I quickly called all the F's and was ready to quit after three wrong numbers when I decided to give this Fiorello a try. What the heck, I figured. No harm in dialing a few more digits.

A woman answered and I asked for Florio. "Hang on." She set the phone down. "Flo! Phone."

I waited to the sound of TV cartoons mingled with dishes being washed.

"Let Pop-Pop get the phone, Bobby," a gentle male voice urged. "Pop-Pop will be right back." I could almost see Florio prying the kid off his leg. "Hello?"

"Florio? It's Lilli."

He didn't answer.

"From the rides?" I prompted, in case he didn't realize who I was.

"Yeah, yeah, I know." His voice had dropped to a hoarse whisper. "How did you find me?"

"Phone book. I'm a real detective."

"Must be." He waited for me to go on.

"Listen, Florio. You left in such a rush last night. Is everything okay?"

"There was so much confusion, I— well, I wasn't exactly an invited guest. I figured the best thing for me to do was get out of the way. Is the old lady okay?"

"She's my father's aunt—my great aunt—and yes. She's fine."

"Thank God for that."

My mind was racing, trying to formulate a plan. "Florio, with everything that happened last night, you never did get to meet Joe."

"I know."

"You need to. And I'd like to make it easy on you both. Can you come to my aunt's house around one o'clock today?"

"Your aunt's house?"

"It's just a little more private than the rides," I said, trying to think fast. "More comfortable. I know how edgy you get when you're talking about that ring."

"It's awfully special to me. I told you, my mother—"

"I know. But why do I get the feeling there's more to the story than you're telling me?"

Again he was silent. I paused, judging whether to say more.

"Florio. The ribbon. You said the ring was on a ribbon. Was it, by any chance, blue?"

He gave a little gasp. My heart galloped.

"It was," he said. "How did you know that?"

"I'll explain it all later. Will you come?"

He answered by asking me the address, which I gave him.

"Do you need directions?"

"I can find it. One o'clock, you said?"

"Right. And Florio? Don't forget the ring."

18 - Connections

By noon my chores were finished and I was showered and dressed in what Stella would call a respectable outfit: jeans and a tee that covered my midriff with sleeves that hid my shoulders. My goal was to avoid setting her off before Florio arrived. While the aim was to keep her calm, I felt a little like an arsonist going for an evening stroll with matches and a can of gasoline. I kept telling myself Florio was only coming to show the ring to Joe, but I felt certain something was going to burst into flames before we were done. I just didn't know what.

At twelve-fifteen the phone rang.

"Baby, your ship just sailed in."

"Khamille?"

"Who else? Jesse just hit the snack bar and I'll clue you he was for sure not looking for Khamille."

I swore.

"What's wrong, girlfriend? He asked how you were. I told him you'd be by later on. Just clean yourself up and hop that bus down here."

"I can't."

"What?"

"I can't. Stella is due home any minute and—"

"And? Get her settled and get on down."

"I can't. I— I need to stay here."

"You're kidding, right?"

I wished I were kidding. I wished I'd never come to the Island this summer, never opened that stupid shoebox, never met Florio, never been born into this bedraggled mess of a family, but here I was. Every nerve in my body was eager to hop that bus to see Jesse, but the pull to stay was even stronger. What was the point in arranging for Florio and Stella to meet if I wasn't here to witness it? Maybe even to direct it?

"I'm serious, Khamille, but I can't explain now. Just tell him..." I didn't know what to suggest. "Tell him whatever you want."

Khamille was quiet for a few seconds. "I'll handle it," she said. I had no idea what she'd do, but I trusted her to do it.

Joe's car pulled into the driveway. "They're home already. I'll see you later."

Joe ran around to open the car door for Stella. He leaned down and tried to help her out but she swatted him away like an annoying fly. It took a few minutes but she managed to heave herself out and stand to her full height. She still wore her flowered dress from last night, which had to be bothering her on principle, but she strode up the front walk with a solid, steady gait, in case any of us had any ideas about her being on her last legs. She came in and looked around the place like she was surprised to find it still intact.

"How much damage did you think I could do in one night?" I asked.

She ignored me and crossed the room to switch on the window AC.

"Hey, kiddo," Joe stepped in behind her. "Doesn't she look great?"

"Terrific," I agreed, reminding myself that my job was to keep her in a good mood. Honestly, it was a relief to see her upright and acting very much like the Stella I knew. She was now ferociously slamming windows shut as the AC roared into gear.

"Freeze to death in that hospital, roast to death in my own home," she huffed. When she bent to close the windows I could see yesterday's wash-and-set was suffering from a serious case of pillow-head. But I wasn't about to mention it.

"It was raining this morning. It didn't feel that hot," I offered, as Joe rushed to help her.

When the windows were closed and the room headed for meat-locker temp, she turned to Joe. "I appreciate the ride and all you've done. But I am desperate to freshen up in the privacy of my own bath." She turned on her heel and headed up the steps.

"I'll just run along, then," Joe said, edging toward the door.

"Wait!" I shouted. Joe stopped, a puzzled look on his face. I calmed myself and tried to think of something persuasive enough to keep him from racing back to the rides. "I got some of those Italian cookies from the good bakery. Why don't you stay and have an iced tea or something while I fix Stella a sandwich?"

Joe started to protest but I guess the lure of his favorite cookies was irresistible. He closed his mouth and followed me toward the kitchen. "Haven't had lunch yet," he explained.

"I can fix you a sandwich," I offered.

"No, no," he insisted. "I'll just have a cookie or two."

It was a quarter to one. If I could keep him hanging around just a little longer he could meet Florio, and by the time they were done talking about the carousel ring Stella would be down. And then?

I wasn't sure what would happen then. I only knew I'd set the clock in motion and the hands were moving fast.

"How'd the party go last night?" I asked. "I mean after— you know."

"Overall, it was a huge success. They all left smiling, the carousel folks and all the honored guests. Word will spread. And it's stopped raining, thank God." He crossed himself. "If the good weather holds today, we'll be mobbed."

I poured his tea. "That reminds me, if you need me later I can come in. I don't really need the whole day off."

He thanked me. "You're a good kid." He sipped his tea. He eyed the unopened bakery box, still tied with its red and white bakery string. "She scared us half to death last night, didn't she? I hope she's really okay. I hate to think—"

The doorbell interrupted him.

"Who could that be?" he asked.

I took a deep breath and excused myself, leaving Joe in the kitchen.

Florio stood on the porch, nervously surveying the block.

"Hey," I opened the screen door. "Come on in."

He just stood there.

"Something wrong?" I asked.

"I'm not sure this is such a good idea."

Geez, this guy blew hot and cold. He was a mess and he hadn't even met my aunt yet. "What? Meeting Joe? He's harmless, don't sweat it." Florio searched my eyes for reassurance, which I must have delivered because he finally stepped in.

Joe jumped when he heard us coming, a guilty look on his face. I glanced at the table behind him and noted the mangled bakery box, the result of Joe's attempts to wiggle a cookie out without cutting the string around the box. I grabbed a sharp knife and slit the twine, smiling. "I told you to help yourself."

Joe bit the head off a chocolate-filled butter man and made a happy sound in his throat.

Florio hung back in the dining room and I motioned him in and pushed him toward Joe.

"Joe, this is Florio. The man with the carousel ring. I asked him to come by today to meet you, so you could talk without the distractions of the park."

The two shook hands, and Joe seemed as fired-up as I expected. A few minutes later when I went upstairs to check on Stella the two men were happily munching cookies and closely inspecting the ring.

Stella's bedroom door was closed and by the scent in the air she was wallowing in a barrel of her favorite powder.

"Hel-lo," I called, rapping on the door. "How are you doing?"

She peered out and eyed me suspiciously. "Fine. Why?"

"Just checking to see if you're okay. I thought I'd fix your lunch, if you wanted it."

Her eyes narrowed. "I won't be coddled. I told you I'm perfectly all right."

"I know. But I'm fixing a sandwich for myself and I figured I'd make you one too. But if you don't want it—" I turned away.

"You got the Boar's Head Ham?"

"And the imported provolone," I sang seductively.

"On a Kaiser roll, with a good smear of butter. I'll be down in a few minutes."

Before I raced back to the kitchen, I ducked into my room and slipped Aunt Helen's poem in the pocket of my jeans. It felt like a loaded gun I wasn't trained to shoot. I took a breath and raised my eyes to the ceiling — and hopefully, beyond. "If you're up there, ancestors, this might be a good time to pay attention. I could use a little help."

"Well?" I asked Joe as I whipped out plates to make the sandwiches. "What do you think of that ring?"

Joe was beaming. "It sure looks like the real thing. Florio was just telling me how he came by it."

"Really? I'd like to hear that story too." I looked him in the eye. "The real story."

Florio's eyes locked onto mine for a split second before he spoke. "As I was saying, this ring belonged to my late mother. She gave it to me on her deathbed."

"And it was on a piece of ribbon?" I prompted. "Blue ribbon?"

He nodded. "Yes, that's right."

Aha. My breath caught in my throat.

Joe clapped his hands together. "That is such a great story! Do you know where she got it?"

Florio's eyes narrowed, clearly considering how to answer. "I'm not entirely sure. I've been curious but I didn't know where to get more information. Mother said she was told it was a carousel ring from the boardwalk. She told me—well, she said it dated back to when I was born. During the war."

"When were you born?" I asked, folding the heavily buttered roll over a thick pile of ham and provolone.

"Nineteen forty-three."

I sucked in a breath and felt my heart drum against my ribs.

"In May?" I asked.

Now it was his turn to gasp. "Why yes. May the seventh."

The poem in my pocket was dated the very next day. If that was a coincidence it was a mighty strange one.

"How did you know that?" Joe asked.

"I'm trying to piece a few things together myself. There seems to be a mystery at hand. Is there anything else you need to tell us, Florio?"

He eyed us both in turn, picked a marzipan Neapolitan cookie from the box, bit, and chewed. "Actually, there is a little more to the story than I told you. It came as kind of a shock to me. It's still hard to talk about." His voice dropped almost to a whisper. "Right before she died, Mother told me that I was adopted."

I nearly sliced my finger in half instead of the sandwich. Thank God, Joe picked up the conversation with something about what a shock that must have been, because I didn't trust myself to say another word.

Was this really happening? All the road signs flashed a warning that this man, this Irish-looking middle-aged Italian grandfather, was somehow connected to my family. And he just verified that the signs could be right. I was the one steering us toward the truth, and after all these years, we might just be racing toward a head-on collision.

I ran to the living room and arranged the sandwich and a glass of orange juice on a tray near Stella's arm chair. There was no time to think, which was probably just as well. The best I could hope was to get Stella comfortable before she laid eyes on Florio. Honestly, I wasn't trying to kill her. I was only trying to get to the bottom of all these dark secrets that clouded our past.

Stella's foot hit the top step and the slow, heavy descent began. I darted back to the dining room, leaning against the wall for a long, steadying breath and another quick prayer to whoever might be listening up there in heaven. I wanted at least to be a survivor if this all ended in a fiery crash.

The stairs continued to creak as Stella came down. The sound of kitchen chairs scraping the floor signaled the two men were standing up.

"I need to be getting back to the park," Joe said. "But why don't you bring the grandson by for a free ride?"

Florio laughed. "After all these years, huh? About time somebody cashed in that ring."

I grabbed Joe's arm as he stepped out of the kitchen and steered him toward the living room, hoping his goodbye would distract Stella and keep her out of the kitchen. Florio started to follow but I waved him back.

"I'll be right back. Need to get my aunt settled. Stay put, okay?"

Florio looked startled but he sat down again.

Stella made it to the foot of the stairs, a bit winded but looking much fresher than when she'd arrived from the hospital. I waltzed over and guided her toward her old gray chair.

"Here you go, Aunt Stel." I hoped her sandwich looked sufficiently enticing.

She shot me a suspicious look— it really was not like me to be so helpful— but she fell obediently into the chair with a whooshing sound, then shook her head at Joe.

"No more merry-go-rounds," she said firmly. "When will you drop off my car?"

"I'll send someone over in a little while."

"Someone responsible, if you please."

"Of course, of course," he said. He rolled his eyes at me. "Hey, kiddo, thanks for introducing me to—"

"You're welcome," I said, cutting him off and practically shoving him out. I didn't want him to mention Florio, but I also wanted no innocent victims in case things didn't go as I planned. Not that I actually had a plan. "Just call if you want me to come in later."

With Joe safely out of the way I sat down across from Stella. Half her sandwich was gone already and she hadn't complained yet, which made me optimistic about her mood. Now that I had more facts, I was wishing I had talked to her about Florio, maybe given her a chance to explain or deny something before he sprang out of her kitchen like a jack-in-the-box.

But it was too late for that now.

"Uh— Aunt Stella?"

She washed down her latest bite with a gulp of juice.

"Joe brought a friend of his over to meet you." It was only a tiny lie, one I hoped would smooth the way enough to get us rolling.

Her eyes narrowed. "He didn't mention anyone."

"He was in such a hurry. Busy day and all." I leaped up, unable to stand this suspense for another second. "He's in the kitchen."

She started to fuss about strangers in her house and who was Joe to invite anyone, but I cut her off. "Let me just get him."

By now, Florio undoubtedly thought I was insane, but he was a good sport and dutifully got up when I beckoned. I led him into the living room.

"Florio Giovanucci, this is my great aunt, Stella Whitaker."

I stepped back and held my breath. The color drained from my aunt's face as Florio extended his hand. When she did not extend hers in return, Florio dropped his hand to his side and sent a nervous glance my way. I nodded my encouragement.

"How nice to meet you," he said, with only the slightest quaver to his gravelly voice. "I'm so glad to see you looking well, after last night. You gave us quite a scare."

Stella managed to set the juice glass on her tray, though her hand shook so badly she banged the side of the plate. Thank God she was sitting on a sturdier chair this time, less likely to keel over into a dead faint. "Forgive my rudeness," she managed. "I— I seem to be a bit more tired than I realized."

"Well, I won't keep you. Your niece has been so kind to me, when she insisted I come over today to meet Joe I felt I had to comply."

"Lilli? Insisted you come? Today." Stella's eyebrows knitted into crossed swords. "To meet Joe?"

I shuffled my feet and averted my gaze.

"Yes. It all seems so silly, really." Florio laughed and brandished the ring. "I've come into this ring, now that my mother's passed on, and I wanted to see if Joe could verify whether or not it's from the carousel at the rides."

"It was on a blue ribbon," I explained, feeling a short stab of disappointment when that revelation drew no reaction from my aunt. "His mother told him it was from when he was born. Well— adopted, actually."

That did it. Stella pretended to give Florio a small nod of passing interest but her head barely nudged on her wooden neck. Something was definitely up here.

"When did you say you were born?" I asked.

"May the seventh, nineteen forty-three." Florio practically sang the numbers.

A small squeak escaped from my aunt. She folded her shaking hands in her lap and forced her quivering lips together.

Florio rushed forward, kneeling at her feet. "Are you all right?"

She peered at me over his shoulder, her eyes blazing. "You have a lot of nerve, inviting this stranger into my home."

"Aunt Stella, he's not a stranger. He's been at the park a lot, and we're kind of friends. And he's—"

"He's what?" Her voice was a raspy screech. "What can you have been thinking, you miserable, wretched child?"

Florio stepped back and looked from me to Stella and back again. "I'm so sorry." He slipped the ring back into his pocket. "All this fuss over a silly ring. I'd better go."

"No! Wait." I reached into my own pocket. "You need to see this first." I handed him the poem.

He puzzled over it for a moment. "It's so smudged. It's nearly impossible to make out."

"Look at the date," I said. "You can read that much."

He blinked several times and shook his head. "I— I don't understand."

I took the worn paper from his hand. "Here, let me. It's something I found in Aunt Helen's things."

"In Helen's—?" Stella edged toward anger, but the struggle to make sense of what was happening was too great.

I plunged on, ignoring her. "Helen was my aunt's sister. She died a few weeks ago. Anyway, listen to this. It's a poem. It's called Blue Ribbon Boy."

In a strong, clear voice I read the words that Khamille and I pieced together this morning.

Oh, bonny wee babe,
Lost to us now,
God's sweet lamb
With an angel's smile,
The memory of thy sweet face
Thy russet curls,
Forever etched on my heart.
I release thee to a life of joy.
Thy father's eyes smile down from heaven
And in his stead, the last brass ring
A remnant of happier days.
May you always know you were born of truest love.

I looked up at the faces staring at me. "Dated May eighth, nineteen-forty-three, with love forever," I paused, "Your Aunt Helen."

Stella took a long breath and made a small mewing sound as she exhaled. "Oh, God, Helen," she whispered. "You silly, romantic fool."

She and Florio turned about the same shade of pink and tears spilled from their eyes. I guided Florio to the couch before he had a chance to fall over, then dashed to the kitchen for a glass of water and a box of tissues.

"Drink," I commanded, and he obeyed.

Stella's face crumpled. Her chin quivered and tears flowed freely. I grabbed a handful of tissues and shoved them at her. She blew her nose loudly, burying her face.

"Stuart," she whimpered. "Oh, my Stuart. You have his eyes. The eyes I fell in love with."

Florio swallowed hard then, and the tears flowed even faster. He opened his palms toward me, then toward Stella and back again. "Can you—can one of you— please explain?"

I shook my head. "Don't look at me. I think my Aunt Stella is the only one who can fit these pieces together. Isn't that right?"

She tried to make an ugly face at me but I could see that, for once, she was beyond that. She had completely lost control.

"It was your eyes. Last night? Those eyes did me in. I thought it was my imagination, being in the park and near the carousel, I thought I must be seeing things." She smiled and looked beyond us then, at something we couldn't see. "And I'll be damned if you don't have the exact same hair as my father had. The bald spot and that tufted red fringe. It's like seeing the old goat alive again." She knotted the tissues with her fingers. "I can hardly believe it. It's too ridiculous after all this time. But I believe it's true. Dear God, it's true. That you might be— that you are — my son." The word croaked out of her throat and she dissolved into a new series of sobs, as Florio continued to sniffle across from her.

That set me off. I felt a knot the size of a soccer ball rise in my chest and my own tears started to fall, tears like I never remembered crying in my entire life. "I'm sorry," I croaked. It was what I was supposed to say, but I wasn't sorry, really, not for uncovering the truth. I just didn't expect the torrent of bottled-up emotion it would release. "I'm sorry."

They both waved their arms in dismissal but neither spoke, raised their eyes, or made any attempt to stem the flow of tears. I guess they were way overdue. I backed into the dining room. Even though I had a hundred more questions, I realized I owed them—both of them— a little space to absorb the possibility of this news.

After a few minutes the sniffling subsided. Florio was the first one brave enough to look up, his lips curved into a shy little smile.

"This is a lot to handle," he said. "I'm sure we can look into— somehow verify— understand what—"

All Stella could do was nod.

"But I think I'd better go now. Give you some time to sort things out." He pulled his tall, bulky frame off the couch, giving his shorts a little tug.

Stella looked him up and down then closed her eyes, as if she still could not believe what she saw. She inhaled deeply and shook her head firmly.

"Sit down," she commanded, her eyes still shut.

He did, instantly.

"I do not need time. I've lived with this for nearly fifty years, and frankly that was plenty of time." She opened her eyes and fixed them on Florio. "What I want is to look at you."

Florio leaned back, blinking his eyes rapidly.

I stepped back into the room. "Aunt Stel, maybe Florio needs a little space. Maybe—"

"Maybe you've done enough meddling for one afternoon." Her eyes remained fixed on her son.

Her son.

It was hard to wrap my head around that one. There was some kind of invisible aura between them and I felt it growing stronger with each passing second. I had taken a huge chance in bringing them together. Now that I had, it was time for me to go.

"See you later, Florio," I said, sidling past them before she had to tell me again.

I wandered out and sat on the stoop. The last clouds had moved off toward the ocean and the sun was beginning to dry the pavement. A bunch of kids clustered near the corner, periodically scattering in all directions, their running followed by the pop-pop-pop of firecrackers. Of course. July 4. The air was thick with the smell of gunpowder on moist concrete.

I sat on the damp steps and tried to find patience. It wasn't easy. I was dying to know the whole story of Florio's birth. I knew Stella had never been married, and it didn't take much detective work to understand why we never knew about this baby. But why had Helen written that poem and kept it hidden all this time? Why hadn't Stella ever tried to look for her son? What would make someone close up so completely?

I wanted to understand, but clearly that wasn't going to happen today. And if it wasn't, I might as well head on down to the rides and see if Jesse was still there.

I stood up to go in for my uniform when I noticed a car driving slowly down the street, like it was searching for an address. As it drew closer to Stella's I realized it was her car. I squinted to see which sucker Joe wrangled into driving the car home and taking the bus back.

My heart thudded. The poor sucker behind the wheel was none other than Jesse.

He parked in front and unwound his lanky frame from the front seat. "Hey," he said.

I returned his casual wave, swallowing hard and ordering myself to get a grip. "Hey yourself. You training to be a cabbie, or what?"

He laughed, that sweet ripple of sound that had slayed me from the moment I first heard it. "Joe was looking for volunteers. Khamille volunteered me."

"That's my friend Khamille." I blessed her silently.

He sat on the stoop, close enough that I felt the heat of his body. "Is your aunt okay?"

I nodded. "She's fine. She's—" I stopped. How would I ever explain this one?

"She's what?" he said, tilting his head with curiosity.

"She's inside. With Florio. The guy with the carousel ring? It's kind of a long story."

He shrugged. "I have all the time in the world."

So I started to explain from the very beginning, at least as much as I knew. At first the words spilled out, but it was hard work to concentrate. I thought I understood what Stella meant when she said she just wanted to look at Florio. Forever wouldn't be long enough for me to sit here just looking at Jesse, letting my heart rest in the peace of his radiant smile.

The kids down the street scattered again, their squeals dissolving into a rapid-fire pop of explosions, and I knew then, the way you know things without really understanding, that as long as I lived the Fourth of July would never, ever be the same.

19 - Family

I'd like to pretend that my Aunt Stella magically transformed into a beloved matriarch, a fairy godmother with a heart of gold, and we all lived happily ever after. But seriously? None of us expected that to happen, no matter how surprised we were by the story Aunt Helen's poem helped to uncover.

That first afternoon when Stella met Florio, there were tears, and more tears, then long stretches of silence and a lot of hugging. Florio was beyond flustered to learn that the brass ring brought him to his birth mother. Once he understood the basic facts he panicked about sharing the news with his own family.

"Maybe we should keep it quiet," he suggested. "Maybe the families don't need to know."

But Stella had enough of the silence and lies.

"No," she insisted. "We must tell them the truth."

It was Florio's first lesson in understanding that Stella always got her way.

On hearing the news, a few of Helen's friends had their own little aha moment, claiming they'd known all along that something was amiss. Stella didn't care what they thought. She'd lived for so long like a hard-shelled crab, their opinion could not harm her. And soon enough all the gossip and speculation converged on one solitary, astounding fact: the pure coincidence of Stella and Florio being reunited after so much time had passed.

Pure coincidence? I knew better. I didn't brag about it to anyone but Khamille, who was convinced my dead ancestors had a hand in it. I tried to argue that it didn't actually work that way, but she wasn't having it.

"Do you have a better explanation?" she asked.

To which I had no good answer.

The week after July Fourth, my new family gathered for a giant meeting with my old family. The Giovanucci's had Florio and his wife

Gina, their grown daughter and son, plus the daughter-in-law and little Bobby, the apple of Florio's eye. The Whitakers included Stella and my dad, Mike and Dette and the kids, and of course, Joe.

And also, there was me. Considering I used to flinch at the very mention of the word family I was now surrounded. Inundated. Nearly overwhelmed.

And to my surprise, it felt just fine.

By then everyone knew the whole story and there were still a lot of hugs and tears and mush that I could hardly stand. After a few champagne toasts, Joe started bragging about how it was his carousel that made this all possible, as if I was just an innocent bystander. Everyone kept hugging and crying and I was starting to wonder if we were going to turn into a family of saps when Stella finally snapped and yelled at Bobby and Patrick for jumping on the sofa. I knew then that things were getting back to normal. Not the same, exactly, but normal.

"Hey, Florio," Joe asked, as we sat around the table after a huge meal of Gina's baked ziti and Stella's pot roast and potatoes. "I've been meaning to ask you this since we first met. I'm Italian, right? But what kind of a name is Florio, anyway?"

Gina, basking in a red-wine afterglow, laughed. "It's really Fiorello." She pinched Florio's cheek. "Isn't that right, sweetie?"

Florio blushed. "That's right. Mother— my other mother, that is," he said, raising his wine glass toward Stella, who nodded in acknowledgment, "named me Fiorello. It means Flower. She always called me her little flower."

My jaw dropped. "No way."

"Way," said Flo's wife, winking at me.

Talk about weird coincidences. "I was my mother's little flower." I looked at Dad. "Wasn't I?"

Dad suddenly found his empty plate totally fascinating. "I— I don't remember," he stammered.

"Come on. That's what Mike told me, that she used to call me that."

Mike leaned across the table at me. "Let it go, Squirt."

"No." This time I was not backing down. "We're all about truth now, aren't we? No more lies, no more omissions and fairy tales. Dad remembers. I know he does. I want him to tell me he remembers."

Everyone at the table held their breath. I didn't care if they turned blue. I wanted to hear it. I had to know.

Dad looked down for a long quiet minute then swallowed hard and slowly raised his head. His eyes were moist and even though that rattled me I held my ground. He nodded, ever so slowly. "That's right," he said. "She always called you her flower."

"Who? Who called me her flower?" I demanded.

"Your mother." His voice cracked. "Celia."

I watched a tear trickle out of his eye and travel down his cheek. I might never get another word from my father about my mother, but hearing that single word, her name— Celia— meant so much. I was dimly aware of the tears welling in my own eyes. No one moved. No one made a sound. We were frozen in place for what felt like a long, long time.

Florio finally stood and came toward me, wrapping me in his big bear arms. I heard everyone around me sigh and their tears flowed, and it felt like I finally had a family I could live with.

I could have gone home any time I wanted after that since Stella wasn't so alone anymore, but I spent the rest of the summer on the Island. The comings and goings of Florio and his family gave my aunt something new to complain about and took the pressure off me. We spent time sorting the treasures in Helen's box, Stella helping me to write names on the pictures. She shared stories about Stuart and their friends. Sometimes she laughed at the memories, and sometimes she grew moody and melancholy. None of us pushed her. She'd been underground for so long, it wouldn't be easy to struggle back to the surface.

As the summer unfolded I saw more and more of Khamille in the neighborhood. She and Ty were an item again, and they mostly hung on his turf. Darlene made some noises at first but when she got the word that Khamille told Ty he was history if he didn't make the grade in school, they high-fived and made peace.

At the end of August when I was packing to go, I dug out Aunt Helen's blue photo album from her shoebox of treasures and quietly removed some of the pictures. I didn't need permission to take what was mine, and I figured Aunt Helen knew— had always known— that nobody needed them more than I did.

A few days after I got home, I took the box from my back-to-school sneakers— my senior-year, swan-song-back-to-school sneakers— and created a treasure box of my own. Inside, I put the pictures, now carefully labeled with names and dates, of my smiling mother and father, and the one of Mike holding me in my little pink blanket. Next to them I laid the gold bead Khamille had taken from her braid to give me the day I went home, and the newspaper article with the photo of me on the carousel. I lightly kissed the small gray shell I found on the beach that Sunday I skipped church, then rested it in the box.

Finally, there was the strip of black-and-whites Jesse and I took in the photo booth at the arcade that Fourth of July night. We both looked a little dizzy and maybe that was from riding the carousel a dozen times in a row.

Or maybe it wasn't.

Smiling, I popped the lid on the box and nestled it in the back of my closet. It's not much of a past, I admit. But at least it's a start.

Acknowledgments

This is a work of fiction and, as they say, any resemblance to actual persons living or dead is purely coincidental.

That's mostly true.

The South Beach Boardwalk and Rides on Staten Island were real places of my childhood. The beach and boardwalk area were a thriving resort in the early part of the Twentieth Century and certainly in the 1940s as depicted in this work. In 1989, when Lilli's story takes place, the rides were still open and being enjoyed by many children. There was a small carousel but nothing like the one depicted in this story.

However, New York City does now have a beautifully restored vintage carousel. Known as Jane's Carousel, it was rescued from Idora Park in Youngstown, Ohio, lovingly restored and placed in the neighborhood in Brooklyn known as DUMBO (Down Under the Manhattan and Brooklyn Overpasses.) The fact that I dreamed up this story long before I ever lived in or even heard of Youngstown or Idora Park is another pure coincidence.

If you believe in coincidences.

I am forever grateful for the encouragement of friends and critique group members at Rocky Mountain Fiction Writers, a fantastic organization that contributed greatly to my work and my idea of how a community of writers might support one another.

Special thanks to those who offered suggestions and encouragement as I wrote and revised this book: Kenn Amdahl, Dea Brayden, Deb Hobart, Alice Kober, Dorsey Moore, Anthony S. Picco, Ruthie Rosauer, and Lorna Wilson. Sincere gratitude to J.E. Sills for providing important input to an early draft. Her solid suggestions saved me from problems I could never have seen through my own eyes and I own any failures to correct the things she pointed out.

Thanks to Matt, for always being willing to listen and not offer too much advice.

Finally, for the blessing of the words I heard so clearly from my own ancestor many years ago at Esalen, thank you: those words set me on this journey and changed the course of my life.

About the Author

Liz Hill grew up in Staten Island, NY and has since lived and worked in six other states. She currently divides her time between western North Carolina and Jalisco, Mexico. Before she retired, she divided her time between work as a business communicator for corporate and nonprofit clients, volunteer work for literary, church, and community nonprofits, and various literary pursuits from poems to plays to novels. See www.lizhill.net for more information.

Typeface

This book has been set using Baskerville fonts.

Designed in the 1750s by John Baskerville (1706–1775), Baskerville is a serif typeface, classified as a transitional typeface, a refinement of old-style typefaces of the period.

Baskerville increased contrast between the thick and thin strokes, making the serifs sharper and more tapered, and shifted the axis of rounded letters to a more vertical position. These changes created a greater consistency in size and form, influenced by the calligraphy Baskerville had learned and taught as a young man. Baskerville's typefaces remain very popular in book design.